The year is 1926

Chaperones and tea parties are passé; petting parties and speakeasies are the latest craze. America is enjoying the Roaring Twenties.

Women are bobbing their hair, shedding their corsets and experimenting with makeup, smoking and sex. Men are sporting raccoon coats and carrying hip flasks brimming with bathtub gin.

People are reading confession magazines, sitting on flagpoles, dancing the Charleston and swooning over Valentino.

It's a dizzying time—of fast music and faster cars, of brief fads and briefer infatuations.

It's a dangerous time—as manners and morals come crashing down, true love is a prayer whispered in the whirlwind.

It is the time of Alice Fontaine and Nicholas Crawford.

Dear Reader,

We hope you are enjoying Century of American Romance, a nostalgic look back at the lives and loves of American men and women from the turn of the century to the dawn of the year 2000. These stories give us all a chance to relive the memories of a time gone by and sneak a peak at romance in an exciting future.

We've traveled from the 1899 immigrant experience to 1906 San Francisco's tumultuous quake to the muddy trenches of France's Western Front in World War I. Now Rebecca Flanders takes us to the Jazz Age—the carefree, decadent Roaring Twenties.

In the months ahead watch for all the titles—one per month—in Century of American Romance, including upcoming books by Anne Stuart and Barbara Bretton.

We hope you continue to enjoy these special stories of nostalgia and romance, written by some of your favorite novelists. As always, we welcome your comments. Please take the time to write to us at the address below.

Here's hoping that Century of American Romance will become part of your most cherished memories....

Sincerely,

Debra Matteucci
Senior Editor and Editorial Coordinator

Harlequin Books
300 East 42nd St.
New York, NY 10017

REBECCA FLANDERS

1920s
THE
SENSATION

Harlequin Books

TORONTO • NEW YORK • LONDON
AMSTERDAM • PARIS • SYDNEY • HAMBURG
STOCKHOLM • ATHENS • TOKYO • MILAN

To my faithful assistant,
Gin, with thanks

Published September 1990

ISBN 0-373-16357-6

Chapter One

"Nicholas who?" Alice Fontaine slid her dress over her hips and stood in her slip and stockings, flexing her aching back. She made up her mind then and there that no matter how far past due the rent became, she would never take another kitchen job.

"Crawford," repeated Jane, glancing up from the newspaper. "Nikki to his friends. Only one of the ten—"

"Five," corrected Alice's roommate, Molly, as she peered over Jane's shoulder at the newspaper.

"—most eligible bachelors in New York City today."

"Rich?"

"Filthy. Honestly, Alice, I don't know how you can call yourself a female and not know these things."

"If I were in the market for a husband," Alice retorted promptly, "I wouldn't care whether he's rich or not. But I'm an actress, and the only thing I'm in the market for is a job. And if the rest of you would spend as much time on your careers as you do chasing down husbands—"

Barbara, who was in the process of painting her toenails a bright orange, groaned out loud. "Don't let her get started again. Read, for heaven's sake, Jane. Read."

Four of the twelve residents of the Handley Hotel for Young Ladies were gathered in the small room shared by Alice and Molly, dressed in loose kimonos and mules, their hair tied up in scarves or twisted around rags to set the curl. The room smelled of fingernail polish, cigarette smoke and perfume samples, which were liberally traded back and forth, and the scene, on that early Friday evening in 1926, was very much like a backstage dressing room.

Almost every evening the girls would gather in someone's room, mostly because Mrs. Handley, combination housemother and landlady who was affectionately known as "Lady Harridan"—always behind her back of course—did not allow her girls to smoke in the downstairs parlor. They spent the hour or two after dinner complaining about their days, looking for jobs and, inevitably, listening to Jane read from the society column, which she followed religiously. To Alice, who treasured the company of show people almost as much as she did the business itself, one of the most exciting things about living in New York was coming home to a hotel filled with women who were struggling to make it on their own, just as she was.

"...what promises to be one of the most exciting galas of the year," Jane was reading now, "hosted at his home this evening by Mr. Nicholas Crawford. Standing as his hostess will be his sister, Cynthia, who reportedly has many of New York City's most elite sobbing in their tea over the exclusivity of the guest list. Among those expected to attend are the illustrious Eugene O'Neill, glittering Greta Garbo, Mr. Tyler Bradford—"

"Tyler Bradford! Let me see that!" Alice lunged for the newspaper and snatched it out of Jane's hand.

"Hey, what are you doing?"

"For heaven's sake, Alice, at least let her finish!"

Alice scanned the column, fatigue fleeing as the kernel of a possibility took root inside her and began to grow. "Tyler Bradford," she repeated with soft satisfaction, and turned to the others. "Do you girls know who he is?"

"Of course we know who he is." Irritably Jane retrieved her newspaper. "A Broadway angel, for one thing—"

"A lech, drunkard and all around dissolute character for another," supplied Barbara, frowning a little as she wiped a trace of stray polish off her big toe.

Molly asked curiously, "Why are you suddenly so interested in the rich playboy type? Didn't you just tell us a minute ago—"

Alice dismissed her with an impatient wave, her face lit with excited determination. "He is also," she informed them, "the man who just last week announced he was looking for a poster girl for his new cigarette company. Do you know what that means? Whoever he picks will be seen all over the city—the world! She'll be the toast of Broadway, the absolute sensation of the decade. And that girl," she decided firmly, "is me."

A chorus of laughter scattered around the room. "There she goes again!"

"Oh, Alice, will you for once be serious?"

Barbara looked up from a critical inspection of her toenails long enough to demand, "And just what makes you think that out of all the girls in New York City—half of whom are sleeping with him, I might add—the infamous Mr. Bradford is going to pick you for his new cigarette posters?''

"Because,'' replied Alice, unfazed, "I'm young and pretty and fresh-faced. Because I need the job worse than anyone else in this city, present company included. Because,'' she added, "I am going to march right up to him tonight at that party and demand that he give me the job.''

Another round of hoots greeted her statement, but Alice turned back to her wardrobe, ignoring them. "All I need is something to wear—''

"All you need is an invitation!''

"And a hyphenated name!''

"And let's not forget cab fare!''

"Just how do you expect to even get in to Mr. Nicholas Crawford's party?'' demanded Molly.

"I'm an actress,'' Alice replied airily, flipping through the dresses on the hook. "I'll just play the role.''

Jane chortled. "Cinderella at the ball. Why not?''

Molly held up her hands for silence, staring at Alice. "Hold it, ladies. I think she's serious.''

"Of course I'm serious!'' Alice pulled out a summer dress of green-sprigged gauze. It was Molly's, and the nicest dress either of them owned, but it was obvious even that would not do. She put it back with a scowl. "When have you known me not to be serious about my career?''

Barbara recapped the bottle of polish, her expression incredulous. "You *are* crazy. Didn't you hear a word I just said about Tyler Bradford?''

"As long as he gives me the job," replied Alice, "I don't care if he has three wives and makes off with the national treasury."

"Lady Harridan will kick you out of here faster than you can blink if she ever found out you were going around with a man like that!"

"Aw, he can't be that bad, Barb—" Molly grinned "—or you would've brought him home a long time ago."

Barbara threw a cushion at her.

Jane sat up on her knees and twisted around to look at Alice, her eyes wide. "You're not really going to crash Nicholas Crawford's party, are you?"

Alice's mouth was set in a determined line none of them could mistake. "Just as soon as I find out where he lives."

A silence that was almost reverent fell as the other three digested the fact that Alice was indeed serious.

For the most part life in the Handley Hotel for Young Ladies was quiet and predictable, and very much unlike what the girls had expected when they had come to New York with dreams of excitement, glory, and perhaps even stardom. Barbara, who was the oldest of the four and who professed to be the most cynical, claimed her best years were behind her and was content to watch life roll by while she paid the rent with an occasional singing job at a private club. Molly was too shy and too easy to please to ever have a career in show business, while Jane made no secret of the fact that the only thing she was looking for was a husband to take her away from all this. It was Alice who made things happen; Alice who stirred things up; Alice who was never content with the mundane—and it was Alice's adventures through which they all lived vicariously, whether they liked to admit it or not.

After a moment Barbara said dismissively, "He lives way over in one of those fancy mansions on Fifth Avenue. You couldn't even get in the gate of a place like that." But her eyes were alight with speculation, as though she were already imagining exactly *how* Alice was going to do it.

"They're having a party," Molly insisted. "The gate will be open. How *are* you going to get in, Alice?"

"That's the least of my problems now." Alice closed the wardrobe door and leaned against it, her brow knit in annoyance. "I've got to have something to *wear*."

"What about Lady H.?" suggested Jane hopefully. "She has a whole trunkful of absolutely gorgeous gowns. I know, because I helped her pack them up one day and—"

The other three quelled her with a look. The main difference between Alice and Mrs. Handley was about fifty pounds.

"Well, we could alter it," Jane said defensively.

"You don't steal a dress and then alter it," pointed out Barbara dryly. "That's a surefire way to get caught."

"Nobody said anything about stealing! I was just—"

"Barbara," Molly said slowly, and turned to her with a light in her eye, which Alice quickly caught.

"Of course!" she exclaimed, and pressed her hands together excitedly.

It took only a moment for Jane to catch on. "You're about Alice's size! We'd hardly have to alter your dress at all!"

"Alter!" Barbara's expression went from incredulity to outrage, but she quickly saw she was outnumbered. She threw up her hands in self-defense. "Now wait just a minute—"

"Oh, Barbara, please!" Alice extended her clasped hands entreatingly. "It would only be for one night and I'd be so careful—"

"I haven't even worn it yet!"

"Barbara, how can you be so selfish? Remember all the times Alice has loaned you her stockings and her bobby pins—"

"But it's not even my dress! It belongs to the club and I can't just—"

She broke off helplessly in the face of the three pairs of eyes that alternately begged and accused her. She turned away, frowning as she patted her rag curls to test for dryness. "I don't know why I have to get involved in this, anyway," she grumbled. "It's a stupid idea and it'll never work. Crashing Nick Crawford's party, trying to meet a man like Tyler Bradford, and *then* expecting him to just walk up and give you a job. What are you all staring at me for? *She's* the one who should have her head examined!"

Jane and Molly exchanged a look, and Alice went over to Barbara. She knelt beside the window seat on which Barbara was sitting and she said, "I know it sounds crazy to you, Barb. Everything I do sounds crazy to you, but you've been in the business a lot longer than I have and you don't have to worry... Don't you see, Barb? I've *got* to meet Bradford, and I've got to make him hire me. I can't keep washing dishes forever. I just can't."

She dropped her gaze briefly and then looked back up at her friend, the old determination flashing in her eyes. "When I came to New York," she said, "I gave myself a year. I'd either make it, or go back home to Tennessee and teach school like my mother wants me to and marry Bart Catlow from down the road. Well, my year's almost up, and so are my savings, and I don't *want* to marry Bart Catlow. So I've got to do something. I'm going to do something, something big, and I just won't take no for an answer from Tyler Bradford or anybody else! I'm going to make it."

Barbara looked at her for a long time. "If you spill anything on that dress," she warned darkly, "or tear it—"

"I won't even sweat on it!" Alice promised earnestly, and crossed her heart with her index finger.

After another long moment, Barbara stood up and went reluctantly to get the dress.

Molly clapped her hands together and squealed with excitement, and Alice couldn't repress a big grin. "You're going to do it!" Molly exclaimed. "You're really going to go to a swanky party on Fifth Avenue with people whose names are longer than this whole building and eat caviar and drink— Goodness, I bet they even have champagne! Rich people can, you know, because the policemen always look the other way—"

"Wait!" cried Jane suddenly, leaping up from the sofa. "I have a pair of silk stockings you can borrow. My brother sent them to me for Christmas, but I haven't had any place to wear them yet."

She hurried off to her room and Alice hugged herself, still grinning broadly. Success was waiting like a big prize wrapped with a bow just on the other side of the door, and all she had to do was cross the threshold and claim it as hers. Just how she was going to open the door she wasn't quite sure yet, but that was a minor detail she would worry about when the time came. The important thing was that after nine months of rejection and defeat—and dishwater-raw hands— she finally had a chance to make something happen in her life. She might not get another one, so she was going to make this chance count.

Alice was not beautiful—not in the way Barbara was beautiful with her cascade of golden curls and her perfectly upturned nose and lips that knew just how to pout without looking silly—but she was pretty. She wore her chestnut-colored hair in a short, wavy shingle, which not only marked her as a woman of fashion but showed off her flawless complexion and big brown eyes to a definite advantage. Her eyelashes were thick and dark, and she plucked her brows so that they framed her eyes in a perfect natural arch. She sometimes wished her nose was more like Barbara's, and she consciously practiced softening the lines of her mouth, which too often looked harsh and determined, or worse, childishly playful when smiling. She was naturally thin, a condition that nine months of irregular meals had done nothing to improve, but a straight figure was fashionable these days, and she never had to starve herself to look good in the short, waistless dresses that were so popular now. For the most part, Alice was satisfied with her looks; if she had not been she never would have had the courage to leave the security of Haven's Hollow, Tennessee, and take her chances in the big city.

When, two and a half hours later, Alice stepped in front of the mirror, she was more than satisfied with the way she looked. She was very nearly astonished.

Barbara's gown was a glittery pink-and-gold satin brocade, dropping from a sleeveless, square-cut bodice to just above the ankles in front, fluttering to a three-inch train in back. A wide sash wound around the hips and ended in a double knot just above the left thigh, loose ends trailing provocatively. Molly had supplied a strand of fake pearls that fell to the waist, and the crowning touch was a headband of the same glittery brocade, which rested low on Alice's forehead and sported a flashy pink peacock feather.

"My goodness," Alice said softly. "I look almost . . . grown-up."

The other three women stepped back to survey their work critically.

"Earrings," fretted Jane. "She needs earrings. Long diamond ones. And a bracelet."

Barbara gave her a withering look. "Not with pearls, she doesn't. And just where do you think we're going to get diamonds at this late date?"

"Zircons, then," insisted Jane.

"No, no it's perfect." Alice backed away from the mirror defensively, careful not to trip over her train. "If I borrow one more thing I'll be so worried about losing something I won't be able to think about what I'm supposed to be doing. What time is it, anyway?"

"Just a quarter till nine. You've got plenty of time. These things don't get started till nine or ten at the earliest."

Alice looked at Jane in dismay. "But if I'm not home by eleven Lady Harridan will lock me out."

Jane shrugged. "So you'll have to work fast."

"Wait, just one last finishing touch." Molly approached her with a patch box that was left over from a costume drama she had done recently. Over Alice's uncertain protests, she expertly applied a small round patch with tweezers and paste to the area an inch away from the corner of Alice's mouth. The effect was to draw attention to Alice's lips, which were already painted a lovely shade of crimson, and to make her look even more dashing and glamorous than she had before. The other girls nodded approvingly, and even Alice had to admit the touch was inspired.

"Don't smile until it dries," Molly warned.

"I feel like a fairy princess," Alice murmured, trying not to move her lips.

"Well," agreed Barbara grudgingly, "the dress doesn't suit you as well as it does me, but you'll do, I guess."

"She looks smashing!" countered Jane energetically. "Absolutely smashing! Nobody will ever suspect she's not one of those hoity-toity East Siders we're always reading about in the papers and, oh, I wish I had thought of this! Promise me, Alice," she insisted urgently, "if you *do* get in, and you *do* meet somebody from society, promise me you'll introduce me!"

Alice held the patch against her skin and tried not to smile. "I promise," she said. "But if I don't get started right now I won't have a chance of getting in. I've got to get there just when everybody else does, not too early or too late, or I'll be sure to be noticed."

"Wait!" cried Jane. "One more thing." She scampered from the room while Alice dumped out the contents of her coin purse and began trying to count out enough money for cab fare.

In a moment Jane returned with a long pink feather boa, which unmistakably did not belong to her. The other three girls stared.

"That's Lady Harridan's!"

"So?" Jane returned defensively. "Do you think she's going to want to wear it tonight? She won't even know it's gone."

Alice looked doubtful, but then Jane arranged the boa around Alice's neck and she caught a glimpse of herself in the mirror.

"Perfect!" Molly declared.

"Very stylish," Barbara agreed, and made a small adjustment to the way the boa draped over Alice's shoulder. "Now it's perfect."

Alice turned to the mirror, and almost against her will, an impish grin tugged at the corners at her mouth. The patch emphasized her smile and made her look more mysterious than playful, sophisticated and even a little dangerous. "Well," she decided, "if I'm going to be a sinner I may as well go all the way." Only a small frown crossed her brow as she added, "My mama would roast me on a spit if she ever found out what I was doing." But then, her mother wouldn't approve of much of anything Alice had done since she had arrived in New York, and Alice had decided a long time ago that it was kinder to keep the dear lady in ignorance.

They crept down the stairway, careful not to rouse Mrs. Handley, who was contentedly listening to a Verdi opera on the parlor radio. They held their breaths until they were safely out on the stoop, and then Alice hugged her three friends enthusiastically. "Thank you! I don't know what I would have done without you!"

"Bring us back something to eat," suggested Molly.

"Don't forget," added Jane, "if you meet anybody important, be sure to mention my name."

And Barbara shook her head dolefully. "You'll never get past the front gate."

Alice waved gaily over her shoulder and hurried down the walk to hail a cab.

ALICE FONTAINE had been born Mary Alice Floyd to hardworking farm people nineteen and a half years ago. She had changed her name from Floyd to Fontaine because even an ingenue like she was could see Floyd was not suited for the stage, and because she couldn't go so far as to break her parents' hearts by *completely* changing her name. So she dropped the Mary, kept the Alice, and added a dash of class with Fontaine. She thought that, as a compromise, her name worked very well.

All her life Alice had wanted to *be* somebody. As the oldest child in a family of eight and the undisputed favorite, she supposed that ambition was as much her parents' fault as her own. She was pretty, she walked away with every prize the small one-room school had to offer, and at nine was reading the devotional at Sunday service. Everyone agreed that Mary Alice Floyd was something special. From a very early age Alice had known she was destined for greatness.

At thirteen she had determined what direction that greatness would take. In addition to taking care of her brothers and sisters, doing her chores and keeping up with her schoolwork, Alice had taken a job at the General Store and saved every penny toward that day when she would leave Haven's Hollow to become a great stage actress. When she finished school at age fifteen she supplemented her income by scrubbing the church floors twice a week and taking in laundry on Saturdays. It sometimes seemed as though Alice had spent half her life with her hands plunged up to the elbows in dirty water. But she didn't mind; she didn't complain. Every diaper she washed, every board she scrubbed, took her one step closer to New York City, and a lifetime of freedom.

When she had stood at the Chattanooga station almost a year ago, with her mother dispensing advice and warnings between sobs and her father looking stern but proud, she'd had an awful feeling of pathos, as though the train that was chugging along the track would bear her off to another world from which there was no return. But then her mother had thrust into her hands a handkerchief-wrapped bundle of money—a collection the community had taken up to see her on her way. Alice knew then that she had to succeed, for the sake of their dreams, as well as hers.

Nine months had passed and she still spent most of her time with her hands in dirty water, but she wasn't discouraged. She had worked too hard, and come too far, to go home in defeat now. She had tasted freedom and it was a potent drug; she was no longer the same girl who had left Haven's Hollow with a mended carpetbag and a headful of dreams, and the folks at home would not recognize, or welcome, her now.

Alice Fontaine was a woman of the twenties, thoroughly liberated, completely modern. She bobbed her hair and wore her skirts up to her knees, and painted her lips and smoked cigarettes. Sometimes, if she was lucky, she got a small part in a strolling musical or a vaudeville show, and once she even posed for a portrait in a magazine. Unfortunately the magazine had suspended publication before the portrait could make her famous, but she earned ten dollars—paid in advance—and she had no doubt that if opportunity could knock once, it could knock twice.

Tonight the knocking was so loud it practically hurt her ears.

It was nine-thirty by the time the cab approached the exclusive parkside address Jane had given her. The gates were open and the big four-story structure was ablaze with lights. To Alice's delight, a line of cars curved down the drive and into the street, and more than one couple, disdaining to wait for their driver to reach the front door and the valet's helpful hand, climbed out of their vehicle and walked up the drive. No one looked twice as the cab pulled up at the end of the line and Alice got out.

She could hear the laughter and music long before she exited the car, and she felt as she had when she was six years old, climbing over the fence into a neighbor's apple orchard: exhilarated with the knowledge that she was somewhere she was not supposed to be, terrified of getting caught, and so excited she didn't care.

Two men in evening dress, accompanied by three women in multicolored silks, were getting out of a white Rolls-Royce. All of them were laughing, and the two men looked as though they had already had more than a little to drink. None of them noticed as Alice fell into step behind them and proceeded up the drive. Along the way they called out to friends as more brightly dressed people got out of highly polished cars, and Alice, wide-eyed, absorbed it all. Bearcats and roadsters painted in colors from fire-engine red to shocking pink lined the drive, occasionally interspersed with a stately black Essex or gold-trimmed Rolls-Royce. The women were mostly young and loud, and their finery for the evening ranged from sweeping floor-length chiffon to above-the-knee sheaths decorated with yards of glass beads and row upon row of shimmering fringe. Headdresses were in abundance: a gold snake coiled around the cropped head of one young deb, a peacock feather draped exotically across the ear of another. Alice, in her droopy pink feather, tried not to feel too dowdy.

As the drive gave way to a flagstone walkway circling the front of the house, Alice dropped back into the shadows of a hedge, pretending to straighten her stocking as she circumspectly examined the proceedings. Light spilled from the house and from lawn torches, illuminating pots of flowering plants and the equally brilliant shades of the ladies' gowns. Diamonds twinkled and feathers bobbed. Bursts of laughter punctuated the tempo of a lively jazz tune from inside the house. The wonder of all that house contained was so rich Alice could almost taste it.

At the door was a rigid-looking gentleman in black tails who must have been the butler. Alice had never seen a real butler before. As each guest approached he nodded without smiling or speaking; they flashed a card at him—probably an invitation—and proceeded inside unmolested. No one got past without that invitation. Why, oh, why, hadn't Alice thought to bring a folded piece of paper that she could wave before his eyes and possibly fool him long enough to allow her to get inside?

But it was too late for hindsight now, and she was undaunted. A fake invitation would have been simpler, but Alice was an expert at improvisation.

She waited until a likely couple walked by, then fell into step behind them. As they approached the door she increased her pace until, on the steps, she was abreast of them. The man reached in his coat pocket for his invitation, and Alice grasped the woman's hand.

"My dear!" she exclaimed. "How lovely to see you again! No one told me you were going to be here. My goodness, how long has it been, anyway?"

The woman blinked and took a small step backward. "I—I'm sure I don't know."

Alice allowed her no quarter. "Oh, you always were such a silly thing with dates—not that I'm much better, mind you. And don't you look lovely? That gown!" And she shook an admonishing finger at her, putting on her best teasing voice. "You've been to Paris, you naughty thing!"

The woman smiled uncertainly and her gentleman friend, presenting his invitation to the butler, cast a curious, though friendly glance toward Alice. "Why yes," the woman admitted. "I have. Do you like it?"

"Why, it's absolutely divine! Do tell me the name of your couturier again. I swear names just fly out of my head."

"Why it's—"

The butler arched a meaningful look at Alice. "Madam, your invitation, please."

Alice pretended not to hear, but wound her arm through the other woman's affectionately and urged her through the door. "Why, we have just *scads* of catching up to do. How is all the old crowd? I've been so frightfully out of touch, you simply must tell me everything..."

Still looking somewhat confused, the other woman allowed Alice to lead her inside. Behind her, Alice thought she heard the butler clear his throat, but she didn't even look around.

She was inside.

Chapter Two

The room in which she found herself was such a cacophony of sight and sound and color that for a moment it took Alice's breath away. It was a long, high-ceilinged room that opened via an arched doorway into another room at the far end, and branched out on either side to other rooms. The floor was black-and-white marble tile, the walls were done in strips of a geometric print that gave the area an exotic, slightly Middle Eastern air, and the ceiling, Alice noticed as she tilted her head back, was a pale blue with painted clouds. The motif—or what little Alice could see of it through the crush of swaying, jostling bodies—appeared to be Egyptian, with low ottomans and chaises, gilded scrollwork and imposing-looking statuary. In the center of the room was a sculpted fountain in which an unmistakably naked man held the waist of a woman whose only adornment was a fluttery scrap of cloth about her ankles. The woman had a water pitcher in her hand that the man's embrace had presumably overturned, and a fountain of water splashed from it into the pool below.

Flowers banked every wall, draped the enormous chandeliers and climbed the fountain pool. The air

was humid and sweet with the smell of hothouse blos-
soms and rich perfume, all of which was underlaced
with the ever present thread of cigarette smoke. The
big room captured and magnified the sound of
hundreds of voices, all chattering and laughing at
once; from another part of the house an orchestra
bleated a jazzy tune. Alice felt as though she had truly
gone through the Looking Glass.

The companion of the woman Alice had used to
gain entry had caught up with her, and the two of
them were engaged in a low conversation that was
punctuated by meaningful glances at Alice. The
woman turned to Alice with a look that was much
cooler than it had been before and said, "My dear,
you must forgive me, but I'm afraid I don't recall—"

At the same moment Alice noticed the butler
speaking to another official-looking man at the door,
who immediately nodded and started to come toward
her. She exclaimed, "Why, I do swear, isn't that Ted
and Celia over there? Forgive me, dearest, I simply
must say hello." She lifted her hand gaily and called,
"Ted! Darling!" Quickly she disappeared into the
crowd.

She insinuated herself deeper and deeper into the
crush of bodies, effusively greeting people she did not
know and calling out fictitious names, ignoring the
puzzled stares that followed her. All the while she was
thinking, *Jane would die. She would simply die!* The
diamonds and pearls that glittered in the hair and
draped the bosoms of these women were real; their
gowns, whether short and fringed, or long and
sculpted, definitely had not come from the costume
box of a back-street club. Alice spotted a pair of shoes

that were painted gold and studded with jewels and she couldn't help staring.

But it wasn't just the way these people looked that captivated Alice; it was the way they behaved. Gay abandon was like an exotic scent in the air, and simply inhaling it made Alice feel light-headed. The way the women were draped suggestively over their male companions, the boldness of their smiles, the careless caresses of hands that had never touched dishwater nor changed a diaper. The lazy gleam of male eyes, the blatant flash of a silver flask, the lazy, sinuous way in which they moved, all of it combined to form a portrait of indolence and self-indulgence that Alice found both mildly shocking and exhilarating. It was clear that these people never worried about overdue rent or skipped a meal or searched behind furniture cushions for cab fare. This was what Alice had come to New York to find. This was where she belonged. And this was where she would stay, just as soon as she found Tyler Bradford and convinced him that she was the newest rising star in the modeling world.

She was so entranced by all the movement and gaiety around her that she had, for a moment, almost forgotten her purpose in being here. Now, shaking off the spell, she determinedly squared her shoulders and turned to begin her search for Tyler Bradford.

And she ran straight into the grim-faced butler.

THE PARTY HAD BEEN IN MOTION for less than an hour and already Nicholas Crawford was bored. Sometimes he was alarmed, in a vague and not very serious way, at how easily he grew bored these days. And in truth it wasn't his own apathy that disturbed him as much as the possibility that his father, who was constantly accusing him of being jaded, cynical and thoroughly worthless, might actually be right.

He leaned against a life-size statue of Nefertiti, sipping a glass of contraband champagne and lazily watching the array of guests pretending to have a good time. He wondered why he had allowed Cynthia to talk him into this. He wondered if it wasn't too late to change his mind about spending the summer in the city. He wondered how many more glasses of champagne it would take to give him the energy to walk away from his own party.

"Well, aren't you the gracious host?" Cynthia sidled up to him, her eyes glinting with dry humor, her lips drawn in a humorless smile. "Having a good time?"

Nick lifted his glass to her. "A veritable orgy, my dear. You've outdone yourself. Nero himself must be spinning in his grave with envy. I wouldn't have missed it for the world."

She drew her feathered fan under his chin idly, causing him to flinch and scowl. "Don't be such a clown. It doesn't suit you. Besides, everyone seems to be having a grand time, and I won't have you spoiling it. You know how we all look forward to your parties."

"Ah, yes. The annual ritual in which we all drink too much champagne, disgrace ourselves in the bushes on the way out, smash up our motorcars and the face of at least one of our dearest friends. What could be more exhilarating?"

She hid an exaggerated yawn behind her fan. "Since when did you become such a god-awful bore? My own brother. How embarrassing."

"On the contrary, my dear. I was just thinking that a good fistfight is just what we need to liven this place up. Perhaps I'll go start one."

He turned as though to set aside his glass, but Cynthia stopped him with a light touch of her fan. "You may not have to." A peculiar smile touched her lips and her attention was directed across the room. "Things may start to get a bit livelier without your help."

He gave her a questioning look, and she explained, "We have a little gate-crasher, I'm afraid. I just set Leeland on her, and it looks as though she intends to put up a fight."

Nick followed his sister's gaze until he found the focus of her attention. The girl in question was doggedly trying to outstep Leeland, pausing to engage in brief snatches of conversation with people she obviously didn't know. Nick felt a small twinge of amusement for the girl's gall, as well as for the confused reactions of his friends, who were too afraid of being considered out-of-step to call her bluff.

"Well, what do you know?" he murmured. "This might turn out to be entertaining, after all."

"Now, Nikki." Cynthia laid a staying hand on his arm as he started to move away, and her tone was laced with a hint of alarm. "I don't like that look in your eyes. You're not going to go off on another one of your crusades, are you?"

Nick grimaced. "Crusades? What a shocking thing to be accused of. If you were a man you wouldn't say it to my face, I assure you."

She frowned impatiently. "You know perfectly well how you are when it comes to your little collection of vagabonds and tramps! Why, the last time you brought a mob of them home, to this very house!''

He chuckled. ''I'd hardly say that three poor men looking for a place out of the snow constitutes a mob.''

''Nonetheless, I ended up sleeping with my door bolted and hiding the silver in my lingerie drawer, and afterward—the smell! Why, we had to air out the whole house, and in the middle of winter! Really, Nikki, you'd think you'd show some consideration. After all, this is my home, too, not to mention my personal safety—'' Suddenly she stopped, the indignation in her face turning swiftly to suspicion. ''*You* didn't invite her here, did you? As one of your wretched little jokes? Because if you did, I swear, Nikki...''

He shook his head, watching in amusement as Leeland stealthily approached his helpless victim. ''Never laid eyes on her before in my life. Upon my honor.''

Cynthia sniffed. ''Your honor! *There's* a joke.''

The butler caught up with the intruder and fastened his hand grimly on her upper arm. She turned in a fair imitation of astonishment. A small crowd was beginning to form.

A smile tugged at the corners of Nick's mouth as the first spark of interest he had felt in weeks kindled inside him. He said, ''Excuse me, sister dear,'' and set his champagne glass in Nefertiti's open palm. Straightening the lapels of his tuxedo, oblivious to his sister's protests, he made his way across the room.

ALICE DREW HERSELF UP to her full five feet three inches and insisted in her most dignified voice, ''I assure you that you are making a dreadful mistake. I've never been so insulted—''

"I'm sorry, miss," replied the butler with a great show of forbearance, "but no one is admitted without an invitation. If you'll just follow me, please."

She gave a light laugh that she hoped did not reveal the desperation she was feeling. To come so close and then be tossed out on her ear! "My invitation? Why didn't you say so? I'm sure I have it here. We'll have this cleared up in the twitch of a whisker if you'll kindly release my arm."

Perhaps if she could distract him for an instant, she could slip away and stay lost in the crowd long enough to find Tyler Bradford. Perhaps she could pretend to swoon or twist her ankle, and the Crawfords would be forced to offer her hospitality until she recovered. But she felt her hopes sink as she gave an experimental tug on her arm and found it held as firmly as before. The butler's stern expression did not ease, and a curious, amused crowd was gathering close, hemming her in. Her situation looked grim and she cast about frantically for a way to improve it.

Just as she was about to resort to a sudden attack of convulsions—difficult to enact, but effective if done well—a male voice exclaimed, "Why, I thought it was you from across the room!"

A young man broke through the crowd, his hands extended, and as Alice stared dumbly, he walked up to her and grasped her hands warmly. "Annabelle, my dear—''

"Alice," she corrected swiftly under her breath.

"Alice," he continued smoothly, "how good of you to come. It's been ages, hasn't it? And how is your dear mother? I was saying at breakfast only the other day..."

The butler cleared his throat softly. "Excuse me, Mr. Nicholas. Do you know this young lady?"

He looked at the butler with an expression that managed to portray an admirable mixture of indulgence, annoyance and surprise all at the same time. "Why, of course. Is there some reason I shouldn't know a guest at my own party?"

The butler looked uncomfortable, gave a stiff little bow, cleared his throat again and walked away.

"Now then, Annabelle—"

"Alice."

"Yes, of course." He tucked her arm amiably through his and began to lead her away. "Do tell me what you've been up to. You've met everyone, I see. How many years has it been? That many? Do you still ride that lovely Arabian of yours—what was his name?"

His hand was folded over hers, holding it in the crook of his arm, his head was bent toward her in a friendly, interested way, and his voice rang with warmth as he led her through the crowd toward a small, relatively isolated alcove. Alice was so taken aback by this turn of events that she actually found herself wondering if she *did* know this fellow, or if he could have possibly mistaken her for someone else, and then she saw the twinkle in his eyes, and relief and gratitude overwhelmed her.

They reached the alcove and she dropped his arm, staring. "Who *are* you?" she burst out.

He bowed deeply from the waist. "Nicholas Crawford, at your service, ma'am."

"Oh...my." A dozen things rushed through Alice's mind, not the least of which was rampant confusion, but still all she could do was stare.

He was, in general appearance, not unlike any other man she had glimpsed since entering the house—impeccably groomed, elegant, with the sort of careless grace that marked him as a breed apart as clearly as a racehorse could be distinguished from a dray. His hair was dark, his face smooth, and he had the most incredible eyes Alice had ever seen. They were pale blue, the color of a clear-cut aquamarine gem, so light as to be almost transparent, and surrounded by a fringe of startling dark lashes so rich they looked as though they had been painted on. When he smiled, as he was doing now, the flesh beneath his eyes did not crinkle and flatten outward, as was common with most people, but puffed upward, narrowing his eyes and giving his face a lazily sensuous, almost dangerous look. Alice was so captivated by his eyes that she almost missed the dimple just left of his full, gently curving lips, and it seemed unfair that one man should have those eyes *and* a dimple. She didn't seem to be able to stop staring.

"Oh, my," she said again, and was annoyed with herself for not being more articulate. Nor was she particularly pleased with the breathless tone of her voice, and she quickly cleared her throat to rectify it. "Well, Mr....Crawford, it was certainly very gallant of you to...to rescue me." And then she stopped, her brief attack of nerves and uncertainty overcome by blatant curiosity. "Why did you do that?" she demanded.

He grimaced a little. "Why," he repeated. "One of my two least favorite words."

She cocked her head at him, aware that he had not answered her question but finding it didn't matter as much as it once had. "What's the other?"

"No," he responded, and the corner of his lips twitched with another one of those lazy grins. "And now, Miss... What did you say your name was again?"

"Fontaine. Alice Fontaine. Actually, it's Mary Alice Floyd, but I changed it for the stage." She had a dreadful feeling that as soon as she stopped talking he was going to take her arm and politely escort her to the door, so she dared not even pause for breath. "It's not that I don't *like* my name—Floyd is a very respectable name back where I come from in Tennessee—but it just doesn't have that ring to it, if you know what I mean. I think it's very important that a name have a ring, kind of a musical quality, because people remember it more easily. Alice Floyd. That's dull. Alice Fontaine. That's memorable. And you have to be remembered in this business, or you're nothing. Of course my parents don't know I've changed my name. They'd probably be hurt if they found out, and I suppose when I become famous I'll have to tell them, but until then I think it's kinder to spare them, don't you? It has kind of a French sound, I think. Fontaine. French is very in." Abruptly, she ran out of things to say, and she simply stood there, waiting for the worst.

But Nicholas Crawford simply bent her a slightly quizzical look, extended his arm to her and said, "Well, Miss Mary Alice Floyd Fontaine, as I was about to say, you have nothing to drink. Would you care for a glass?"

Alice repressed a small gasp. "You mean... you're going to let me stay?"

"That depends." He pretended thoughtfulness. "Are you wanted by the police?"

"Certainly not!"

"That's too bad. Harboring a fugitive would be interesting. But I think I shall let you stay anyway."

Alice giggled, relaxing a little as she let him lead her through the crowd. "You're a very strange man."

"Thank you."

"Not," she hastened to add, "that I'm not grateful—I am, truly more than you can know—but you're still . . . strange."

Nick laughed. He could not remember the last time he had laughed so freely and on so little to drink, and it felt odd. But there was something about the earnest, apologetic look on her face as she called him "strange"—she, who had crashed a party so exclusive not even his own parents could get in, who had gone to battle with his butler and given him a three-minute lecture on nothing more consequential than the origin of her name. Considering that and looking at her, he found laughing seemed the only natural thing to do.

She was so different from the other women of his acquaintance that she stood out like a beacon, and Nick was amazed that he hadn't noticed her before. He didn't claim to be an expert on fashion, but even he could tell that the dress she wore was out of a costume trunk, the feathered headdress was beginning to wilt, and her shoes were a little shabby. Her face, though too heavily painted and rouged, was pretty, but he could turn half a degree in either direction and find women who were just as attractive, perhaps even more so. On the street he would not have looked at her twice. But here in the midst of this frantic crowd whose familiarity had become deadly to him, she was like an exotic bird in a nest full of wrens, and he found everything about her delightful.

Of course Nick was aware that he had a notoriously short attention span, and that his fascination with the young lady would probably not outlast the next glass of champagne. But even a few moments' relief from ennui was better than none, and for now she was exactly what the doctor ordered.

"Oh, look!" Suddenly she grasped his arm and pointed toward the fountain, her eyes bright with excitement. "Those people are holding their glasses under the water pitcher! Is it... Do you have *champagne* in that fountain?"

"A very poor quality," he admitted, "and it tastes foul. The real wine is being served at the buffet, this way."

He started to turn her toward the adjoining room, but she held back, exclaiming, "Oh, no, I'd rather have it from the fountain. That is, if you don't mind. Jane would never forgive me if I told her there was a champagne fountain and I didn't even taste it!"

Nick shrugged, amused, and headed toward the fountain. "Who is Jane?"

"A friend of mine at Mrs. Handley's. She's always reading about fancy society goings-on. She says you're one of the top five most eligible bachelors in the city."

Alice wondered if that was quite the proper thing to say, especially since, looking at him, she could easily understand why he was among the top five. Anyone with that combination of good looks and easy suavity could not possibly need to be reminded of his status.

But Nick only replied, "Oh, really? I thought I was much higher."

Alice didn't know how to respond to that.

He edged his way toward the base of the fountain, where the laughing crowd was so thick that he had to slip his arm around Alice's waist to keep her with him. In view of everything else going on, that minor familiarity seemed not only acceptable, but positively chaste.

Someone was trying to balance a glass of champagne on the female statue's naked breast. A man had his companion draped backward over his arm and was pouring champagne into her laughing mouth. When the liquid splashed on her neck and down the loose fitting bosom of her gown, he licked it away with his tongue. Another couple was posed on the basin of the fountain, engaged in an embrace almost as lewd as that struck by the statue above them. Alice liked to think of herself as a sophisticate, but she knew she was gaping like a schoolgirl unable to avert her eyes.

Nick, however, hardly seemed to notice as he scooped up two glasses from the ledge of the pool and handed one to her. Champagne splashed into her glass and over her hand, and Alice giggled, forgetting her awkwardness as she tasted the effervescent liquid.

"Well?" Nick's expression was amused as he looked down at her. "Would Jane approve?"

"Definitely." Alice wrinkled her nose and sipped again, growing accustomed to the sparkly, dry flavor. "I like it," she decided. "It's not as good as cola, but I like it."

Nick laughed and slipped his arm around her waist again as someone jostled up against her. This time the gesture did not seem so much protective as intimate, and Alice felt a little thrill travel along the base of her spine. No, Jane would *never* believe this. A house full of glamorous people and Egyptian statuary, champagne from a fountain, and Nicholas Crawford with those magical blue eyes glinting down at her and his arm around her waist. They would live on tales of this night for weeks. Months.

Abruptly Alice realized that, for the last few glorious minutes, she had been so entranced by her good fortune that she had forgotten her purpose in being here. Quickly she swallowed the sip of champagne she had just taken and said, "You're very kind—"

"Nonsense. I'm a complete degenerate, as anyone in this crowd will be happy to tell you. Come along, let's get out of this crush before we're trampled to death."

Alice had some difficulty keeping up with him and balancing her half-full glass of champagne, because he held her so closely that they were like one body instead of two. She found herself repeatedly bumping into people and murmuring "Excuse me" and "So sorry" to men and women who didn't even turn around.

"What I mean is," she managed a little breathlessly, when they had cleared the crowd around the fountain, "it was good of you to let me stay and give me champagne and all, and you've been so nice I really hate to ask another favor—"

"Don't be absurd," he interrupted negligently. "If I had thought it would be more entertaining to kick you out than to let you stay, I would have kicked you out. So you see there's nothing good about me at all, and if I'm nice to you it's only for my own selfish pleasure, I assure you. Now, what is this favor?"

Alice looked at him, more than half-convinced he was serious. What did she know of the wild, cavalier

world in which he lived? He was perfectly capable of
using her for his own enjoyment and then turning on
her when he grew bored, which meant that she could
find herself on the street again at any moment. Obviously she had best act on his good humor while she
still had the chance.

She said, "Actually, I didn't crash your party just
for the fun of it."

"How disappointing."

"I came here to meet someone."

"Not a man, I hope? I'll be crushed."

She saw he was flirting with her and the knowledge
made her cheeks tingle with excitement, but she
couldn't afford to be distracted. Gamely, she pushed
on. "A...a Mr. Tyler Bradford. Do you know him?"

"Know him, yes. Don't like him much, but I know
him. Why?"

"I was hoping you could point him out to me."

"Aha." His smile was teasing. "So he wasn't
expecting you any more than I was?"

"No, actually, the fact is—"

"Then I say forget about him. You'd only be disappointed, anyway. Bradford's not half as charming
as I am, and not even in the top ten."

She was about to open her mouth to object or explain, but the words were swept out of her head before they could even form. Nick had led her to the
banquet room and she stopped on the threshold, staring. "Look at all that food!" she breathed.

Three long tables, draped in white cloth and decorated with fresh flowers and greenery, formed an open
square along the three walls of the enormous room.
One entire table was devoted to breads and pastries—
rolls with gleaming brown crusts were fashioned into

birds and fishes, cakes shaped like swans were decorated with creamy white frosting and delicate pastel
flowers and ribbons, an arrangement of multicolored
tarts formed a carousel in the center. On another table were two turkeys, several ducks, a ham and an
enormous fish molded out of some sort of pâté. The
third table contained an array of delicacies so vast
Alice could scarcely begin to catalog them all—strawberries and fresh oranges and bowls of frothy cream,
tiny sandwiches cut into flower shapes and decorated
with green peppers and red tomatoes, a spiral of sau-
sages wrapped in pastry, a huge lobster shell over-
flowing with shredded pink meat, silver bowls of red
and black caviar... The mere spectacle was almost
more than the eye could take in; the rich aromatic
scents made Alice's knees week and her mouth water
shamelessly.

Nick was watching her with undisguised amusement. "Alice in Wonderland," he murmured.

Alice shook her head, trying to break the spell of so
much plenty in the face of so much need. "No," she
managed dazedly. "Cinderella at the ball." She gestured vaguely at her costume, her attention still mostly
on the tables of food. "Borrowed gown, make-believe
pearls, a surly cab driver instead of a coach-and-
four..." *And,* she thought but did not say, *a Prince
Charming all my own, and who would have believed
this could happen to me?*

Nick smiled and touched her back. "Come along.
Put away that nasty glass of sludge and taste some real
champagne."

Alice wasn't particularly interested in champagne,
but the aroma of the banquet tables drew her like a
lure, and she followed Nick willingly to the end of the

pastry table, where a waiter was pouring champagne from a towel-wrapped bottle into crystal glasses.

Alice could not bring herself to waste the champagne that was already in her glass, so she swallowed it quickly when Nick offered her a fresh glass. Watching her, Nick winced. "Not even bad champagne should be guzzled," he pointed out, "not as hard as it is to come by these days."

"I'm sorry." She took the fresh glass of champagne and sipped it. Truthfully, she couldn't tell much difference between that and what she had previously consumed. And she was still much more interested in the victuals than the libations. "I wouldn't think a man like you would have much trouble getting anything."

"One just has to be a little more creative sometimes. I generally manage to get what I want."

"I've never known a man who actually dealt with bootleggers before," Alice confessed. "I mean, not right up front like this." She found it somewhat awe-inspiring to realize that all this opulence was due, in a great part, to the offices of gangsters, and decided after the briefest of moments that it was probably best not to think about that at all.

His eyes narrowed with a sparkle of amusement. "I believe Al Capone was recently quoted as saying, 'When I haul it on the back of my truck it's called bootlegging; when your host serves it on a silver tray it's called hospitality.' There's a fine distinction, my dear. You should be careful not to offend your host." He was looking at her with a peculiar glint in his eyes, but if his words had a double meaning Alice was too naive to understand it, and too hungry to care.

Seeing the way her eyes wandered, Nick took a china plate from the arrangement by his elbow and handed it to her. Alice accepted it gratefully. Nick followed her down the buffet line, occasionally nibbling at a selection himself, watching in increasing amusement as she piled her plate high. At last, when it became obvious she was either going to have to stop before she reached the third table or ask for another plate, he groaned, "Oh, Lord, don't tell me you're a starving waif. How depressing."

"I'm not a waif," Alice responded, wondering if she could possibly balance one of those elegant-looking sandwiches on the edge of her plate without spilling everything and embarrassing herself beyond redemption. "But I am, at the moment, starving."

Remembering her promise to be careful of Barb's dress, she decided to forgo the sandwich, though with obvious reluctance. She wished she had pockets, because it hardly seemed fair to enjoy all this luxury without bringing some delicacies home to her friends. Perhaps she could sneak a few pastries into her evening purse when no one was looking.

Nick handed her a rolled napkin of silverware, his delight with her growing by the moment. "Don't they ever feed you at that place where you stay?"

"Oh, yes. But nothing like this. Besides, I'm usually working at mealtimes, which is a blessing in a way because Mrs. Handley's not a very good cook."

Balancing a bottle of champagne and a glass in one hand, and a platter of caviar and toast in the other, Nick gestured her toward a small table that was drawn up before a love seat next to the garden door. It was still too early for most of the guests to be interested in solid refreshments, and the room was relatively uncrowded. The little niche he had chosen was almost private, which suited Nick perfectly.

The band struck up a swinging rendition of *Bye-Bye Blackbird* and she tapped her foot to the rhythm. She hoped Nick would ask her to dance—and she hoped he would wait until she had finished every morsel on her plate before doing so.

When they were seated side by side on the love seat, Nick said, "So, you are an actress. Might you have been in anything I've seen?"

Alice thought for a moment, her fork poised over her plate. "There was a vaudeville show about six weeks ago. I was the one who cleaned up after the duck."

Nick smothered a smile in a sip of champagne. "I'm afraid I missed that one."

She shrugged, scooping up a big forkful of salmon mousse. "Don't feel bad. You didn't miss much."

Nick chuckled, spreading a wedge of toast with caviar. "Here, try this."

When Alice looked up she was surprised to see he had moved much closer, with one hand resting on the back of the love seat and his fingertips brushing her bare shoulder, the other hand holding the morsel of toast before her lips. The only polite thing to do was to part her lips and accept the bite he offered her. It seemed a very intimate thing to do, and the way his eyes lingered on her mouth, the way his fingertip brushed across her lower lip as though removing a crumb, made Alice's throat go so dry she could barely swallow, much less taste the delicacy. Now those pale aqua eyes held a lazy, confident light, and the slight, tilting smile on his lips reminded Alice of the way a man might look when he was watching a woman undress... Not, of course, that she had any practical experience whatsoever with that look.

She swallowed quickly and took a rather large sip of champagne. "That was very good."

"Your first caviar, and your first champagne." His fingers crept around her neck and traced a light pattern at the tip of her spine. "Before the evening's done, I shall have utterly corrupted you."

Alice dabbed her lips with her napkin and picked up her fork again. The touch of his fingers on her neck was making her skin prickle all along the length of her back and down her legs. It was not an entirely unpleasant sensation. "I doubt that."

"Oh?" A spark of amusement—or perhaps challenge—came into his eyes. "Are you incorruptible, then?"

"No." She dipped a piece of crispy duck into a red sauce with her fork. "It's just that I don't have much time."

His fingers paused in their delicate caress of her neck.

"You see," she explained to him earnestly, "if I'm not home by eleven Mrs. Handley will lock me out, and I really have to find Mr. Bradford so I'll have time to talk to him before—"

Nicholas Crawford dropped his hand, sat back against the love seat and laughed. "You are the most incredible young lady," he declared, his eyes snapping.

Alice wasn't sure that was a compliment. And though she was sorry he had dropped his hand, she was also a little relieved. Now it was much easier to keep her mind on her real purpose in coming here. She cleared her throat and said a little uncertainly, "Well, it's nice of you to say so, I'm sure. But about Mr. Bradford..."

The mirth left his face and his eyes narrowed a fraction as he lifted his champagne glass. "It's not very flattering of you to crash my party in search of another man, you know. I feed you caviar and champagne and all you can talk about is Tyler Bradford. If you're not careful, I might take offense."

"Oh, it's nothing like that at all!" she assured him quickly, although the bored tone with which he uttered the words made her doubt he was serious. "It's purely business. But very important business, so if you could just point out Mr. Bradford to me I'd be very grateful and won't bother you again."

Nicholas shrugged, refilling his glass. "I don't think he's here. Tyler usually has better taste than to come to my parties—that's one thing we have in common. He will be late, if he arrives at all."

Alice's disappointment was so great that she could actually feel her spirits sinking, deep down in her stomach. How was it possible that, after all this trouble, after getting in the door, outlasting the intrepid butler, even winning the favor of Nicholas Crawford, the object of her quest could elude her now? The paper had said he would be here. She had been so certain that all she had to do was get inside this house and everything would fall into place. Oh, how could her luck desert her now?

But Nicholas had said he might be late. She held on to that small hope. "How long do your parties usually last?"

He was thoughtful for a moment. "I'm not really sure. I can't say that I've ever stayed awake till the end of one."

Seeing her crestfallen features, Nick added, topping off her champagne glass, "Cheer up. If he does show, I'll wave him over, if it's that important to you. Meanwhile, you're in much better company than you would be if he were here."

Alice smiled wanly. "I'm sure I am."

But her words did not sound very convincing, and Nicholas noticed with a reproachful shake of his head. "You *do* know how to flatter a fellow, don't you? Come along, drink up while I see if I can think of something to get your mind off the inestimable Mr. Bradford."

Alice smiled, more genuinely this time, and lifted her glass. "You drink a great deal, don't you?"

"One of my many vices. Do you disapprove?"

Alice thought of her teetotal father and Bible-quoting mother, then she thought of all the laughter and gaiety that surrounded her now, and she frowned a little, confused. "I'm not sure."

"Good," he responsed, and lifted his glass again. "Because it wouldn't matter if you did. I'm thoroughly unredeemable, you know. I'm told so constantly."

Alice did not know whether to feel envy or pity for the elegant Nicholas Crawford, whose freewheeling life-style was all she had ever dreamed of, and whose smooth negligence had an air of desperate disillusionment about it. In the end she decided men like him were not meant to be judged, but enjoyed. Besides, the champagne must have started to go to her head because she found it difficult to concentrate on anything of consequence for very long—not even her disappointment over the possibility of missing Tyler Bradford.

Or perhaps it was only Nick's charm that made her so light-headed. She had a feeling it would be impossible to take anything seriously in his company.

He said pleasantly, "So, Mary Alice—"

She grimaced. "Please don't call me that. Only my mother calls me that. Do they call you Nikki?"

"Only my relatives, and then at great peril. All right then. Alice, is it?"

She nodded, breaking off the corner of a butter-soaked roll and popping it into her mouth.

"Tell me what life is like in— Where did you say you were from?"

"Haven's Hollow, Tennessee." She swallowed quickly and took a sip of champagne. "It's a very small town and absolutely nothing happens there. That's why I came to New York."

"To be the next Sarah Bernhardt."

She smiled at him. She had, Nick observed, one of the most enchanting smiles he had ever seen. It covered her whole face and made her look very young.

"Any reason I shouldn't be?" she tossed back at him coquettishly.

"None at all. Except of course . . ." He took a long sip of champagne. "And you mustn't take this personally, but having had an opportunity to view your performance up close, I must say there does appear to be room for improvement."

She frowned. "Like what?" she demanded. "I got in here, didn't I? My performance was good enough to fool your fancy friends."

"Yes, but only for a short while," he pointed out, "and you didn't fool my sister at all. She spotted you as a fraud immediately."

Alice settled back, the frown between her eyes
smoothing into lines of thoughtfulness. "That's true,"
she admitted after a moment. "But it still isn't very
nice of you to say so."

He laughed softly, blue eyes flashing. "I assure you,
being nice is one thing I've never been accused of."

She looked at him for a moment longer, uncertain
whether or not she should be insulted, and then decided it wasn't worth spoiling her meal over. She
picked up her fork. "You have a funny house," she
said. "All these statues and drawings on the walls. It's
not like I pictured at all."

"This?" He glanced around and waved a negligent
hand. "It's all plaster and paper and will be thrown
out tomorrow. Cynthia just got back from Egypt and
thought it would be clever to have an Egyptian theme
for the party."

"Oh." Alice tried not to sound as dismayed as she
was. She didn't quite know what to think of people
who would redesign an entire house for the sake of a
party and then throw it all away when they were finished.

But Nicholas caught her expression and his eyes
twinkled. "You disapprove?"

"Well, no," she assured him quickly. "I mean, I'm
hardly in a position to disapprove of anything and it's
none of my business but, well, it just seems so waste-
ful." She thought of her mother, mending and hand-
ing down worn-out articles of clothing through
generations, carefully drying seeds from this year's
garden for next, and even the girls at Mrs. Handley's,
sharing the laundry tub to save soap and turning
threadbare stockings eight or ten times before throw-

ing them out. She had to ask earnestly, "Don't you ever worry about running out of money?"

Nicholas laughed, and though it sounded exactly like the carefree laugh of any other young man in the room, there was a hard edge to it and there was no smile in his eyes. "My dear, there are many things I may be short of—patience, virtue, even good sense— but the one thing I need never fear running out of is money." He lifted his glass in a salute to the room in general. "Money is the one constant in my life, the only thing that can be counted on. Long may it reign." Then he glanced at her and there seemed to be a glint of challenge in his eyes. "I suppose that sounds terribly decadent to you."

"No," she replied, skewing a bit of tenderloin with her fork. It practically melted in her mouth. "I think it's marvelous. I expect to have loads of money myself one day. But I wouldn't like it to be the *only* thing I had. I'd prefer to depend on something a little more trustworthy, I think."

"Like what?"

"Myself," she answered immediately, and bit into a juicy section of orange.

The amusement in his eyes faded, and he seemed to look at her a little more closely than he had before. "You say the oddest things," he murmured, and that intent, examining look in his eyes was beginning to make Alice a little uneasy.

"In fact, you are an altogether odd girl," he decided. "I think I must be enchanted." Abruptly he put down his glass and stood. "Have you had enough to eat? Will you dance?"

Alice looked at her plate, somewhat disconcerted by his sudden change of mood and subject. In the other room, the musicians were striking up a Charleston.

"Well..."

"Surely an up-and-coming young actress like you knows how to do the Charleston!"

"Well, of course I do, but—"

"Come along then."

He grasped her hand, and sparing only one longing look backward for the delicacies remaining on her plate, Alice allowed herself to be pulled onto the dance floor.

Chapter Three

In only a matter of moments the abandoned pleasures of the palate were forgotten in favor of the heady gaiety of the dance. Nick led her into the midst of the crowd of laughing, jostling people, their hands touched and separated, and as one they fell into the jaunty steps of the Charleston. Around her, jewels glittered and women tossed back their heads and rolled their shoulders, men strutted out the steps with defiant playfulness; they danced with champagne glasses in their hands, they shouted their approval, they danced as though if the world ended tomorrow they would have no regrets. And for a time Alice was a part of those people and all they represented: freedom, gaiety, the single-minded celebration of the sensations of life.

She danced the Black Bottom and the shimmy, and the exhilaration of movement was almost as heady as the sips of champagne she took from Nick's never empty glass between dances. Sometimes another young man would try to cut in, but Nick always sent him away, and Alice was absurdly flattered by his possessiveness.

When Nick whirled her into his arms after the last steps of a particularly frenetic dance, Alice leaned against him, her face hot and her head spinning, gasping for breath between gulps of laughter. "Oh, please—I have to rest! I'm exhausted and I promised Barb I wouldn't perspire on her dress."

Nick chuckled and slipped his arm around her waist, holding her tightly as he moved through the crowd toward an open set of terrace doors. "By all means we mustn't allow that to happen."

The terrace was wide and deeply shadowed, lit only by the reflection of light from the inside. Flowering trees in pots decorated the corners, and more than one couple had decided to take advantage of the starlit night. Alice could hear soft female moans and giggles coming from one corner, and in another, clearly silhouetted by the light from the room behind, was a couple in a fierce embrace, the man's hands exploring parts of the woman's anatomy that made Alice blush and quickly look away.

Nick entwined the fingers of one hand with Alice's and led her to the edge of the terrace, where a stone half-wall overlooked a darkened garden. Alice tilted her face up to catch a cooling breeze and inhaled the scent of roses.

With his free hand, Nick took a handkerchief from his pocket and surprised her by gently blotting the perspiration from her face. Alice smiled and reached to take the handkerchief from him, but his hand trailed down, touching the cloth to her neck, her collarbone, and then to her chest just above the cut of her gown.

His touch, and the lazy intent in his eyes, made her heart beat faster. She was not unfamiliar with the ways of the world, and she knew he had not brought her out here to simply take the air. What she didn't know was what, exactly, she was supposed to do about it.

Her heart tapped a light, rapid rhythm against her rib cage and her breath came shallowly as Nick let the handkerchief flutter to the ground and his fingers traced a light pattern over the bare portion of her chest. When his fingertips dared to dip a little inside the material, just brushing against the top curve of her breast, Alice closed her hand around his.

"Are you trying to seduce me?" she inquired breathlessly.

He smiled. "It seems the natural thing to do."

Alice was giddy with the thought. What would it be like to be kissed by Nicholas Crawford? One of the top five most eligible bachelors in the city, the man with those magical eyes and full sensuous lips, and hands that felt like silk against her skin. One kiss, the appropriate ending to her Cinderella night. Surely that couldn't hurt.

"I think you must have had too much to drink," she said.

He laughed low in his throat. "And?"

"And..." She caught her breath as the hand still entwined with hers moved to his own body, arranging her fingers against the back of his neck. His other arm slipped around her waist, drawing her close. Alice did not try to move her hand or step away, enjoying for one brief intoxicating moment the sensation of his smooth warm skin against the palm of her hand, his abdomen brushing against hers, his scent enveloping her. It was with great difficulty that she remembered what she wanted to say.

"And...there are lots of other women here. You should be with one of them. You don't know what you're doing."

"Those other women bore me." His index finger traced her earlobe and sent tiny shivers down her spine. His eyes examined the shape of her face as though he had never seen anything more fascinating. "I know exactly what I'm doing."

Whatever resistance or common sense Alice might once have had was melting rapidly. She swayed toward him. She whispered, "I'm very flattered, I'm sure, but..." A horrible thought occurred to her. She stiffened in his arms. "What time is it?"

He stared at her. "You aren't serious?"

"Please!"

"Oh, very well. Stop squirming." He released her long enough to take out his pocket watch. An expression of definite impatience crossed his face as he flipped open the gold lid and held the watch up to the light. "It is...exactly ten forty-five. The shank of the evening."

"Oh, no!" Panic gripped Alice as she glanced desperately back toward the house. "I have to go—Mr. Bradford! I didn't even get to see him!" But it was too late to worry about that now. "I have to go!" she repeated, and turned quickly toward the steps that led into the garden, a quicker way to the street than going back through the house.

"Wait!" Incredulity and amazement marked Nick's face as he caught her hand. "You can't just— At least let me drive you home!"

"Oh, no, I couldn't possibly let Mrs. Handley see me come home at this hour in a motorcar with a man!" She pulled her hand away, took a few steps, then turned back quickly and said, "Thank you, I had a wonderful time, you've been very gracious. Good night!"

And without another moment to spare, she ran down the steps.

Nick started to go after her, then stopped at the head of the steps, bemused. "Even Cinderella left a slipper behind!" he called.

Alice grinned and waved back at him, but she did not pause. She ran toward the street where, with any luck at all, she would find a cabdriver who could make the twelve-minute drive to the Handley Hotel in ten.

"I STILL THINK you should have taken off one of your shoes and tossed it back to him," Molly said dreamily.

"With my luck, it would have hit him in the face and knocked him out cold," Alice replied. "Besides, that was the only good pair of shoes I have."

Late the next afternoon the two girls lounged on the bed, taking respite from the heat that, in July, was almost unbearable in the third-story room they shared. Alice had stripped down to her cami-knickers and lay on her stomach, searching through the Help Wanted section of the newspaper. Molly, who was so modest she undressed behind a screen even when no one but Alice was in the room, wore a cotton robe buttoned up to her chin and sat with her legs tucked primly to the side as she counted out the rent money.

"Still," sighed Molly, "it would have been so romantic. Not that it wasn't already romantic," she added. "It's practically the most romantic thing I've ever heard. Imagine, Nicholas Crawford and *you*."

Alice frowned a little and tried to concentrate on the newspaper. As far as she was concerned, the episode was over and the least said about it the better.

She had arrived on the doorstep the night before just as Mrs. Handley was turning the key in the lock. With much pleading and apology through the door panels, Alice had persuaded her landlady to unlock the door. At that point Mrs. Handley stared her down coldly for a good thirty seconds, snatched the borrowed feather boa from Alice's neck with enough force to leave a rope burn, and stalked away. Now not only was Alice behind on her rent, but she had made an enemy of her landlady, which was not a desirable thing to do under any circumstances.

It all would have been worth it, of course, if only she could have met Tyler Bradford. Her rent problems would be solved, she could *buy* Mrs. Handley a feather boa, and she might even have been able to afford to do something gaily extravagant, like leaving one of her slippers behind for Nicholas Crawford. Now she was not only right back where she started, but even worse off: she was out both cab fare and her landlady's goodwill.

Her friends seemed not in the least distressed by the failure of her mission, however. They had kept her up until two o'clock in the morning, whispering and giggling over her adventure and making much more over the incident with Nicholas Crawford than was necessary. To them it was a fairy tale; to Alice it was... depressing.

Perhaps the most depressing part was that, for a brief moment, she *had* been swept up in the fairy tale, she *had* been carried away by Nicholas Crawford's attentions and mesmerizing blue eyes; she had danced

with him, flirted with him, almost let him kiss her—
and in the midst of all this she had let the importance
of her meeting with Tyler Bradford slip into the back-
ground. She was as bad as Jane, as foolishly romantic as Molly. She was angry with herself, and every
time her wandering mind conjured up a picture of
Nicholas Crawford's lazy smile she grew even more
annoyed.

"It wasn't romantic at all," she said now, and her
tone was short as she firmly pushed that disconcert-
ing picture out of her mind. "He was drunk and he
didn't mean a thing he said—or did. How much are we
short on the rent?"

Molly looked as though she wanted to argue with
that first statement, then caught Alice's expression and
turned back to the bills and coins she was counting.
"One dollar and five cents," she announced.

"Maybe I could *sell* Nicholas Crawford one of my
shoes," Alice grumbled, and snapped out a crease in
the newspaper.

"Molly!" The door burst open and Jane burst in,
breathless and excited. "Thank goodness you're here!
You've got to do me this one favor and if you do I'll
owe you a dozen, I promise! Please say you will!"

Jane bounced on the bed and grasped Molly's
hands. Alice hastily scrambled to gather up the coins
Jane had displaced. "What in the world has gotten
you into such a dither?" she demanded.

Molly inquired, confused, "What favor?"

"I just heard that Rudolph Valentino is arriving on
the afternoon train and I've just *got* to see him, but
I'm supposed to start that job at Gimbels in an hour
and if I don't show up I'll be fired, so please, *please*
take over for me!"

Everyone knew, of course, that Rudolph Valentino would be in town for the premiere of his latest film, *Son of the Sheik*; Jane had been frantically scrambling for tickets for weeks to no avail. Standing in line for three hours for tickets Alice could understand—she was a Valentino fan herself and sometimes fantasized about playing opposite him in one of his moving pictures. But what she couldn't understand was why Jane felt it necessary to skip work in order to meet the actor at the train station.

As soon as Jane paused for breath Alice exclaimed, "That's the stupidest reason for missing a job I've ever heard. You don't even know Rudolph Valentino."

Molly, still confused, protested, "But . . . Gimbels! I don't know anything about sales slips and I'm not very good with figures and—"

"It's not a sales job," Jane explained quickly, "it's a singing job—some kind of promotion they're doing for bath soap or something. All you have to do is dress in a costume and stand outside the door and sing a little jingle—just to draw the customers in. Anyway, it won't be for long, I'll be there as soon as I can, less than an hour, really. All I want to do is get a glimpse of him."

Molly drew her hands away, her eyes growing wide. "You mean, stand on the sidewalk and sing? With all those people wandering by and staring?"

"You've done it on stage."

"Oh, no, that was different. There were a lot of other girls singing with me and it was dark and I couldn't see the people. Oh, Jane, I don't know. Why can't Alice do it?"

Jane didn't even glance Alice's way. "Because they want a *singer*."

Alice protested indignantly, "I can sing!"

"I'd ask Barbara," Jane went on, "but she's getting ready for the club and, oh, Molly, it would mean so much to me if you could just do me this one tiny favor. And," she added, "it pays a dollar fifty."

"You'd let me have the money?"

"If you'll do this," Jane said earnestly, "I'll give you anything you want!"

Molly's brow puckered worriedly. "But it hardly seems fair, for me to take your pay, especially if I'm only going to be there for a short while—"

"She'll do it," Alice said eagerly, and grabbed Molly's arm before she could protest. "The rent," she reminded her.

"Alice, I'm not sure—"

"I'll go with you. You'll be fine." She turned to Jane. "What time do we have to be there?"

Jane looked hopefully at Molly.

Molly sighed. "Well, all right. We do need the rent money, and if you're sure it will only be for a little while—"

"Oh, thank you, thank you!" Jane fell on Molly and kissed her hard, then kissed Alice for good measure. "You're the sweetest girl in the world. Just go through the back entrance and ask for Mr. Epworth. Be there by three. Here are the lyrics." She pulled a scrap of paper from her purse. "And it's sung to 'Camptown Races'—you know that, don't you? I'll be back before you even known I'm gone, I promise. Rudolph Valentino!" she cried as she skipped out of the room. "I'm going to see Rudolph Valentino!"

ALICE'S MOTHER was fond of saying "God never closes a door without opening a window somewhere," and today Alice thought there might just be some truth in that. Of course, it was a very small window—watching Molly sing on the sidewalk for a bathsoap promotion was not the same as being Tyler Bradford's new poster girl—but at least the rent would get paid. And in her present circumstances Alice had to be grateful for whatever small favors heaven was inclined to dole out.

"I don't know why anyone would go to all this trouble to hire somebody to sing about soap," Molly fretted, looking anxiously around the dusty, warehouselike back corridors of Gimbels department store. "I mean, how much soap can they expect to sell, anyway?"

Brisk-looking women with stenographer pads and anxious-looking young men in bow ties brushed by them on their way to some important meeting or other; the shouts and clatter from the loading dock were clearly audible, and more than once they had to move out of the way of a man carrying a pile of boxes or pushing a loaded cart. Clearly Molly was intimidated by the strange surroundings. Alice found them fascinating.

"I told you," Alice replied, scanning the corridor for some sign of the office to which they had been directed, "it has nothing to do with soap—it's just a way of getting people into the store. A crowd gathers to watch you sing, people start coming inside, and pretty soon they're buying all sorts of things they don't need."

"Then why do I have to sing these silly lyrics? Why can't I just walk down the street with a sandwich board?"

"Because singing is more interesting."

"I suppose it's just as well. My ankles would never hold up under a sandwich board."

Alice grabbed Molly's arm and quickly pulled her out of the way of an oncoming cart loaded with a tall, double stack of towels. Molly pressed her hand to her throat and closed her eyes. "I'll never get through this," she moaned. "I shouldn't have told Jane I would do it. I'm too nervous. I'm going to make a mess of it."

"No, you won't," Alice said firmly. "You have a lovely voice. Everybody's going to adore you. You'll do fine."

The sound of raised voices behind a closed door alerted Alice, and she stepped forward, peering at the lettering on the door in the dim light of an overhead bulb. "Here it is. Epworth." She knocked loudly on the door, then noticed that Molly was still cowering several feet behind her. "Come *on*," she urged impatiently, just as the door was jerked open.

A short, bald man glared at her. Huge semicircles of perspiration stained his white shirt from armpits to midchest, and his brown slacks were rumpled and brushed with dust. "You the girl for the soap?" he demanded.

Alice grabbed Molly's hand and quickly pulled her forward. "She is."

But he was already turning away. "You're late." He had a gruff voice that seemed to bark rather than speak, and he seemed to Alice the kind of man who was angry all the time about everything. He strode into the narrow, cluttered office and Alice, urging Molly along, followed a few steps inside.

A cloud of cigar smoke hung over the room, and the entire place smelled like a spittoon. A nervous-looking young man stood beside a big metal desk, eyeing the door as though wondering if he could make an escape. He jumped when Epworth spoke to him. "When I say a gross I mean 144, can you remember that? Twelve times twelve, can you count that high? Now do you want to tell me what I'm going to do with 144 *gross* of copper teapots? I don't even have room on the loading dock to store them!"

The young man said miserably, "I'm sorry, Mr. Epworth—"

"Sorry ain't gonna sell teapots!" Epworth jerked open a wooden file drawer, rummaged through some papers and came up with a handful of blue serge, which he tossed to Alice. "Here's your costume," he said. "Get in it and get around front in three minutes or you're fired. They're already bringing the tub out." He turned back to the young man. "Now let's just get one thing straight—"

"Tub?" Alice repeated, clutching the bundle of blue serge in astonishment. "What tub?"

Epworth swung on her with a scowl that would have sent a lesser woman scurrying for the door. It did cause Molly to shrink behind Alice until she was almost invisible. "Didn't they tell you *nothing*?" Epworth demanded. "It's soap, ain't it? You sit in a tub full of bubbles and sing about *soap*! Now get to it!" He swung on the young man again, continuing his lecture, but Alice didn't hear what he said.

Slowly Alice shook out the costume, staring in dismay as far less of it was revealed than she had expected. Held up by the shoulder straps, the hem, even when stretched down as far as it would go, barely covered her thighs.

Molly gasped softly behind her. "A bathing costume!" she whispered. "He wants me to sit in a bathtub on a public street in a *bathing* costume!"

Alice nodded soberly. "It certainly looks that way."

Molly clutched Alice's arm so tightly that Alice winced. "Oh, Alice, I *can't!*" she whispered. Her eyes were terrified and miserable. "I can't go out there in that. I'll simply die of mortification. I—"

"Don't be silly, Molly," Alice whispered back urgently. "Lots of people wear them. Why, I saw a picture in the newspaper just the other week..." She swallowed hard as she remembered that the picture she had seen had been of women being arrested at a public beach for wearing just such a costume. But that, of course, had been in the deep South, and this was New York, and everyone knew nothing shocked New Yorkers. "Besides," she went on quickly, "no one will see you anyway if you're in a bathtub."

Molly's eyes were bright with tears. "I can't!"

"You have to. You promised Jane, and the money—"

"You still here?" This time Epworth's bark did cause Alice to jump. "I'm not paying good money for you to stand around and gab. You want this job or not?"

Alice cast a quick look at Molly, whose face was red and whose eyes were brimming and who, even now, was inching for the door. She thought of Jane, who was counting on them, and the rent that was overdue. She clutched the costume to her. She looked at Epworth and took a breath.

"Where do I change?" she inquired calmly.

As NICHOLAS CRAWFORD went down the steps of the Handley Hotel he was aware of half-a-dozen wide female eyes following him from behind half-drawn curtains, and the knowledge amused him just enough to take the edge off his annoyance at not finding Alice at home. Of course Nick was accustomed to being followed by female eyes almost everywhere he went; rarely did he give it a second thought. His friend Stuart, on the other hand, who was short, a little pudgy and not very distinguished looking, was obviously uncomfortable.

"I felt like a bloody monkey at the zoo," Stuart grumbled, casting a self-conscious look back at the rambling brownstone with its gay windowboxes and leaning front rail. "Lord, they're still looking at us. Do I have food on my face or something?"

Stuart stepped in front of Nick and earnestly thrust his face forward, and Nick chuckled. "Behave yourself, Stu. Do you want the young ladies to think we have no manners?" He stopped, turned and blew a big kiss toward the house. He saw several window curtains flutter closed.

"Well, if this is your idea of a swinging time," Stuart grumbled, "all I can say is you must be in pretty bad shape. Can we go home now?"

"Nonsense, old man. We haven't gotten what we came for yet."

Stuart sighed. "I was afraid of that."

Nick launched himself at his yellow roadster, which stood at the curb with its engine idling noisily, and sprang gracefully over the door and into the driver's seat. Stuart managed a little less smoothly. He looked at Nick warily as he settled himself into the seat. "I suppose now we're going to Gimbels department store?''

"Do you have anything better to do?"

Stuart's expression was martyred. "God help me, no. And if you ask me, the world's come to a sorry state when two fashionable young men-about-town like us can't find anything better to do on a Saturday afternoon than chase some wayward little actress through the slums and villages—"

His words were cut off as the roadster sprang into traffic, one wheel bouncing off the curb as the car careened wildly to avoid a middle-aged woman with a shopping bag. The woman stopped and shook her fist at them, and Stuart waited until the car was safely on the road again before continuing, "Do you want to tell me again why we're doing this?"

Nick leaned back and guided the wheel with one hand, enjoying the flutter of wind across his face and the feel of the automobile's power at his command. "Because it annoys the hell out of my sister for one thing," he responded easily. "For another, why not?"

Stuart, who had been Nick's best friend for most of his life, seemed to accept that explanation as no more than typical, and Nick was glad. He wasn't sure he could have justified his behavior any further if pressed, for in fact there *was* no rational explanation.

He only knew that he had awakened at noon feeling as though he had something exciting in store for him, and it had been a long time since he'd felt that way. Alice Fontaine. A woman called Handley. It had been fun tracking her down. It was even more fun now that the plot had been complicated by her unexpected departure to Gimbels. He didn't know what he was going to do when he found her, for Nick rarely thought that far in advance, but he was sure that would be fun, too. There was no doubt she would be surprised to see him, and he enjoyed surprising people.

But as he approached the front of Gimbels and noticed the crowd that had gathered, fully blocking the sidewalk and a good portion of the street, he had a feeling he was the one who was in for a surprise. That delighted him even further.

He pulled up as close as he could without mowing a path through the pedestrians, and Stuart climbed out and onto the running board.

"Can you see anything?" Nick called.

"No— Wait!"

Nick turned off the engine and started to get out of the car himself. He became aware, over the murmur of the crowd, of a strange warbling sound he could not identify. He stood up on the seat.

"Nick, you won't believe it." Stuart strained on tiptoe to see over the crowd. "There's this woman in a bathtub, up to her neck in bubbles, and she's singing!"

"It's her." Nick grinned broadly and began to clamber over the windscreen. "It's got to be."

He stood on the bonnet of the roadster and laughed out loud at what he saw. Mary Alice Floyd Fontaine, her hair covered by a ruffled bathing cap, bubbles of soap twinkling on her lashes and cheeks, was sitting in a bathtub on a raised platform, singing her heart out about the benefits of a facial soap. "Didn't I tell you this would be worth it?" he called to Stuart, still laughing.

Behind him there came a stir of movement and commanding shouts. "Ho, there! Out of the way now! Break it up! Coming through!"

He looked around and saw six uniformed policemen pushing their way through the crowd. Apparently no one had told Miss Alice Fontaine that singing in the bathtub was not something one did on a public street, and it looked as though Nick was about to be witness to another first for Alice—her first glimpse of the inside of a jail.

"Hello! Jimbo!"

The policeman whose name Nick had called paused and looked around. He spotted Nick immediately, waving from the top of his car. He grinned and pushed back his hat, letting his fellow officers precede him as Nick jumped down from the automobile and made his way toward him.

"Well, if it ain't the fine Mr. Crawford," he greeted him. "What brings you down to this side of town?"

"It was a choice between Gimbels department store and a steamer to Greece, and I couldn't get my passport ready in time."

The other man laughed, letting the crowd surge around him. "Hot enough for you?" He blotted his forehead with the back of his sleeve.

"Tolerable." Nick nodded toward the front of the store. "What's all the commotion?"

"Some crazy female took a notion to take a bath on the street, can you figure that? As if we didn't have enough to do with Valentino in town."

Nick shook his head woefully. "These are hard times we live in, my friend."

The officer started to agree, then caught the twinkle in Nick's eyes and grinned instead. "Harder for some than others. Now, if you'll excuse me, I've got my duty to do.''

Already Nick could hear indignant squeals from the front of the crowd, and he had a very good suspicion they came from Alice. Stuart, he could see, had taken his place on the bonnet of the roadster, and was straining to see for himself just what a woman might look like when pulled from a bathtub on a public street.

Nick caught Jimbo's arm. "You're not going to arrest her, are you?"

"Have to," Jimbo called back, using his nightstick to gently force an opening through the milling bodies. "Creating a public disturbance."

"To say the least," Nick murmured, though to himself now, as Jimbo was too far away to hear.

He stood there for a moment, tapping his chin lightly with his forefinger, and knew that, all things considered, his best option would be to move back and let the excitement dissipate. Stuart would never forgive him for dragging him into another melee, and this thing could get nasty before it was over. Besides, it was hot and getting hotter and he had half promised Cynthia he would be at home this afternoon to supervise the cleanup crew from the party while she had her hair done.

But the last thing he wanted to do was to play the dutiful brother, and it was utterly against his nature to retreat from any kind of excitement. He rushed back to his car and extracted a blanket from the back seat.

"Wait!" he called to Jimbo, and pushed recklessly forward to rescue the damsel in distress.

Chapter Four

The water was cold. It was so cold that Alice's limbs were numb and her fingertips ached, and it was all she could do to keep her teeth from chattering in order to sing more or less on key. She waved her arms a lot and belted out the tune—mostly to keep warm—but every time she moved, bubbles splashed into her eyes and mouth. She began to understand why this job paid a dollar fifty.

She was only vaguely aware of the crowd that had gathered in front of the elevated bathtub, women whispering behind their hands and men grinning boldly as they shuffled forward for a better view. She wasn't embarrassed—how could she be, sunk to her neck in icy water, with nothing but her ruffled bathing cap and the tip of her red nose showing between the bubbles?—but she *did* think it was rude of them to stare so, and she was extremely glad it wasn't Molly who was being subjected to this humiliation. As it was, Molly was huddled in the shadows of the building behind the bathtub, clutching Alice's clothes and looking mortified. Every once in a while Alice tried to remember to send her a bright smile of reassurance, but it was almost as hard to smile without allowing her teeth to chatter as it was to sing.

And then Alice saw Jane, pushing her way forward and waving to her. Relief energized her and she sang louder. Jane reached the edge of the tub just as Alice finished the chorus and, improvising, she cried gaily, "Come on in, folks! Ten cents a bar for soft skin and shining hair! Good for laundry, too!"

She leaned over the edge of the tub and, dripping bubbles, glared at Jane. "There were a few things you didn't tell us about this job."

Jane curled her fingers over the edge of the tub and stood on tiptoe. "He was gone by the time I got there!" she cried. "All those mobs of women and he came in on an earlier train!"

Molly scurried forward, looking around anxiously. "Jane, thank goodness you're here! Please, can we go now? I mean, it didn't seem right to leave without you, but now that you're here you surely didn't mean for Alice to do *this!* Let's go, can't we?"

"You don't understand!" Jane wailed. "Now I'll never get to see him! The picture show is sold out for three weeks and you can't even *steal* a ticket—"

Molly tugged at Jane's arm. "Please, Jane, tell Alice she can get down now."

There was a disturbance in the crowd and Alice glanced around quickly. "Look, do you want your job back or not?"

"I can't sing! I'm too upset to sing!"

"Well, somebody's got to. People are starting to leave, and if Mr. Epworth finds out—"

"Oh, good heavens!" Molly gasped. "That must be him now!"

Alice drew a quick breath, stretched a smile over her face, and began to screech out soapy lyrics to the tune of "Camptown Races" at the top of her wobbly voice—but the man who broke through the crowd was not Mr. Epworth. It was a uniformed policeman, and he was followed by another, and another, each of them waving a nightstick and shouting things like, "All right folks, break it up, show's over!" and, "Out of the way, now! Move back!"

It took Alice a long time to realize what was happening, and afterward she would never be quite sure she had the sequence of events right in her memory. The closer the policemen came the louder she sang, holding some incoherent notion in the back of her mind that Mr. Epworth had called the police because she had stopped singing in the first place. Then one of the policemen tried to push Jane away from the tub and Jane cried out angrily, "What are you doing?"

The policeman made a reply Alice couldn't hear and began to climb onto the platform that supported the tub. Molly stuffed both fists against her mouth and let out a muffled cry of horror. Jane, who had endured more frustration that day than any woman would reasonably be expected to, began to swing at the policeman with her handbag, crying, "You get down from there! What do you think you're doing? Leave my friend alone!"

Molly began to sob. Another policeman tried to pull Jane away, but she broke his grip, flailing with her fists. Alice, trying to follow the plight of both her friends without missing a beat in the song, didn't know what was happening until she felt herself grabbed roughly under the arms and pulled upward. She let out a yell and twisted away, then slipped and

splashed into the water over her head. She came up
sputtering and wiping soap bubbles from her eyes, and
a policeman, red-faced and sweating, declared, "Now
you come along peaceable and don't make a scene.
You're under arrest."

Alice barely had time to gasp "Arrest!" before her
arms were grabbed again and, from the other side of
the tub, her ankles grasped by another policeman, and
she was lifted bodily out of the water. Bare arms and
naked legs thrashing, she had a tilted view of the excited crowd below her: of Jane, furiously pummeling
a policeman with her fists and, incredibly, of Mr. Epworth, standing a little to the side of the crowd with his
arms folded across his chest, looking on benignly. She
twisted around just in time to see Molly press her hand
to her throat and slide to the ground in a dead faint.
And then the worst happened.

Alice instinctively flung out a hand toward Molly
and caught one of the policemen on the side of the
jaw. He stumbled backward and lost his balance, and
still a good five feet above the ground, Alice felt herself begin to fall. She muffled a shriek between her
teeth, squeezed her eyes shut and kicked out wildly.

Her bare feet thudded painfully against the side of
the tub, her knees grazed the platform, and then another pair of arms caught her. When she opened her
eyes she was held securely against a man's chest, and
looking straight into the laughing eyes of Nicholas
Crawford.

"And so," he murmured, "we meet again."

Around her the crowd surged and milled. Jane,
struggling against the grip a policeman had on her
arms, was shouting Alice's name, Molly lay in a
crumpled heap on the sidewalk, one of the policemen

was angrily declaring something about assaulting an officer, and all Alice could do was stare, dumbfounded, at Nicholas Crawford's smiling face.

At last she became aware of his crisp linen suit growing damp against her wet body, and worse, of his arms encircling her unclothed thighs and bare shoulders. She struggled frantically to right herself and he politely set her on her feet—though not as quickly as she would have liked. "What . . . what are you doing here?" she stammered, and at the same time pressed her knees close together and tried rather awkwardly to cover her chest with her arms.

"Permit me," Nicholas drawled smoothly, and shaking out the folds of a blanket he held draped over his arms, he arranged it around Alice's shoulders. The gesture would have been a gallant one if his eyes had not traveled so boldly from the tip of her collarbone down the length of her legs, and Alice jerked the blanket from his fingers and wound it tightly about her.

A round-faced man in a tattersall suit, puffing with exertion, clutched Nicholas's arm and said, "Now look what you've got us into! It's turning into a bloody riot! One woman's swooned already and—"

"Molly!" Alice cried, her own troubles forgotten as she turned toward her friend.

"You wait just a minute." A policeman grabbed Alice's elbows from behind. "We're taking you in, young lady!"

As Alice struggled, she saw Jane suddenly kick the shins of the red-haired policeman who held her and break away. "Alice!" she cried, rushing over to her. "Are you all right? Can you believe the nerve—"

"Molly's fainted," Alice replied, trying to free her elbows. "And this . . . this brute—" she tugged again at her elbows "—won't let me go to her."

"Oh, for heaven's sake!" Jane whirled and ran straight into the arms of the red-haired policeman from whom she'd just escaped.

"All right, miss," he said grimly, "that's the last straw. You're under arrest." And before either of them knew what was happening, he had snapped a pair of handcuffs on Jane's wrists.

"How dare you!" Jane cried. "You take these things off immediately. You can't do this!"

But the policeman was already dragging her away. "Oh, for the love of—!" Alice began to struggle in earnest now, twisting around to face the policeman who was trying, so far unsuccessfully, to fit her squirming hands into a pair of metal cuffs. "You've got to let me go! My friend is ill."

Nick looked amused as he said, "Looks like the ball is over, Cinderella."

His mockery, at that moment, was the last thing Alice needed, and she turned on him furiously. "You stay out of this! What do you know about it, anyway? You've had your fun. Now just go away and . . . and stop looking at me!" The policeman had succeeded in snapping on the handcuffs, and in the process, the blanket had fallen down around her knees. To her dismay, Alice felt tears of frustration and embarrassment and, yes, even a small amount of fear, sting her eyes as she stood half-naked for Nicholas Crawford and all the world to see.

Nick reached down to pick up the blanket and tucked it securely around her shoulders as he admonished the policeman, "Please, a little consideration for the lady's modesty."

To Alice's absolute astonishment, the officer looked a little abashed as he muttered, "Sorry, Nick, but she's a wildcat, this one is."

"Aren't they all?" Nick turned to the round-faced man, who was earnestly entreating him to leave, and advised, "Why don't you go see what you can do for the girl who swooned? We don't want her trampled, and this could be your chance to be a hero."

Somewhat reluctantly, it seemed to Alice, his friend went over to Molly, pushing his way through the small crowd that had gathered around her, and then Nick turned back to the policeman who held Alice. "Well," he said pleasantly, "don't let me hold you up." He touched two fingers to the brim of his straw hat and said to Alice, "It was nice running into you again. You must look me up sometime, when you have more time to visit."

The policemen tugged on Alice's upper arm, and she opened her mouth to say something to Nicholas, but no words came out. She simply stared at him, openmouthed, until the policeman jerked on her arm again and she was forced to stumble after him.

The crowd parted to make way, and Nick called after her, "Make them put you in cell number three. It's the cleanest!"

She twisted around to look at him, but she only got a glimpse of his laughing face before she tripped over the folds of the blanket that had once more fallen to her feet. Only the policeman's strong grip on her arm saved her from a bad fall, and when she looked again, Nicholas Crawford had been swallowed up by the curious crowd. But she could still feel him watching her, amusement snapping in those azure eyes, and she determinedly squared her shoulders and lifted her head as she marched toward the paddy wagon.

ALICE WAS NOT PESSIMISTIC by nature, but after an hour in the sweltering jail cell with two sullen, middle-aged prostitutes for her only companions, it was hard to think cheerful thoughts. Jail. She, Mary Alice Floyd, who read devotion in Sunday school at age nine and sang in the church choir and was always first in Bible class. What if her mother found out? Worse, what if her *father* found out? She would be dragged home by the hair and forced to live out the rest of her life in small-town disgrace.

She worried about Molly. Abandoned on the street corner in a dead swoon, what would happen when she came to? And Jane. What had become of Jane? They were all in trouble because of Alice and she was locked in here, helpless. She could have beat her head against the bars in frustration, but she would not give her two narrow-eyed companions the satisfaction.

How was she ever going to raise bail money? A chill came over her as she realized the full consequences of today's escapade. She could be locked up here for days, weeks. And when Mrs. Handley found out, she'd never be allowed back into the hotel, and then what would she do? Live on the streets? Fleetingly, the thought came to her that she never should have left Haven's Hollow, she should have stayed safe at home where she was loved and where bad things never happened. Where nothing at all ever happened.

Her skin had long since dried, but the bathing costume was clammy against her body and the wool blanket made her skin itch. The cell smelled of unemptied slops and dirty bedclothes. Alice sat perched on the edge of the cot even though she was sure it was full of lice, because there was nowhere else to sit. The other two women lounged on the opposite ends of the cot where it met the wall, and Alice was trapped between them.

Dear God, she thought, *if only you'll get me out of this...*

It was perhaps fortunate that she never got to finish the prayer because she didn't have the first idea what desperate promise she was about to make. One of the women spoke to her abruptly.

"You a friend of Nick's?" she demanded.

Alice stared at her, not certain she had heard right. "Wh-who?"

"You know, the Duke," the other one replied. She had a chipped front tooth and bad skin. "That's what we call him around here." She chuckled. "The Backstreet Duke." At Alice's stupefied expression, she explained earnestly, "On account of him being so rich, you know."

Alice managed, "You *know* Nicholas Crawford?"

The woman shrugged. "He's a regular around here. Everybody knows Nick."

"Anyway, honey," the first woman said, and Alice tried not to flinch as she reached forward and patted her knee, "if the Duke's on your side, you got nothing to worry about. He don't let his friends down."

Alice was saved from a reply by the rattling of gates and slamming of doors. She got quickly to her feet as an officer approached and turned a key in the cell door. "All right, Miss Fontaine, you're free to go."

"What'd I tell you?" the prostitute declared smugly. "Hey," she added as Alice hurried through the opening door, "tell Nick Lilly says hello!"

And the other woman called after her, "Ask him if he's got any cigarettes!"

Alice cast a harried glance over her shoulder, and pure relief at being on the outside looking in caused her to stammer, "Y-yes. Yes, I will."

The officer thrust a bundle of clothing at her. "Come with me."

Alice looked down at the tightly wadded bundle in her hands. "My clothes! Then Molly must have gotten here. Thank goodness she's all right."

The policeman walked in long strides down the corridor and Alice picked up the trailing corners of the blanket and hurried to keep up. He opened a wooden door and gestured her inside. "You can change here. Knock on the door when you're finished."

Alice stepped inside what was obviously a storeroom, dusty smelling and hot, and piled high with boxes and cast-off furniture. When the door closed, the only light came from a high barred window, which was so dirty even the sunshine looked like mud. Alice didn't care. She lost no time stripping out of the wet costume and pulling on her clothes—clothes that were so badly wrinkled Mrs. Handley would have never let her leave her room wearing them—but they were hers, and they covered her decently from neck to knee. She pulled on her gloves and set her cloche firmly on her wildly curling hair, checked the top button on her dress and straightened the seam of her stockings before knocking on the door. Now she felt ready to face anything.

The officer led her down another twisting corridor and through a set of double doors, where the first thing Alice saw was Molly, who hurried to fling herself into Alice's arms. Alice hugged her hard.

"Molly, I was so worried about you—"

"I feel just awful, it's all my fault—"

"I was scared to death when I saw you faint and then they wouldn't let me go—"

"But I told them the whole story, about that awful Mr. Epworth and how he made you put on that embarrassing costume and get in the water and they sent a man over to talk to him and, do you know, I think he *knew* this was going to happen! He wasn't even sorry, he said it brought people into the store and that's all he wanted and—" She pushed away from Alice, her face indignant. "He wouldn't even pay what he promised. He said you didn't finish the job!" And then a slight stain of color crept into her cheeks as she added, "That is, until that nice Mr. Bainbridge went over to talk to him and...well, here!" She dug into her handbag and triumphantly produced a folded handkerchief, inside of which were six quarters. "I think," she confided, "Mr. Bainbridge threatened him. He was really magnificent—Mr. Bainbridge, that is, not that nasty Mr. Epworth!"

Alice looked from the quarters to Molly in confusion, trying hard to follow her explanation. "Mr. Bainbridge? Who is he? How did you get here? Where is Jane? And how did you raise the bail money?"

Molly gave a nervous, high-pitched giggle and cast a quick glance over her shoulder. "Mr. Bainbridge is Mr. Crawford's friend and they both brought me over in their motorcar. Well," she demanded defensively, "what else could I do? Here you were in terrible trouble, and the police had taken Jane and I had to get here somehow, didn't I? And even if they were strangers they were nice, and..." A shadow of anxiety crept into her eyes. "You don't think it was really bad of me, do you? I mean, that I was fast or anything?"

Alice looked over Molly's shoulder, scanning the room until she located the round-faced young man in the tattersall suit, who was standing rather stiffly in a corner, looking very out of place and uncomfortable as he surreptitiously mopped his gleaming forehead. There was a big desk in the center of the room around which several policemen were gathered, laughing and telling jokes. On the corner of the desk sat Nick Crawford, twirling his straw hat on the tip of his finger as he exchanged witticisms with the officers. Alice quickly jerked her eyes away before he noticed her looking at him, fighting a prickle of unwelcome heat that came to her cheeks. It was bad enough that he should have seen her in that ridiculous costume and witnessed the humiliation of her arrest, but did he have to follow her to the police station just to see the outcome of the fiasco? For all she knew the jokes they were exchanging were about her, for obviously there were no limits to the lengths the man would go in his desperate search for amusement.

"Alice! There you are!"

Just as Alice was beginning to think she might creep away unnoticed and put this entire dreadful episode behind her, Jane's voice caused every head to turn. She was crossing the room with her hand raised in jaunty greeting, her cheeks flushed with excitement. To Alice's absolute amazement, she was pulling along behind her the red-haired policeman—the very one Alice had last seen Jane kick in the shins.

"The most incredible thing!" Jane exclaimed breathlessly. "Officer Williams—that is—" she corrected with a quick, almost flirtatious glance at the policeman beside her "Jim—is on guard duty tonight at the theater, and he offered to get me in *free* to see Valentino! Can you just imagine? I was merely explaining to him how this all got started, with standing in line for the tickets and then rushing down to the station when he wasn't even there, and the next thing I know I'm going to see Valentino on screen *and* in person and all because you got arrested for taking a bath in public! Isn't it just marvelous the way things work out?"

Jane cast a look of adoring gratitude toward the officer she had called Jim, winding her arm tightly through his, and the florid-faced policeman went even a shade redder, looking enormously pleased with himself. Alice could only stare.

"Well, Miss Alice," drawled a smooth voice at her elbow, "how do you like Wonderland so far?"

Alice turned, rather dazed, to meet Nicholas Crawford's gaze. Wonderland, indeed. Molly, who had last been seen swooning on the street, had not only roused herself but come to the rescue with a man in a tattersall suit *and* the rent money. Jane had turned a charge of assaulting an officer into free tickets to see Valentino and had apparently gained an admirer in the process. And Alice, who only moments ago had been facing a grim future in a six-by-six cell, was now standing beside one of the top five most eligible bachelors in New York City and listening to him make jokes. She couldn't help wondering whether things like this always happened when Nick Crawford was around.

She cleared her throat, determinedly trying to shake the fog from her brain, and turned back to Jane, then to Officer Williams. "Um, excuse me, but what do I do now? I mean, I don't have any money for bail and..."

"Oh, well, I don't think you have to worry about that, miss." Looking a little embarrassed, the officer tore his gaze from Jane's and reluctantly disengaged his arm. "After uncovering all the facts in the case it appears you were a victim in this matter and not a perpetrator."

"Yes, indeed." Nick touched her elbow and turned her smoothly toward the desk, where an officious-looking gray-haired man sat smoking a cigar that smelled so rich it could have only come from Nick Crawford's pocket. "After all, you were decently covered until the policemen pulled you from the tub and you didn't *mean* to sock the officer in the jaw, now did you? I think we've decided to drop all the charges, isn't that right, Chief?"

The chief, who'd been engaged in a grinning conversation with another officer, removed the cigar from his mouth and immediately arranged his face into stern lines. "That's right," he affirmed. "Providing—" he jabbed a finger at her "—you've learned your lesson and nothing like this happens again. If I see you back here again I'm going to throw the book at you, do you hear me?"

"Yes, sir!" Alice breathed, clutching her hands tightly together. "I mean, no, sir, you'll never see me again."

"Good." He nodded curtly and impatiently waved away the officers who were lounging around his desk. "Now, let's get back to work here. This is still a police station, you know. Let's see if we can't make it look like one."

The officers quickly began to look busy, and Alice stepped out of their way, still feeling dazed. There was not a doubt in her mind that she had Nick Crawford to thank for her good fortune, and she looked up at him, puzzled. She opened her mouth to express her gratitude, but found herself demanding instead, "Why did you do this?"

He shrugged. "My life is a quest for adventure." He touched her arm lightly and gestured toward the door. "Freedom awaits. Shall we go?"

But Alice stood her ground, still staring at him. And though she had been warned all her life about the dangers of examining the teeth of a gift horse, she felt compelled to add, "I, um, met some friends of yours back there."

"Is that right?"

She watched him closely. "Yes. What you might call . . . ladies of the evening. Lilly says hello."

His face was perfectly bland. "Hello to Lilly."

"And they want to know if you have any cigarettes."

Without missing a beat, he removed a gold cigarette case from his pocket and tossed it on the desk. "Hey, Lou, take these back to the ladies, will you?" He seemed to reconsider for a moment, then removed the cigarettes and picked up the case. "It was a gift from my sister," he explained, leaving the cigarettes on the desk as he returned the case to his pocket. "She might not understand if I lost it."

Then he smiled and crooked his arm for Alice. "Now then, shall we go?"

Chapter Five

Alice stared at his smiling face, at his politely offered arm, and she was suddenly quite convinced that the smartest thing to do would be to thank whatever fates prevailed for her narrow escape and get out of this place as quickly as possible. Nicholas Crawford, with his winning ways and effortless ability to work miracles, was definitely beyond her scope and she simply wasn't up to trying to figure him out today. For all she knew, he had bribed the policemen to drop her charges and if she wasn't careful she might end up right back in jail again.

Abruptly she extended her hand and shook his firmly. "Well, thank you very much. Goodbye."

She had just a glimpse of his startled expression before she turned and called, "Molly, Jane. Come on, we can go now."

"Wait," Nick said quickly. "I'll drive you home."

"Thank you," she said, "but I've had enough adventure for one day. I'll walk. Jane!" she repeated, more loudly. "We're leaving now."

Jane looked up from her conversation with the smiling young Officer Williams and said, somewhat dismissively, "Oh, you go ahead, Alice. Jim gets off in a few minutes, and he'll see me home."

And before Alice could reply, Nick turned to his friend and suggested, "Stu, drive Miss Molly home, won't you? She really shouldn't be walking in this heat. I'll catch up with you later."

Stu, looking enormously pleased, turned to Molly, and it was obvious from Molly's shy smile that she did not object to the arrangements in the least. Nick fastened his hand firmly on Alice's elbow. "There. Everybody's taken care of and you won't escape me this time."

"You're very good at arranging things, aren't you?"

"One of my many talents. Shall we go?"

Alice looked at him for a moment, but there seemed no point in fighting the inevitable. "It's a long walk," she warned him.

"I'm in the very pink of health."

She met his determined expression for just a moment longer, then shrugged. "I suppose I can't stop you. It's a free country, after all."

"There's nothing more heartwarming than the gratitude of a gracious lady for my concern on her behalf."

"Oh, it's not that I'm not grateful for what you've done," Alice insisted, stepping back to allow him to push open the door for her. "I just don't understand why you did it."

"To annoy you, of course." He gestured her through the door, then paused to replace his hat as they stepped out into the bright sunshine. "I woke up this morning wondering what I could do to make Alice

Fontaine's life miserable. Then I thought, I know! I'll go downtown and get her out of jail.''

Alice tried, rather unsuccessfully, to repress a smile. He *was* charming. "I guess I do sound ungrateful," she admitted. "And I do appreciate all your trouble, really I do, it's just that it doesn't make sense."

He tucked her arm through his as they descended the wide steps. "It was no trouble. I didn't have anything better to do."

And that, Alice decided, was what bothered her about him. He never had anything better to do, and if he had she might well still be sitting in a cell biting her fingernails and counting off the days of her future behind bars. It wasn't logical to resent the whim of fate that had brought a bored young playboy to her rescue, but that was the way she felt.

They turned west on the busy street and Alice tried to sound noncommittal as she commented, "You certainly do seem to know your way around the police station."

"Yes, I suppose I do."

She glanced at him warily. "The, uh, girls said you were a regular."

A flash of amusement sparked his sun-narrowed eyes. "Does that bother you?"

Alice thought about that for a moment. "Well, my mother always said that the only thing in life we can really choose is our companions."

"Ah. And your mother wouldn't approve of me as a companion."

"No," Alice decided seriously. "But then again, she wouldn't approve of having a jailbird for a daughter, either, so I don't suppose I can be too picky about my companions."

His eyes fairly snapped with repressed amusement, but he kept his face perfectly sober. "Jailbirds of a feather, so to speak."

Alice grinned. She couldn't help it. She was really beginning to like him. "So to speak."

They reached an intersection, and Alice gestured to the left. "It's shorter this way." They turned into a street that was crowded with neat row houses and children playing on handkerchief-size scraps of grass. There were more horses than automobiles traversing the dusty road, and it was a little quieter. "So," she asked Nick after a moment, "what did your mother used to say?"

He was thoughtful for a moment. " 'Don't be late for dinner,' " he replied, and Alice chuckled.

"Where are they now? Your parents."

"In Newport. Or Greece. I don't really remember."

Alice decided to reserve judgment on a man who couldn't even remember where his parents were. There would be no point to it. "And you live in that big house all by yourself?"

"With my sister, when she's home. When I'm home. Sometimes the folks come home, too, but frankly, we all get on better when we're not in the same place at the same time."

"That's sad."

He gave her an odd look. "Do you think so?"

"Of course it is. What's the point of having a family if you can't enjoy them? I miss my family, even though they used to get on my nerves sometimes."

"Then why did you leave?"

"I told you, you can't be a star in Haven's Hollow, Tennessee."

"Ah, yes, of course. The search for stardom. And how is it going? Not much progress since last night, I suppose."

She sighed. "No. And it looks like there isn't going to be. When I came to New York, I thought all I'd have to do is work hard and keep trying and eventually I'd make it to the top. Well, I've worked hard and Lord knows nobody tries harder than I do, but it's beginning to look like the only way you can even get *noticed* in this town is if you have someone who—"

Suddenly Alice stopped in midstep. An incredible idea had just occurred to her. "You!" she exclaimed. "You could do it!"

An expression of puzzled wariness came over his face. "Do what?"

"Of course you could!" Her mind was racing and with every second she grew more excited. "You have plenty of money and you never have anything to do, you said yourself you're always looking for adventure, and what could be better? All you'd have to do is back a few shows, introduce me to the right people, and in no time you could double your money! People do it all the time!"

"Do what? What on earth are you talking about?"

"You!" she declared, delighted. "You can be my sponsor! You can make me a star!"

He shook his head, chuckling softly. "Thank you, my dear, but no."

Her astonishment was followed quickly by suspicion. "Why not?"

He tucked her arm into the crook of his elbow again and resumed walking. "Quite simple. I've heard you sing, remember?"

Dignity demanded that she drop his arm, glaring at him. "That's the second time you've said something uncomplimentary about me. You don't think much of my talent, do you?"

"I merely don't believe in nurturing false hopes," he assured her blandly. "Besides, I do have a great many other complimentary things to say about you."

It was only curiosity that persuaded Alice to swallow her pride and allow Nick to take her arm again. "Like what?" she demanded ungraciously.

"Like you have an adorable nose and enchanting eyes and very kissable lips, and the most exciting pair of legs I've seen in a long time."

The matter-of-fact way he cataloged her features left Alice dumbfounded, surprised by the erratic beating of her heart and the tingling of her cheeks. She stared at him, but his expression remained pleasant and unaffected, and he appeared to be thinking about nothing more consequential than the weather.

With difficulty Alice regained her equilibrium and replied, "Well, that's all very nice, I'm sure, but it doesn't do me much good on the stage."

"Why not forget the stage?" he suggested. "Become my mistress instead."

This time Alice's response was immediate and adamant. "Don't be ridiculous. If I wanted to do *that* for a living I'd go back home and marry Bart Catlow."

She thought she detected an undertone of laughter to his voice as he said, "Now I'm hurt. I make you a perfectly legitimate offer and you reject me out of hand."

Alice was not amused, and she walked faster. "There's nothing legitimate at all about your offer."

"It's as good as anything you'll ever get on the stage—except, of course, you'll have a much more secure career with me than by casting yourself into the hands of a fickle public."

"I'll take my chances with the public, thank you."

"You're making a big mistake. I treat my ladies well—ask anyone. You'd have your own apartment, a generous allowance, and your clothes would come from the smartest shops in town."

"I half think you're serious."

"Of course I'm serious, my dear. There are two things I never joke about—love and money."

She frowned, growing a little uneasy. "You don't know the first thing about love."

He stopped, and took her shoulders lightly, turning her to face him. His eyes were lit by a gentle sunwashed glow, and his face had been remarkably transformed into something that almost resembled sincerity. It occurred to Alice in that moment that *he* should be on the stage. "Perhaps," he suggested softly, and with just the faintest hint of an entreating smile, "you could teach me."

The heat rose from the sidewalk and thickened the air between them. Across the street a group of children laughed with faraway voices; a black and white cat ambled out into the street and sat down to preen itself in a patch of sun. And for a moment, caught by the play of light and the whisper of promise in his fantastic blue eyes, Alice was almost drawn in.

Abruptly she began walking faster, away from him. "Thank you, but I don't think so."

"What?" He pretended astonishment as he hurried to keep up with her. "Can it be I've stumbled upon a woman of virtue? Or, rarer still—" his eyes twinkled as he bent his head to peer at her "—a true innocent?"

Alice scowled, her cheeks stinging, and walked even faster. "It has nothing to do with virtue," she informed him curtly, "or innocence, either. It's just common sense. Why should I go begging to a man for every favor when I can make my own fortune and have men come begging to me?"

Nick burst into laughter and Alice's face flamed. She said quickly, "Let's walk through the park. It's cooler there."

Her pace was so rapid that, for the next block and a half there was no time—or breath—for conversation. When they reached the shady avenue that led into the park Nick was laughing. "All right, enough. I said I was in the pink of health, but I didn't know I'd be competing with a professional. Come here, sit down. It's too hot to be dashing around like this." He caught her arm and guided her over to a bench set in the shade. "I always did say it was a mistake to take women out of corsets."

"What?" Her own cheeks were flushed with exertion and her breath was short, but Alice could not let that pass. She stared at him, wondering if the heat had gone to his head.

"Corsets," he explained simply. "A woman who's wearing one can't run as fast as a man and therefore never gets away. In my opinion, all the problems of the modern world can be traced back to undergarments."

She stared at him for a moment longer, incredulous, then burst into laughter. "You are outrageous," she declared, sinking onto the bench. "It's a wonder they let you wander around loose."

He grinned and removed his hat, running his fingers through the damp curls that clung to his forehead. The gesture gave him a suddenly boyish look. "I wouldn't be," he pointed out, "if you'd take me up on my offer. Sure you won't reconsider?"

"It's nothing personal," she assured him.

He sat beside her, fanning his hat between them, sharing the breeze. "A pity," he mused. "If you'd cast your lot with me you could be taking cabs home instead of hiking cross-country."

"A small sacrifice to make for independence."

He slanted her a curious look. "And it's that important to you—independence?"

"As important," she countered, "as it is for you to try to seduce every young lady you come across."

He shrugged modestly and leaned back against the bench. "I can't help it. Seducing young ladies is the only thing I know with absolute certainty I do well."

Alice could not restrain herself from commenting, "I'm not at all sure that's something I'd want to boast about."

Alice thought she saw the playful light in his eyes grow briefly shadowed by bitterness. He stopped fanning his hat. "No," he murmured. "I suppose it's not."

And then he looked away and resumed his lazy fanning. "You know, you have an irritating habit of being right about the damnedest things. I should probably stay away from you. You make me think too much. Would you like to go to see Valentino with me tonight? I have a date, but I can easily beg off."

Alice gave a startled laugh; it seemed at the moment the only thing she could do. Trying to keep up with him reminded her of the time she and her brothers had tried to negotiate the rapids of a nearby river in a sawed-off barrel. She had escaped with only three broken ribs, but her oldest brother still bore a scar across his forehead as a memento of the escapade.

She said, "Are you serious? You have tickets? And you want *me* to go with you?"

"I said so, didn't I?"

"But you already have a date."

He shrugged. "I'd rather go with you."

She looked at him carefully. "And you always get just what you want."

"There's no reason I shouldn't."

Of course Alice wanted to see Valentino. Of course she wanted to go with Nicholas Crawford. Of course she wanted to pull up before the theater in a big Rolls-Royce wearing a corsage that was so big it draped over her shoulder, and have everyone staring at her in envy as she strolled up the aisle to a private box seat with the most eligible man in town. What girl wouldn't want that? And for almost a full three seconds she allowed herself to fantasize. But no more.

She frowned. "I'll tell you why you shouldn't. Because it's selfish and inconsiderate and irresponsible and . . . and shows an alarming lack of moral character!"

He sat up straight, his brows drawn together in annoyance and bewilderment. "Moral character? I didn't ask you to sleep with me, just go to the moving-picture show!"

"And what about the other girl?" she demanded.

"What other girl?"

"The one you've already asked!"

"What about her?"

"There, you see?" Alice declared, frustrated. "You don't even care, and that's exactly why I won't go with you!"

Nick fell silent. "I see," he said thoughtfully, after a moment. "If I take another girl instead of you, you'll approve of me."

"Well, I'd have more respect for your integrity, yes."

"And that would give me moral character?"

She shifted uncomfortably. "Hardly. But—"

"And if I take this other girl to the show tonight, will you go for a drive in the country with me tomorrow?"

For a moment Alice was speechless. And then, because it was apparent that explaining things to him was utterly pointless, she gave the simplest reply. "No."

"Why not?"

"Because." She focused her eyes on her knees, pleating the material of her skirt neatly over them. "I have to look for a job tomorrow."

"Sounds dull."

She shrugged. "I have to make a living."

"How about the next day, then?"

"No."

"All right, if you don't want to go driving how about dancing? Or to a matinee? Or the opera? I enjoyed that once. Is it opera season? I'll have to find out."

She looked up at him in exasperation. "Why?" she demanded. "Why do you want to go anywhere with me?"

He smiled engagingly. "Because," he replied, "I have a feeling you're going to be very bad for me, and that's one thing I never could resist."

"And because," Alice supplied dryly, "you have nothing better to do."

He chuckled. "That, too."

Alice sat there for a moment, torn between amusement and despair. The truth was, it was he who was very bad for her, and she knew the warning signs when she saw them. The trouble was, her resistance was not what it used to be, and the longer she lingered with him the greater the temptation grew. After all, he was charming and fun to be with, and what harm could there be in enjoying his company? But then, she had used exactly the same kind of reasoning when she had decided to go down the rapids in a sawed-off barrel.

She stood, determined to take no chances. "I have to get going."

He joined her more lazily. "You didn't give me an answer."

"Yes, I did."

"I didn't like it."

She increased her pace. "Oh, Nick, really, what's the point? I said no. Just leave it at that."

He caught her arm. "Don't start running again. I've got my second wind and you don't have a chance. Now," he demanded, tucking her arm firmly through his, "tell me why you said no."

She sighed impatiently. "Because I have too much to do to waste time being seduced by you."

"Waste time?" His eyebrows shot up. "Well, I like that. I don't believe any girl has ever accused me of wasting her time before. Besides, who said anything about seducing you? Maybe I just like to be with you."

She looked at him uncertainly, and then she laughed. "For a minute there, you looked almost sincere."

He stopped walking. "I am sincere," he said quietly. "I like you. I like spending time with you. What's wrong with that?"

She shouldn't believe him. She knew she shouldn't believe him. But there he was, his dark hair sprinkled with sunlight, his handsome face bent toward her with every appearance of earnest entreaty, his eyes as blue as a mountain pool in summertime, and the last of Alice's common sense disappeared like dew.

"Besides," he added, when she continued to hesitate, "I could be a help to you, you know. I'll make sure you're seen in the smartest places and introduce you to the right people."

"Show people?"

"Of course."

He obviously knew how to make himself difficult to refuse. "Even Tyler Bradford?" she suggested.

"If you insist."

She tried to think of all the reasons she should stay away from him. Only one came to mind. "I'm not going to be your mistress," she warned him.

"All right," he agreed. Far too easily, Alice thought. "You can be something else."

Suspicion prickled. "What?"

He smiled. "My companion."

She had never known a smile that was harder to resist than his. She started walking again, although much more slowly. "Well, I suppose that would be all right. If, from time to time, you wanted to go to a show or a museum or something and you needed a . . . companion."

"How about tomorrow?"

"No, not tomorrow."

"The next day?"

"You will have forgotten me completely by then."

"I'll call for you at three on Monday."

Alice smiled to herself. She didn't believe, even then, that he would, but it was nice to think he might.

Chapter Six

"This is the screwiest idea you've ever had," complained Jane, surreptitiously slipping one shoe off and wiggling her stockinged toes. "I can't believe I let you talk me into this. We've been here three hours already."

The sign at the front of the Forty-Second Street theater announced: Now Auditioning George and Ira Gershwin's Newest Musical Comedy OH, KAY! The line of hopefuls stretched from the stage-door entrance, around the building and almost to the next theater. The crumpled paper Alice had been given when she first arrived was marked 51, and the line was moving with maddening slowness. Her hair was limp beneath her cloche and her feet were burning, and she was quite sure that by the time she did make it inside she would be so wilted with perspiration that she would look more like a drowned cat than a candidate for a Gershwin extravaganza. She wished Molly were here. A nice public swoon would be just the thing to distract this crowd long enough for Alice to sneak to the front of the line.

"That's what open auditions are for," she replied, trying to peer over the heads of the shifting bodies in front of her. "Anyone can come."

"Well, it's stupid," pronounced Jane flatly. "There are over a hundred girls here, and what makes you think either one of us has a chance? At this rate all the chorus parts will be filled before we even get to the door! I mean, it's *Gershwin,* for heaven's sake!"

"That's just the point," Alice insisted enthusiastically. "Once you've been in a Gershwin or Kern production, your career is made! Do you have any idea where we'd be now if we'd gotten in *No, No, Nanette* last year?"

"Some of these women *were* in *No, No, Nanette,*" Jane replied sourly.

"So maybe the producer's looking for fresh faces," answered Alice, undeterred. "Everybody's got to start somewhere. And do you know what kind of run this play is going to have? We won't have to worry about looking for work for months. Years! And even after it closes, producers will be knocking on *our* doors, begging *us* to come fill their lead roles, no more standing in line or scrubbing floors or wondering how we're going to pay the rent. Now then," she finished breathlessly, "isn't that worth standing out in the sun for a little longer?"

Jane took a handkerchief from her purse and dabbed at her face, disgruntled and unimpressed. "I just hope the play runs longer than the casting call."

"Don't be such a pessimist. Don't you want to be in a Gershwin musical?"

"Of course I do. I also want a dozen Worth gowns and a yacht with my name on it and a villa in Spain, but I don't think I'm likely to get any of them this afternoon. Besides," she added, avoiding Alice's eyes as she smoothed down a spit curl at her cheek, "I've got a date tonight, and if I stay here much longer I'm going to be too wrung-out to enjoy it."

"A date? With who?"

Jane brushed an imaginary piece of lint off her white cuff. "Oh, nobody special. Just Jim Williams."

Alice lifted an eyebrow. "Is that right?"

Jane looked defensive. After the *Son of the Sheik,* she had come home to declare that Valentino, in person, was rather disappointing, but Officer Williams was "really a nice man." She had said nothing about having another date with him.

"We're just going to see a picture," she replied with a deliberately casual shrug of her shoulders. "It's something to do."

Then she glanced at Alice curiously. "What happened to you and Nick Crawford the other day, anyway? You never did say."

"That's because there's nothing to tell." There was a disturbance toward the front of the line and Alice stood on tiptoe to see what it was, but it turned out to be a false alarm. Conversation around her settled back to its normal pitch and she continued, "He walked me home, that's all. Or partway home. He wasn't wearing his spats and I think he was afraid of getting his shoes dirty when I took the shortcut through the alley."

Jane stared at her. "And that was it? You just let him get away? You're not going to see him again?"

"I doubt it. What would a man like him want with me, anyway?" Still, she remembered his promise and there was a funny little tingling sensation along her skin when she did.

Jane looked disgusted. "Well, I'm not sure about that, either, but I can think of a lot of things a girl like you would want a man like him for."

"I did ask him if he'd be my sponsor. He wasn't interested."

Jane rolled her eyes. "That's all you can think about? Your career? For the love of Pete, Alice, did you ever stop to think that if you would just once use what the good Lord gave you, you wouldn't have to be standing out in the broiling sun waiting for some addlepated stage director to call your number—"

The stage door opened and the crowd surged. Jane yelped as someone trod on her heel from behind, pushing her into the woman in front of her, who promptly stepped backward and planted her heel on Jane's toe. "Ow! Dammit!" Jane hopped on one foot, rubbing her injured toe, while the woman in front of her cast an offended look over her shoulder at Jane's language.

"Look at that," Jane exclaimed. "My best pair of pumps! All right, that's it. I've had it." She thrust her number in Alice's hand. "Enjoy yourself."

Alice caught her arm. "You're not leaving?"

"That," replied Jane, tugging her arm away, "is exactly what I'm doing. Look," she added impatiently, "if you want to spend your afternoon wrestling with a bunch of sweaty Shebas just for the chance to have the door slammed in your face by the stage manager, I wish you all the luck in the world. Personally, I have better things to do."

"Wait!" Alice caught her arm again as she started to walk away.

"Alice, cut that out. I'm not staying, I tell you. My feet are killing me and I've got a headache and—"

"I don't want you to stay," Alice insisted. And, at Jane's startled look, she added more charitably, "Not if you don't want to, that is. But if you're leaving anyway, and you're sure you don't want to audition, well, I have a plan."

Disregarding Jane's skeptical look, Alice pulled her closer and whispered in her ear.

Jane's eyes narrowed with every word until finally she pulled back in alarm. "Are you crazy?" she whispered. "I can't do that!"

"It'll work!" Alice assured her excitedly. "All you have to do is—"

"I don't do things like that! *You* do things like that!"

"Then I'll start."

Jane shook her head adamantly, taking a step backward. "Leave me out of this. I'm going home."

"I got arrested for you," Alice reminded her.

Jane's expression clouded doubtfully. "But I wouldn't know how to begin. It would never work. I couldn't—"

"You're an actress, aren't you? Just do it!"

She could see Jane begin to weaken, and taking advantage of the opportunity, Alice cried, "Valentino!"

Heads turned, and after only a second's hesitation, Jane took her cue. "It's him!" she exclaimed, grabbing the arm of the women in front of her. "It's Valentino, I saw him! Walking down Broadway—this way!"

A ripple of excitement broke through the crowd as Jane ran toward the corner, several people following.

Alice moved up in line, grabbing shoulders and shouting, "Valentino! It's Rudolph Valentino himself. I saw him—that way!"

The bored girls in the queue, restless for any diversion at all, began to break up—cautiously at first, and then with more enthusiasm as others picked up the cries of "Valentino!" and joined the mob Jane was leading toward the corner. Alice ran back and forth, gesturing excitedly, always returning closer to the head of the line until, when the last back was turned, she pulled open the stage door and slipped inside.

She paused to let her eyes adjust to the dim interior, her heart beating hard. The smell of dust and greasepaint infused her senses like an intoxicant, and she took a moment to breathe it in, reveling in her triumph. First Nicholas Crawford's party and now this. She was invincible. And this was only the beginning.

She followed the tinkling of a piano down the corridor and up a short flight of stairs, emerging in the wings. She peered through the curtain to see a blond girl—too short, Alice thought, and too plump—just finishing her audition. From the darkened rows of seats in front of the stage a bored male voice said, "Okay, sweetie. Check back with us Thursday."

"Y-yes, sir," the girl stammered, backing into the wings. "Thank you, sir."

She rushed past Alice, clutching a sheet of music to her chest and murmuring excitedly to herself, "They liked me! They liked me!"

Alice did not even spare her a glance. She took a deep breath, straightened her cloche and stepped onto the stage.

She stood blinded by the glare of the floodlights, looking toward the vast emptiness of the shadowed seats beyond, and wondered if anyone was out there at all. And then a harsh, disembodied male voice demanded, "Who the hell are you?" and Alice jumped.

She cleared her throat and inquired innocently, "What number did you call?"

Another voice, also male and also irritated, replied, "I didn't call any number."

"Well," Alice replied cheerfully. "I'm next."

She waited anxiously through a mumble of consultation and then the first voice spoke, sounding bored again. "What's your name?"

"Alice Fontaine." She pronounced it very carefully.

"Okay, dollface. Let's see your gams."

Alice hesitated, then lifted her skirt an inch, another inch, then two, then almost up to her knickers, and turned a full, dramatic circle. The response from the audience was singularly unimpressed. Slowly she let her skirt drop and turned to face her unseen judges again.

The silence stretched out. Then: "Let's hear your number."

For a moment Alice was taken aback. "W-what?"

"Your number!" the voice barked. "This is a damn musical, isn't it? You do plan to sing, don't you?"

"Oh. Of...of course." Alice overcame her momentary sinking of spirits and hurried to the pianist, giving him the tune and the key. Of course she would sing. It was a musical, wasn't it?

She returned to center stage, waited for her intro, missed it by half a bar, then gestured to the pianist to start over. On cue, she launched into a rousing rendition of "I Found a Million-Dollar Baby in the Five and Ten Cent Store."

It lasted about thirty seconds. The piano kept drowning her out, and when she tried to sing louder her voice cracked. She was two beats late coming into the second measure and never did catch up. She tried to compensate with an improvisational dance routine, but before her first fan kick the director was shouting, "Next!"

They did not ask where she could be reached in case of an opening. Alice was not surprised.

Jane was waiting for her when she came out. She took one look at Alice's face and slipped her arm around her shoulders. "Rough, huh?" she inquired sympathetically.

Alice nodded wordlessly.

Jane squeezed her shoulders. "Well, it was a good plan."

"Yeah," Alice sighed. "It was a good plan."

They walked silently toward Broadway.

Then Alice stopped, bleakness fading away into new hope at what she saw. "Look," she said, pointing at a billboard. "'Opening Soon This Theater—*The Girlfriend*.' I wonder if they're auditioning."

Jane laughed. "You never give up, do you?"

"'Rodgers and Hart,'" Alice said, reading further. "Who are they?"

"Who knows? Anyway, look—casting is closed. It's stamped right there on the poster."

"Well, it won't hurt to go in and leave our names, will it?" Alice grabbed Jane's hand. "Maybe the lead actress's understudy will get sick!"

Jane laughed, running a little to keep up with Alice as she dodged traffic to cross the street. "And maybe," she declared, panting as they safely reached the other side, "a knight in shining armor will come along and sweep you away from all this!"

Alice grinned. "Maybe!"

She pushed open the door of the theater.

The lead actress's understudy did not get sick, and there were no uncast parts in *The Girlfriend*. But within forty-eight hours, a knight in shining armor did come along, and Alice's life, for a few short weeks, was turned inside out.

"I WISH YOU'D STOP making it sound like a grand romance," Alice insisted, "because it's not like that at all. Nicholas Crawford is just a bored playboy with nothing better to do. He told me so himself."

The girls in the hotel rotated housekeeping duties because, Mrs. Handley insisted, hard work built character, but they all knew the real reason was that she was too cheap to hire outside help. That Saturday afternoon Molly, Jane, Alice and Barbara were assigned to scrub the kitchen, and the talk had turned, as it almost always did when they were together, to men. There had been a time when Alice had quickly grown impatient with such idle chatter, but since Nicholas had made himself such a presence in her life her attitude had changed. A great many things had changed.

He had shown up promptly in the downstairs parlor at three on the Monday he had promised, with a bouquet of posies for Mrs. Handley and enough charm to make certain that the good lady—as well as every other resident of the hotel—would welcome him gladly whenever he chose to call. And if that weren't surprising enough, he had brought along his friend

Stuart, and suggested that Molly accompany them on a picnic in the park. There was something devious about that, and Alice still had not quite decided whether he had chosen to make it a foursome in order to reassure Alice about his honorable intentions or because he had known that Alice wouldn't dare disappoint Molly by refusing at the last minute. One thing she knew for certain: a picnic in the park could not possibly be Nick Crawford's idea of high entertainment. He was playing some sort of game for his own amusement, and wondering when he would grow tired of it made Alice more nervous than she would have liked.

But over the next ten days Alice had to admit Nick's threshold of boredom was much higher than she had imagined. She saw him almost every day, sometimes for something as simple as an ice-cream soda at the local sweet shop, sometimes for a full-course dinner at Sherry's or the Waldorf. Occasionally he brought Stuart along and Alice began to like the young man, because, as shy and awkward as he was, he was gentle with Molly and made her eyes glow for hours after he had left.

The four of them went to the beach, and Nick teased Alice mercilessly when she told him she did not own a bathing costume. They had crisp white wine under a fluttering umbrella, and as the sun began to set they walked along the dunes. Nick held her hand, and that was the closest he had come to an intimate gesture with her.

She met no celebrities, producers or influential show people. Nick took her to the picture show and argued with her spiritedly about the charms of the young Greta Garbo. They went to a cellarlike speakeasy called Bearnie's to hear a ragtime band and Nick introduced her to the taste of gin, laughing at the face she made. He took her to the elegant Puncheon Club, where all the waiters knew him by name and made a great fuss over him, and he seemed to take singular delight in watching Alice's reaction to the luxury that surrounded her.

The next day he seemed to be equally delighted by the jugglers in the park, and spent an hour of apparent contentment doing nothing more than watching Alice feed popcorn to the ducks. If there was one thing Alice was quickly learning about Nick it was that there was nothing consistent or predictable about him, except that when she was with him she always had fun.

Barbara's voice brought her thoughts back to the present. "Well, if it isn't a romance, you're a fool for not turning it into one," she said. "And quick, before he gets away."

Barbara sat on the edge of the stepladder, examining the results of her manicure, and Alice gave her a dry look as she nudged her out of the way. For appearance's sake, Barbara pretended to put in her stint at kitchen duty, but household chores were obviously beneath her.

"He can't get away if I never had him in the first place," Alice pointed out, and lifted the bucket of wash water onto the top of the stool. Hitching up the skirt of her housedress, she climbed onto the stool and bent to wring out the washrag. "Besides, I told you, it has nothing to do with romance. All Nick wants is—" She paused, frowning a little as she applied the sopping rag to the dusty doorjamb. "As a matter of fact, I don't know what he wants."

And that was what bothered Alice most about her new relationship with a leading member of New York's fast set. When they talked, it was never about anything important. He teased her a lot, and she laughed a lot. He needled her and she gave him back his own and he seemed to enjoy that, too. He had not, since that first night at the party, made one improprietous move toward her; he played the perfect gentleman with the enthusiasm of a child trying out a role for the school play, but that was all it was—pretense. She had known him for over two weeks, yet she didn't know him at all. That bothered her, more than it should have.

Barbara grinned. "Well, if it was me, I'd sure let him have what he wants soon enough."

"Oh, Barb, honestly, you have a one-track mind." Jane rattled the lids of the stove impatiently. "Did it ever occur to you that there might be one or two men in the world who are just *nice*?"

"Like your policeman?" Barbara teased her.

"Well, yes," Jane replied a little defensively. "Jim is nice. I mean, he's not the man I want to marry or anything, but he's...nice." And she scrubbed the stove lids even harder, bending her head to hide her face. The other girls exchanged knowing smiles.

"It's funny," mused Molly. "Mr. Crawford is supposed to have such a desperate reputation, but in person he doesn't seem at all like that, does he? I mean, he's always so polite to me, and Stuart says—" She blushed. "Well, Stuart says he's a 'right regular fellow,' and Stuart should know."

Alice would not dream of disillusioning her friend by pointing out that Nick's charm was only a practiced facade, and that Stuart, to put it gently, was not the brightest man Alice had ever met. What would Molly say if she knew that Nick Crawford was an intimate of prostitutes and regularly spent time in jail? That he boasted about his prowess with the female sex and had propositioned Alice twice within twenty-four hours of meeting her? That he drank too much and cared too little and had a cruel streak he didn't always bother to keep hidden? She suspected that Stuart was just as naive about Nick as Molly was, and it was not her place to enlighten either of them. In fact, if there was one genuinely good thing about Nick Crawford it was that he had brought Stuart into Molly's life, and Alice would not do anything to jeopardize their blossoming relationship.

"He's a hard man to figure out," she said noncommittally.

"And you know a man who's *easy* to figure out?" Barbara challenged, and they all laughed.

But Alice's mirth was a little forced, and she wished they would all just change the subject. Far too much of her time was spent thinking about Nick Crawford, talking about Nick Crawford, having fun with Nick Crawford. In the past week and a half she had ridden down Broadway in a yellow roadster, had dinner at the Ritz and gone canoeing on the lake with a handsome, attentive gentleman at the paddle. But she had not found a permanent job. She had tasted the glamorous life of the very rich but was no closer now to making it on her own than she had been a year ago. And as for Nick...what was there to figure out? He was indolent, selfish and disreputable. He was distracting at the least and dangerous at the most. A man like him could bring her nothing but trouble, and the smartest thing she could do would be to politely refuse his next invitation and get on with her life.

Jane was saying, "That's for sure. Do you know what Jim told me about him?"

Alice told herself she didn't care what Jim had said about him, and applied the washrag with more vigor to the dusty doorjamb.

"Do you remember last Christmas when the papers all ran that story about the mysterious Santa Claus who set up a big table filled with turkeys and fruit and all kinds of goodies in the middle of the street for the poor? You'll never guess who Santa Claus was."

"Not Nick Crawford?" Barbara said incredulously, and Alice paused to look at Jane.

Jane nodded adamantly. "Jim says he's always doing crazy things like that. Bringing cigarettes and stockings and wool sweaters—not castoffs, either, but the genuine article—down to the people in jail. Even wine. And going to those awful slums and giving out candy to the children—can you just imagine? They even have a nickname for him—"

"The Backstreet Duke," Alice supplied softly, and the other girls looked at her expectantly, waiting for her to finish the story.

But Alice turned back to her work, hiding a secret smile and reveling in the rush of warmth that went through her. And that, she realized slowly, was only one of the reasons she couldn't just put Nick Crawford out of her mind and get on with her life. Without him, life would have no more surprises.

The Backstreet Duke, she mused, and the smile she had been trying to repress turned into a full-fledged grin. She would have to tease Nick about that the next time she saw him.

But Alice didn't see Nick that day, or the next. By the time a week had passed she began to wonder if she would ever see him again, and she told herself it was probably just as well. But it wasn't, and she had never missed anyone more in her life.

NICK SHIFTED in the lawn chaise, turning his face to better catch the sun. Down the parklike expanse of neatly manicured grass several couples played croquet, and in the distance the waters of Cape Cod glistened. Nick was in his tennis whites, and his racket lay abandoned on the grass beside him. He had come down that afternoon with every intention of playing, but had lost interest before he'd even reached the court.

He reached for the cool glass at his elbow and sipped it lazily. So far the only thing he had really enjoyed about his stay was the glass the well-trained servants kept perpetually filled at his elbow.

The invitation had come unexpectedly; some of Cynthia's friends were opening their house on the Cape and it had seemed as good an idea to go as to stay. He had always liked sailing, and several interesting females of his acquaintance were going to be there, and for good measure he had brought Stuart along. He could not recall ever in his life having been quite so bored, or completely at odds with himself.

Stuart came up, sweaty and puffing from the courts, and plopped down in a lawn chair beside Nick. "I lost," he announced, without Nick's asking. "Never was any good at the game."

"Then why do you play?"

Stuart shrugged. "Everybody does."

"That's the trouble with you, Stu." Nick took another sip of his drink and gazed out over the lawn. "You spend too much time worrying what everybody else does. Why don't you do what *you* want for a change?"

Stuart looked uncomfortable and didn't answer. The son of a banker who actually worked for a living, Stuart was a member of that rare social class that didn't seem to belong anywhere: too rich to be ignored but not quite prominent enough to be completely accepted. Sometimes Nick envied Stuart his uncertain position; at least it gave him something to strive for.

Then Stuart surprised him by saying, "You know, I was thinking I might go back to the city."

Nick glanced at him. "What for? There's nothing to do there, either. All the interesting people have made for the shore by now."

Stuart glanced self-consciously at his pudgy hands. "Not all of them."

After a moment of incomprehension, Nick gave a short laugh of astonishment and delight. "You can't mean Molly Mouse!"

"Don't call her that."

The sharpness of Stuart's tone caused Nick to throw up a hand in self-defense. "It was meant with affection and highest respect," he assured him. But his amusement became mixed with curiosity as he looked at his friend. "Be serious. You can't mean you're stuck on the girl?"

Stuart looked around, grumbling, "What do you have to do to get a drink around here?"

Nick lifted his hand, and in a moment a servant appeared with a pitcher of fruity chilled wine and several glasses on a tray. And when Nick continued to fix him with a waiting gaze, Stuart sipped his drink and replied, "I like being with her, that's all. She's different."

"She is that," Nick agreed. He turned back to his own drink, smiling. "What an interesting development. I think I rather like playing Cupid. Maybe I'll have a new career."

"You don't have to look so smug. I noticed you weren't exactly sitting on your hands back in the city, either."

Nick shrugged and refilled his glass from the pitcher. "A mere flirtation. I've forgotten her already."

Then Nick was irritated because the words didn't sound nearly as flip as he had meant them to, and it was embarrassing to be caught in a lie over something so inconsequential.

"She was fun," he amended casually. "Funny. She made everything seem new and it was a kick taking her around. But there's only so long a woman like that can hold a man's attention, isn't there?"

"Look at the two of you. What a couple of flat tires." Cynthia dropped to the ground beside Nick and helped herself to a piece of fruit that floated in his glass. "You must be talking about that dreadful little actress of yours, Nikki. I could smell the ennui all the way to the stables."

Nick retrieved the fruit from her fingers and pointedly tossed it away. "Why don't you run along and play, dear? This conversation is for adults."

"Not even an actress, really, just a cheap little hoofer from what I hear." Cynthia fluffed the ends of her short blond hair at the neck and leaned back on her palms, surveying the croquet game below. "At least an actress would have some sparkle. You could show her off."

"You're starting to sound like a brat, Cynthia."

"Not that it's any surprise. Everybody knows how screwy you are—we've come to expect it, enjoy it, really. But really, Nikki, this is so dull. It shows no imagination whatsoever, and I'm starting to worry about your reputation. I think you may be slipping." She picked up a glass from the tray and filled it. "I mean, if we want to talk about escapades, my particular favorite was in Portugal year before last—or was it three? You remember, Stuart, when he—"

"You *are* a brat," Nick said, and drained his glass.

Cynthia shrugged. "The point is, you used to be much more entertaining."

Stuart inquired curiously, "What happened in Portugal?"

Nick did not even bother to glare at him, nor was he the least bit interested in the story Cynthia began to recite. He lifted his glass, noticed it was empty, reached for the pitcher, but that was empty, too. He started to call for another, but then changed his mind. He was starting to get a headache from drinking so much; since he'd known Alice he'd gotten out of the habit. That realization both amused and dismayed him. The girl *was* bad for him, just as he'd predicted.

But she was also a great many other things. Quirky, energetic, oddly naive and exhaustively determined. Surprising. Always surprising. Seeing the world through her untutored eyes made even the most commonplace thing seem extraordinary, and when he was with her Nick felt renewed, curious, almost enthusiastic, and those were emotions he had not known in too many years. Her innocence delighted him, her seriousness both baffled and intrigued him, her stubbornness exasperated him, but she never, ever bored him.

Of course he had never known anyone like her before, and the initial attraction was easy to understand. What puzzled him was why it had not faded away by now. Except for one passionate infatuation with an upstairs maid when he was sixteen, Nick had never before been able to maintain an interest in any woman—or anything, for that matter—for so long a duration. He did not understand it, and was unsettled. And if he were completely honest with himself, he would have to admit that was why he had decided to leave the city. What Nick did not understand, he was accustomed to ignoring.

But ignoring Alice Fontaine, oddly enough, had not made her go away. Perhaps that was what disturbed Nick the most, for he had an uneasy feeling that it wasn't healthy to be quite so fascinated by one woman. And he was irritated because there was a small part of him that agreed with Cynthia: it wasn't a bit like him to throw himself so wholeheartedly into any enterprise, and he didn't like to think he might be losing control.

On the other hand, he'd had fun with Alice—a hell of a lot more fun than he was having here, with the members of his own so-called set. And having fun was what life was all about, wasn't it?

"A bunch of us are driving up to Coney Island tonight," Cynthia was saying, and Nick wondered when she had finished her story about Portugal. Lazily she picked a piece of fruit out of her glass and popped it into her mouth. "Should be good for a giggle or two if nothing else. We can count on you boys, can't we?"

Stuart hesitated. "I don't know. I was thinking about going back to town tomorrow. I'd like to catch the early train."

"Oh, applesauce," Cynthia replied dismissively. "There's nothing to do in town, and if you leave we'll be a man short. There's nothing more irritating than being left with an odd girl at the dinner table. You'll stay."

Stuart cleared his throat, glanced at Nick as though for support, then said, with far more conviction than Nick had ever heard him use with Cynthia, "Matter of fact, I really can't. Pressing business, you know. Someone's, well, sort of expecting me."

"Expecting you? Who could be expecting you? Everyone who's anyone is here."

Stuart's color rose and Cynthia eyed him narrowly as understanding dawned. She turned an accusatory look on Nick. "Now see what you've done. You've convinced poor Stuart that running after a cheap little Sheba is the latest fashion, and first thing you know he'll be a laughingstock. I mean maybe you can get away with it, kiddo, but you ought to have more consideration for your friends. Get him back on track, Nikki, before he makes a complete fool of himself."

Nick glanced at Stuart. His friend's face was beet red, but Nick couldn't tell whether it was from anger or embarrassment.

"There's a train leaving tonight, isn't there?" Nick said.

Stuart looked startled. "I think so, but—"

Nick rose, stretched lazily, and started toward the house.

"Where are you going?" Cynthia demanded.

"To pack."

After a moment, Stuart hurried after him, and Nick took particular satisfaction in his sister's open-mouthed stare as the two of them left her alone.

"ALICE! ALICE, wake up!"

Molly's frantic whisper barely penetrated Alice's heavy slumber, and Alice pulled the pillow over her head and rolled over.

Molly grasped Alice's shoulder and shook her hard. "Alice, wake up! There's something at the window."

Reluctantly Alice pushed away the pillow and batted open her eyes. "What?" she murmured sleepily.

"The window! There's something out there."

And then Alice heard it. A splattering, crackling sound pelted the windowpane, too random to be rain, too loud to be the wind. She sat up, frowning.

Molly clutched her arm, her whisper frightened. "What do you think it is? Should we call Lady Harridan? Do you think it's some sort of animal?"

Alice pushed aside the bedclothes and pulled down the hem of her wrinkled cotton shift as she got out of bed. Cautiously she made her way across the darkened room and lifted the curtain a fraction.

"It's an animal, all right," she announced grimly after a moment. "A low-down, long-tailed lounge lizard. And he's throwing rocks at our window."

Molly crawled quickly across the bed and came to stand beside Alice. "Why," she exclaimed softly, "it's Mr. Crawford!"

Scowling, Alice watched as Nick bent down to the ground, and suddenly realizing what he meant to do, she pushed open the window. It screeched loudly enough to catch Nick's attention and, Alice was very much afraid, that of everyone else in the building.

She leaned out the window and whispered angrily, "Nick Crawford! What do you think you're doing?"

He grinned up at her, sweeping off his hat. "Alice, Alice," he chanted softly, "can you come out and play?"

"Are you crazy, coming here this time of night? You must be completely ossified!"

He threw up a hand in mock insult. "I haven't had a drop in—" he pulled out his watch and squinted at it in the dim light of a distant streetlight "—almost eight hours. See what a state you've brought me to?"

"Then you're mad as a hatter! Go home, for heaven's sake, before someone sees you!" But the heat that flushed Alice's cheeks was not entirely from anger, and the light, skipping rhythm of her heart felt more like excitement than alarm. He had disappeared for over a week without so much as a tip of his hat and now he stood pelting stones at her window in the middle of the night, and was there anything surprising about that? She didn't know whether to slam the window shut or throw back her head in laughter.

"I shan't leave until you come out."

Though he spoke in a normal tone of voice, it seemed to Alice his voice was loud enough to echo. She made a frantic shushing gesture, and even Molly glanced with alarm over her shoulder toward the door, as though expecting Lady Harridan to burst through it any moment.

Suddenly Nick dropped to one knee and extended his hand upward dramatically. "Juliet, Juliet, wherefore art thou, Juliet?"

"Go away!" Alice whispered, and started to draw the window shut. But it was very hard not to grin.

He sprang to his feet. "Shall I sing you a serenade, then?"

"No!"

He tucked his fingers into the front pockets of his trousers and tilted his head back to better view her. Though it was far too dark to clearly see his face, Alice imagined that his light eyes were snapping with mischief.

"Then," he suggested, "I suppose I'll just have to stroll around to the front door and knock until someone lets me in."

"Don't you dare!"

"Come out with me."

"No." She tried to make her voice firm. "Good night."

He lifted his shoulders negligently and turned toward the corner of the building. "I'll go knock."

"No!" She leaned frantically out the window. "Wait!"

He paused obligingly, tilting his head toward her.

Alice looked at Molly. Molly's eyes mirrored her own helplessness.

"I don't think he's going to go away," Molly ventured timidly after a moment.

Alice took a deep breath. "I've got to go down."

"You can't!" Genuine alarm tore at Molly's features. "If you get caught—"

"I won't get caught. I'll slip out the back and be back in bed before Lady Harridan even cracks an eye."

Quickly Alice went over to the window and leaned out again. "I'll be right down," she cried in a stage whisper. "Stay there!"

She hurried to the wardrobe, snatched a dress off its hook and pulled it over her shift.

Molly was wringing her hands with distress. "But what if someone hears you? What will I say? How will I explain—"

"Nobody's going to hear me. I'll be quiet as a mouse." She slipped on her shoes without bothering with stockings and paused only to give Molly a quick hug. "I'll just get rid of him and be right back. Go back to sleep."

And as quickly as she possibly could without making a racket, she stole out of the room and down the stairs.

She ran silently through the dark alley and, breathless and flushed, reached Nick, who was standing where she had left him. He turned to her, arms extended, and just as she had suspected, his eyes were laughing.

"Darling!" he exclaimed.

She slapped his arms away, fuming. "How dare you? Don't you know the kind of trouble you could get me in? What kind of crazy person goes running around this time of night throwing stones at windows? Are you crazy?"

"And this is the thanks I get for traveling half the night to see you?" He was laughing softly, and he reached out to clasp both her hands. This time he did not release her when she resisted—or perhaps she didn't resist with quite so much enthusiasm this time.

He looked wonderful. Perhaps it was the streetlights, perhaps it was merely absence that made him a welcome sight, but he looked taller, fitter and more dashing than she remembered. His hair seemed thicker and richer as it resisted its part and shadowed his forehead, his lips seemed fuller and his eyes more magically hued than ever before. The foggy distant glow of the streetlight softened the planes of his face and deepened the dimple when he smiled, and in that moment Alice did not understand how she could have ever determined so casually to put him out of her mind.

For that was exactly what she had done. She had always known that men like Nick Crawford tended to fade from one's life with far less ceremony than they burst into it, and from the beginning she thought it would be only a matter of time before his attention wandered. When she did not hear from him by the second day, and then the third, she had decided to forget him.

Of course it hadn't been that easy. For a shining space of days she had been Cinderella, and it was hard to settle down to being a scullery maid again. And she couldn't help being piqued that he had forgotten her that easily, or tired of her so quickly. But most irritating of all was that she had missed *him*. She'd missed his smile and his unpredictable impulses and his sly cynicism and his quick wit. She missed being around him and she'd missed waking up in the morning full of expectation for what Nick might have in store for her that day.

Until he was gone, she had not fully appreciated how much of her life had been taken up with him, how much of her thoughts revolved around him. When he was gone a great expanse of empty hours stretched before her; in a hotel filled with friends she had no one to talk to, and the life that had once seemed so rich with challenge was a dull and unsatisfying routine. *That* was what Nick Crawford had done for her, and all the while when she couldn't stop thinking about him, she kept telling herself she was better off without him.

Now here he was, smelling of bay rum and cigarettes, blue eyes twinkling and hands wrapped warmly about hers, and she was both wildly happy and perversely sorry to see him. And while she debated whether to stamp her foot hard on his toe or fling her arms around him, curiosity overcame her. He was as difficult to resist as ever.

"Where have you been?" She inquired grudgingly.

"Around the world and back. Did you miss me?"

"Like I'd miss a sore tooth. And you came here in the middle of the night just to tell me about your trip?"

He took her hand and tucked it possessively through the crook of his arm. "I came to show you something quite spectacular."

Alice refused to budge. "What?" she demanded suspiciously.

"You have to come with me."

"This time of night?" She tried to pull her arm away. "I can't go anywhere with you! You've got some nerve, dragging me out of bed in the middle of the night and just assuming I'd be at your beck and call."

But then curiosity crept insidiously to the forefront again and she had to ask, "Come with you where?"

He smiled benignly. "It's a surprise."

"What kind of surprise?"

"You'll have to come with me to see."

Alice looked back at the darkened house and knew the only smart thing to do would be to creep back inside as silently as she had left, pull the covers over her head and forget that this bizarre interruption of her night's sleep had ever happened. But then, without meaning to look at him at all, she caught a glimpse of Nick's eyes, deep with mystery and twinkling with promise, and she knew she'd never had a choice.

"This better not take long," she warned.

He chuckled softly and led her toward the street.

Chapter Seven

Waiting at the curb was a horse-drawn carriage, the old-fashioned kind with a canopy and a seat for the driver on top. Alice stopped in astonishment when she saw it. "Where's your car?"

"It's too noisy for this time of night," he said, gesturing her toward the carriage step. There was a sly curve to his lips as he confessed, "I didn't really want to wake everybody in the hotel if I could help it."

The leather seat squeaked as Nick got in beside her; the driver flicked the reins and the carriage swayed forward. Alice felt her first stab of trepidation as her own familiar block disappeared from view. "We can't go far," she warned Nick. "Molly will be worried, and if Mrs. Handley ever finds out I'm gone—"

"Then we'll make up some daring and elaborate tale that will be so impossible she'll have no choice but to believe it."

Alice looked at him dryly. "Like the one you made up to explain where you've been for the past week?"

He shrugged. "I was at the Cape with some friends."

"Why didn't you stay?"

"I never stay anywhere for long."

Alice promised herself she would remember that about him.

The carriage turned toward the manufacturing district, and the streets were deserted and silent except for the clip-clop of the horse's hooves. The night air was balmy and faintly moist with the breeze off the river, and Alice was enchanted by the stillness of it all. She had never been out this late before, never seen the city shrouded in the mysterious hours of predawn, never known the heady feeling of being the only living creature in a city of millions. But every time she was with Nick she experienced something new. Every moment with him was an adventure.

She sat back against the seat with a sigh. "I wish you had stayed away. I was just getting used to missing you."

There was a moment of silence in which it seemed that Nick, uncharacteristically, had no ready reply. Then he said simply, "But I couldn't stay away." He reached for her fingers and held them lightly. "You see, I couldn't grow used to missing you."

Though his tone was playful and the shadows of the carriage hid his face, Alice felt a slight quickening in the rhythm of her pulse. She thought he meant it.

The carriage pulled up in front of a tall, deserted brick building, and Alice peered out cautiously. "What is this place?"

"A shirt factory." Nick came around the carriage and extended his arms to help her out. "My father owns it."

Alice hesitated. The place looked spooky in the dark. Haunted, if not worse. "You brought me all the way out here to show me a shirt factory?"

"Shh," he admonished her. "It's a surprise, remember?"

Nick grasped her waist and Alice had no choice except to brace her arms against his shoulders as he swung her down. She stayed close to him as he led the way into the shadows of the building, glancing repeatedly over her shoulder to reassure herself the driver was still there. Suddenly she found she wasn't as adventurous as she had always pictured herself, and she tugged at Nick's sleeve. "I really think I'd like to go back now. I've been gone too long and—"

"And you might as well be hanged for a sheep as a lamb, hadn't you? Don't you want to see what's inside?"

"I know what's inside," she replied, looking back nervously as she thought she saw something move in the shadows. "Shirts."

He chuckled softly and took a key ring from his pocket. Then the wooden door swung open with a screech after he inserted the key. "Come on in," he invited, extending his hand to her.

Hesitantly Alice stepped over the threshold. The room smelled of machine oil and cotton dust, and it was as black as tar when the door closed behind them. Nick caught her hand. "Come on. Don't worry, I know this place as well as my own parlor."

As her eyes gradually adjusted, the darkness began to reveal lumpy, crouching shapes that were far from reassuring. "Should—should we be here? I mean, isn't there a night watchman or something? What if he shoots us?"

"There's not a night watchman in sight. Besides, I own this place, remember? More or less," he amended, and started forward, pulling at her hand.

Alice hung back. "Maybe," she suggested, "I could just wait here."

"Suit yourself." He dropped her hand. "Watch out for rats."

Alice scurried to his side and Nick laughed as he draped an arm around her shoulders.

He led her through a door and up a narrow flight of stairs, then another. Alice counted five more flights before he opened a final door and gestured her through it. A gentle breeze tossed her hair and cooled her heated cheeks, and Alice caught her breath at what she saw.

"Oh, Nick!"

A blanket was spread out on the rooftop, surrounded by enough cushions to make the Sheik of Araby's tent look squalid in comparison. In the center of the blanket was a picnic basket from which protruded a champagne bottle and a loaf of bread, and two merrily dancing candles illuminated the whole with a soft glow. Below her all of Manhattan was spread out like a wonderland, electric lamps glittering on the East River and looping like lace through curving streets.

"Oh, Nick," she said again, and hugged her bare arms with delight. She ran to the wall and peered over, drinking in the view and the smell of the river and the breeze through her hair like an intoxicant. Then she laughed out loud, twirled, and flung herself onto a pile of cushions.

"Do you like it?" Nick dropped down beside her, smiling.

"It's wonderful! It's absolutely the most incredible thing I've ever seen! A picnic on the roof. Who would ever have thought of it?"

"I used to come here when I was a boy." Nick reached for the champagne bottle and his face grew oddly thoughtful as he worked the cork. "It seemed like a magical place then, a secret castle where, for a time, I was king of the world. I felt . . . safe here."

And then he shrugged, as though embarrassed to find himself in the midst of a surprising sentiment. "If my father had ever caught me, of course, he would've skinned me alive, but I suppose that was half the fun of it—the danger."

Alice looked at him closely, tantalized by the hint of discovery—the first clue she had ever had as to who Nick Crawford might really be. "Funny," she said slowly, "I can't picture you as a boy."

The cork loosened between his hands with a muffled pop, and he flashed a smile at her. "I haven't changed much."

"Oh, I know you still act like a boy sometimes." She found the glasses in the picnic basket and held one out to him. "But that's different. I just can't picture you wearing knickers or rolling a hoop or laughing and playing like other children. Being . . . I don't know. Happy. Innocent."

He filled the first glass, and she held out the second. "Maybe that's because I was never innocent. Come to think of it, I'm not entirely sure I was ever happy, either."

"Not even here, on your rooftop?"

He looked thoughtful as he put away the champagne bottle and took his glass from her. "Maybe here," he agreed, leaning back on one elbow against the cushions. "All by myself, imagining things."

"What kind of things?" Alice prompted softly, unwilling to shatter the odd mood that had come upon him with something as mundane as the sound of her voice.

His smile was one of secret, distant reminiscence, and there, for the first time, Alice got a glimpse of the boy he must have been. "Oh, that this was my fortress, and the East River was my moat, and below me were the peasant villages, under siege by a slew of fire-breathing dragons. Not one, mind you, but a whole army of them. And I alone would be called upon to save the day."

He gave a short shake of his head, visibly pulling himself away from the world of childhood fantasies and into the present. "Of course," he added lightly, lifting his glass in a small salute, "I always did. An illustrious start for a somewhat less-than-illustrious career, wouldn't you say?"

"I would say," Alice replied slowly, "that it's a shame you grew up."

He looked uncertain for a moment, as though he would like to say more, or didn't know quite what to say. Then, abruptly, he stretched forward and began to unpack the picnic basket. "You must be sleepier than I thought, girl, to waste time talking when there's food to be had. And after I went to all the trouble to order your favorites. Except ice cream." He glanced at her with mock apology. "I couldn't quite think how to manage ice cream."

"Well, if you were any kind of gentleman at all you'd run right out and rob a soda shop for some."

"What a splendid idea! I think I will."

He made as though to rise and she caught his hand, laughing. "The trouble is," she said ruefully, "you'd probably do it."

He declined to answer.

The basket was filled with soft and hard cheeses, wafer-thin slices of ham; strawberries dipped in powdered sugar. A feast like that in the middle of the night was intoxicating enough; to indulge in it on a rooftop beneath a canopy of stars with the city glittering below her seemed the most delightfully decadent experience that had ever been conceived.

"Do you know what the main difference between you and me is?" Alice said contentedly, cradling the champagne glass as she leaned back against the cushions. "My fantasies aren't even as good as the things you do every day. Oh, Nick, this *is* a magical place. And this—" she smiled at him "—is the best time I've ever had."

"So far." He stretched out, placing a pillow under his head, and crossed his legs at the knees. "There's always tomorrow."

Of course, for people like Nick there was always tomorrow, but Alice was only a working girl and could not afford to get tangled up in his games, delightful though they might be. She took a sip of champagne, trying not to spoil the moment with mundane reality. Tomorrow was another day of searching the city for a job, of counting pennies for stockings and lipstick, of beating on doors in hopes of an audition. But tonight, here on the rooftop with Nick, was a moment to be savored for its own sake, and she would not let tomorrow intrude.

She said, "See that star up there? Right over the river, the big twinkly one? That's a wishing star."

An indulgent, half-cynical smile touched his lips. "How can you tell?"

"I just can. Go ahead, make a wish. See if I'm not right."

"I don't have anything to wish for."

She looked at him. "Everybody has something to wish for."

"Nope." He settled his head more comfortably on the cushion. "What I don't have, I know how to get, or else I don't want it at all."

Alice could not decide whether he was to be envied or pitied. "I'm not sure I'd like it very much if I didn't have at least one thing to wish for."

He sipped his champagne, then made a lazy skyward gesture with his glass. "Be my guest. Make a wish."

She hesitated, then turned her face toward the star, closing her eyes. When she opened them again Nick was looking at her curiously.

"Well?" he prompted.

"Well, what?"

"What did you wish for?"

"I don't have to tell you."

"You certainly do. It was my wish, remember?"

"If I tell you, it won't come true."

"If you don't tell, I'll take back my wish."

"Anyway—" she twirled a strawberry by the stem in her champagne as she had seen Nick do, and popped it into her mouth "—you already know what I wished."

Exasperated, he got up on one elbow, turning toward her. "If I did I wouldn't ask, would I? Come on, what did you wish for? A shiny new roadster? Riches beyond the dreams of avarice? My hand in marriage? What?"

She slanted a glance toward him, a small smile tightening the corner of her lips. "Well," she said, "I don't know how to drive, so a roadster wouldn't do me much good. And I certainly don't want your hand in marriage."

"A grave mistake," he observed. Then, as though an afterthought, he added "Why not?"

"First," she replied, "because I don't want to get married."

"Every girl wants to get married."

"Second," she continued, oblivious to his interruption, "because you'd make a dreadful husband."

"So true."

"And third—" she popped another strawberry into her mouth "—you haven't asked me."

"Count your blessings."

She laughed. "Why? Just because you ask doesn't mean I have to say yes."

"But I'm very persistent. I'd keep after you until I wore you down and eventually you'd have to say yes, and then we'd both be miserable."

But at that moment, feasting on strawberries and champagne in the balmy summer night, Alice could not imagine being miserable with him, no matter what the circumstances. And she found the direction of the conversation, playful though it was, had caused a fluttering in her rib cage that was perfectly pleasant.

He said, "Not a roadster, not me... You must have wished for riches."

Alice finished her champagne and put the glass aside. She placed her hands behind her and straightened her elbows, leaning back and gazing up at the sky. "Not riches, exactly, though I expect to have those, too. But fame. Success. Stardom."

"Ah, that again."

"Yes, that again." A slight note of irritation crept into her voice that threatened to spoil the perfect night.

"I know you don't think much of my ambition, but I assure you it's very important to me. And I don't intend to fail."

"Why?"

He reached across her knees to help himself to a strawberry from the bowl at her side, and perhaps it was a sudden awareness of his warmth, or the brush of his sleeve against the bare portion of her lower leg, or the fact that when he settled down again his hip was pressed lightly against hers, that caused Alice to miss the question. She stared at him blankly.

"Why," he repeated, "is being a star so important to you? There must be easier ways to get a fortune."

"I told you, it's not the fortune." She gathered her thoughts with difficulty. "It's doing something special, *being* someone special—not just some man's wife or mother or—" she glanced at him meaningfully "—mistress. But doing something that only *I* can do, and being remembered for it. Like Clara Bow or Sarah Bernhardt or Jenny Lind. I want to be important, cause a stir, be *somebody*. Do you know what I mean?"

He chuckled softly. "Not much to ask for."

"You think I'm foolish."

"I think you're adorable, and I just remembered what I missed most about you."

That was a surprising thing for him to say. When she turned to look at him she found that his face was very close to hers, and that, too, was surprising. She wanted to move away, but didn't know how to without being rude. Besides, there was a part of her—a very insistent, though not very wise, part—that didn't want to move at all.

She tried to keep her voice from sounding as breathless as she felt as she inquired, "What?"

He smiled, teasing her. "That remarkable ability you have of letting your reach exceed your grasp."

She frowned a little, disappointed somehow that he hadn't taken better advantage of the moment—and yet contrarily relieved to have the conversation back on more familiar ground. "I don't think I've ever known what that means, but I guess it's your way of telling me—again—what you think of my talent."

"What do *you* think of your talent?"

She replied promptly, "I think talent isn't important if you have heart. And that's what I have. Lots of heart."

He laughed, his eyes sparkling in the starlight. "I won't deny that. And coming from a man who's known far and wide to be completely heartless, you may take that as a compliment."

"Heartless, are you?" She shot him a glance of smug enjoyment, feeling he deserved some retaliation for the teasing he had given her. "Is that why they call you the Backstreet Duke?"

His face immediately composed itself into bland lines. "Who told you about that?"

"Oh—" she shrugged elaborately "—word gets around."

"Jimbo. I'll lay my fortune on it. Remind me to stop by the commissioner's office in the morning and have him fired, will you?"

"Now *that* would be heartless." She looked at him curiously. "Why do you make such a big secret of it, Nick? No—why do you do it at all?"

He reached for the champagne bottle and poured the last quarter-inch into her glass. "The same reason I do everything," he replied casually. "For sport."

She looked at him thoughtfully, ignoring the glass he offered to her. "No," she said slowly, watching him closely. "I think it's because somewhere inside you there's still a little boy fighting dragons from a rooftop."

"And still believing he can always save the day," Nick added softly, without looking at her.

The moment between them was so poignant that a frisson touched Alice's spine, a prickle of awareness and anticipation so certain that she caught her breath with the sweetness of it. She touched his hand. He looked at her.

"I always thought there must be more to you than meets the eye," she said.

"Most of it's not worth knowing."

"But a lot of it is."

His expression was sober. "Don't expect too much of me, Alice. I'll only disappoint you."

She did not know what she expected from him. She only knew that when he lifted his hand to touch her face she did not turn away; when the backs of his fingers lightly stroked a pattern down her cheek she moved instinctively toward the caress. There was a subtle change in the atmosphere between them; tenderness was charged with expectation, warmth with anticipation. Alice could feel the light, jumping motion of the pulse in her throat, and she dared not draw a breath for fear of breaking the spell. His eyes were steady, soft and gentle, not questioning or hesitating, merely gazing into hers. And Alice met that gaze, feeling heat creep into her cheeks with each passing second. But she could not look away. Not if it meant her soul, could she look away.

His hand slipped around her neck and his face moved closer. His lips clasped hers lightly, more of a promise than a kiss, and a warm shiver rushed down Alice's spine. Another whisper of a kiss, and another, until Alice's lips, hungry for a taste of him, formed a response. Their lips clung together for a brief, exploratory time, and Alice's breath shortened in her throat; a strange weakness drained through her muscles.

His smile curved against her lips and his breath cooled the moisture there. He murmured, "There. Was that so bad?"

Somehow she managed to whisper, "I never thought it would be."

His hand tightened slightly on the back of her neck, supporting her as his weight gently urged her back to rest upon the cushions. His mouth covered hers slowly and she tasted him, rich with strawberries and champagne; she felt his moisture merging with hers; she felt all will and restraint seep out of her as she gave herself over completely to the sensation.

She lifted her arms around his neck, she caressed the thick, springy texture of his hair and the strength of his back. His nearness was an intoxicant, his kiss caused her senses to spiral, enticing her to painfully new heights of awareness of her own body—and of his, pressed so close to hers.

His hand slid down to her waist in a long, caressing stroke, slipping beneath her back and lifting her gently upward, pressing her closer. At the same time his lips parted hers to the moist, warm invasion of his tongue.

Never had she been kissed like that. Heat rushed to every pore, her heart clamored against her ribs, rich vibrant colors swirled behind her closed eyes. She drank of him and felt filled with him, swept along beyond control or reason. Her muscles trembled and her skin was on fire; she did not know how it was possible to endure such an intense influx of wild sensation, of aching desire and blinding pleasure.

She felt the pressure of his thigh against her hip, the heat of his neck beneath her fingertips, the caress of his hand against her bare leg. She heard a moan from far away and thought it must be hers. His lips touched her cheek and she could feel his uneven breathing. He whispered, "Ah, love. So many delights I could show you. So many sensations we could share..."

Alice's head spun, her strength of will fading like a pinpoint of light into the night. He was the exotic sheik and she was the Arabian princess, swept away into the desert and held captive in his tent, helpless against his passion. The Sahara winds caressed her skin and silken curtains fluttered in the candlelight and she was his... Except that the wind smelled of the East River and the cushions upon which she lay were chintz, not silk, and he was not a sheik but Nicholas Crawford, more real, more exotic than even the grandest fantasy could be. And she was still helpless against his passion... and her own.

He took her hand and brought it to his face. His warm breath tickled her palm; the touch of his tongue caused a tingle of sensation to settle in the back of her throat. He brought her hand down, across his face and his neck, loosening the buttons of his shirt as he did so until her fingertips brushed the light matting of hair upon a male chest—damp, heated flesh against her palm. Her heart was beating hard, and his eyes, drowsy-bright and gently commanding, held her mesmerized. She moved her hand over the smooth planes and tight muscles of his chest and saw his eyes narrow with pleasure. The wonder of discovery was heady.

He dipped his head and placed a kiss near her ear, then took the lobe gently between his teeth. The sound of his breath was like the rush of an ocean tide, and a tingling jolt of current traveled from the sensual caress of his tongue to the pit of her stomach. Her hand tightened against his chest; then, as he dropped his mouth to her throat, her fingers moved greedily around his back, searching to explore more of him, drawing him closer.

He murmured, "Ah, Alice. What music we could make together...."

His hands cupped her waist and slid slowly upward, pausing to caress each rib, to trace with gentle, tantalizing strokes the indentation below her breastbone, and in the back of her mind Alice did hear music, sweet and high like the sigh of the wind. She thought senselessly, *This is what it's like, then. This is what it's like to know a lover....*

Tightening spirals of anxiety tugged at her abdomen and caught in her throat as his hands cupped her breasts, so lightly that his touch was almost a shadow, hesitant and teasing. Then with slowly tightening fingertips he molded her shape to his hands, pliable flesh becoming heated, aching. A part of her knew that they were moving inexorably toward that point where harmless petting ended and serious lovemaking began, and common sense urged her to pull back. But there was a deeper urgency that blurred her senses, and she was not entirely sure she wanted to pull back. Not yet.

She had pulled her dress on over her nightgown, and nothing separated her swollen, aching breasts from the touch of Nick's lips except two thin layers of material. She moaned in dizzy protest as Nick expertly unfastened the top buttons of her dress and pushed the material away, baring one shoulder to the night air and the warmth of his breath. Her hand, trapped against his bare chest in the warm nest between their bodies, tightened convulsively. Her heart leapt and thundered as his tongue played lightly over the exposed curve of her bosom, and then in a flood of heat and moisture, he moved lower, opening his mouth against the tingling, distended center of her breast.

The vague knot of need in her abdomen suddenly tightened into a distinct ache that left her breathless. He took the material of her nightgown between his teeth and moistened it, then flooded her skin with a wordless whisper as he closed his mouth around her nipple, tugging gently. The ache blossomed into a tingling between her thighs, a helpless wanting that frightened her. His hand slid down to caress her bare leg, sliding upward under her skirt across her knee, and her thigh, and instinctively she moved her hand to stop him.

"Nick—"

"Hush, love." His voice was like a murmur, only more breathless. His face was heated against her chest, his fingertips traced a light circular pattern on her kneecap. "Don't let me frighten you. Open your eyes," he whispered.

His face was a sculpture in passion against the starry sky. Dark hair tousled from the play of her fingers, darker eyes that seemed to capture her very soul. Shadowed planes, the flush of desire, lips that were meant to mold themselves to hers. "Feel this," he said softly. He drew his hand down the length of her leg, a feathery touch that made her skin tighten and tingle. "And this." He placed a kiss deep within the hollow of her throat. "Feel my heart beat against your hand. That's all that matters. The way we make each other feel, this moment. And it only gets better, I promise. Let me show you...."

She wanted to say, *Yes. Show me, teach me, take me on a grand adventure and let me be yours. For a moment, an hour, forever, I don't care.* She wanted to turn her mouth to his and drown in him again, let him sweep her away in mystery and magic as only Nick could do. She wanted to cast all else aside and revel in the sensation of it, fill herself with it, to sate herself with it.

But as he made to draw her close again she brought her hand up, unsteadily, and laid her fingers against his lips. "Nick," she whispered. "No. Please."

He took her fingers and kissed them gently. His eyes were the changing colors of the moon-kissed sea, dark and light, utterly hypnotic. "Let me be your lover, Alice," he said softly. "I will try to be as good for you as you are for me."

Her fingers tightened around his. She was aching and burning inside, but the ache, as she spoke, was more than physical. "No, Nick. Not yet. Not now."

She sensed a slight tensing within him, as though he were reaching for self-control, and the silence that followed seemed to stretch across the night. Then he moved away, drew the gold cigarette case from his pocket and opened it for her. She accepted a cigarette with unsteady fingers, and she noticed, when he struck a match and held it to her cigarette, a faint, almost imperceptible tremor in his own hands.

He brought the flame to his own cigarette, shielding it against the breeze, then shook it out and tossed it away. Leaning back in what gave every appearance of casual disregard, he drew on the cigarette, exhaled, and asked after a moment simply, "Why?"

"Because—" she fixed her gaze on the glowing tip of the cigarette between her fingers "—there are things that are more important to me than . . . just the moment. And you are entirely too much of a temptation."

After a moment he spoke, and though his voice was still husky with the residue of passion, there was a hint of his old playful tone. Alice was grateful for that.

"Is that bad?" he asked.

"For me it is." She spoke softly, looking at her knees. "I can't afford to grow used to you. It would be too easy to depend on you." She brought the cigarette to her lips, but still could not draw a deep breath. She inhaled and exhaled lightly. "I don't want to be just another one of your girls, Nick."

Nick did not reply, smoking silently for a while and gazing out over the shadowed rooftop. His voice had an odd tone to it when he spoke, one that Alice had never heard before, and still he did not look at her.

He said quietly, "Alice, I want you to listen to me, because this may be the last completely true thing I ever say to you. I've spent a lifetime perfecting the art of indifference. I'm cynical and careless and selfish and I work hard at avoiding intimacy or concern. I am probably the worst misfortune that could cross your path."

He looked at her, and his voice softened. "Yet I'm touched by you," he said slowly. "You make me see things in myself that I don't often think about, and when I'm with you I don't feel quite as worthless as I probably am. I care for you in a way that I have never cared for any woman. No..." he corrected slowly, as though the truth surprised him, "for anyone, ever. And for that reason—" he tossed aside the cigarette and stood "—I am taking you home now."

His smile seemed a little forced as he extended his hand to her, but it was reassuring nonetheless. Alice placed her hand in his and allowed him to pull her to her feet. And there was a moment, looking into his eyes and feeling the effects of his smile, that she wanted to say something, to touch his face, perhaps even to change her mind.

But in the end all she could do was smile at him, and walk away from the rooftop.

Chapter Eight

Nick paced restlessly in front of the building, his hands clasped behind his back, his hat pulled low on his forehead. Occasionally he would stop to pull out his watch, or to reread the shingles that hung from the post outside the door. Harvey Hillman, Attorney at Law. Reginald Forest, Real Estate. Capris Enterprises. Seymour F. Kahn, M.D. He doubted whether Alice had any business with a lawyer or a realtor. What if she was ill?

For the second time since knowing her, Nick had reason to be glad that the residents of the Handley Hotel were required to inform their landlady of their destination before leaving the building. Mrs. Handley couldn't remember the name of the person Alice was going to see, however, only the building number. The name of Seymour F. Kahn, M.D., kept leaping out before Nick's eyes.

For three days Nick had called himself every kind of fool for the episode on the roof. He had known then, as he knew now, that he was only a breath away from sublimity with Alice; a whispered word, a gentle caress, and her protestations would have melted away. She was not, after all, the first woman to say no, only to realize later that what she really meant was yes, and Nick was practiced in the art of persuasion. Then why had he pulled away?

And even more unsettling was the fact that he wasn't certain whether his biggest mistake had been in trying to seduce her in the first place, or in giving up so easily. He had wanted Alice Fontaine from the first moment she caught his eye, and he'd made no secret of it. The little game he had played of being the perfect gentleman "companion" had been a diversion, adding spice to their relationship and whetting his appetite for the conquest he had always been certain would come. Or at least, that was what he had been telling himself all these weeks. The truth was, as time passed he had almost forgotten it was a game, and he had begun to enjoy the experience of having a woman as a friend for the first time in his life. And that was why, when the crucial moment had come, he discovered that he cared too much for her to put his own desires before hers.

He had tried to put it down to too much champagne, or excessive fatigue or any number of other pallid excuses. But the simple fact was that he cared for her and that was an experience so new and so shocking he simply did not know what to make of it. He had done more soul-searching over the past three days than he had in his previous twenty-six years and had found no answers. The only thing that was clear was that he was in the midst of a novel experience, on the verge of the discovery of something important about himself, and he had not felt so excited about being alive since he'd been a boy. Whatever peculiar power Alice Fontaine had over him demanded to be explored, however cautiously, to its natural conclusion.

Of course, he had been more than half-convinced that natural conclusion would be nothing more than a waning interest with the passage of time; he might even see her today and find himself wondering what all the fuss and furor had been about. Then he had arrived at this address and had seen the shingle with Seymour F. Kahn, M.D., written on it and his stomach had knotted with fear.

He checked his watch again. He had been walking up and down for twenty minutes now. Perhaps he should go inside and make inquiries. Maybe she had already left. Maybe that silly woman had the address all wrong and Alice had never come here at all.

And then he saw her. The door opened and closed behind her, and she stood on the top step. She pressed a handkerchief to her eyes and the slump of her shoulders was so dejected that Nick felt an actual stabbing pain in his chest with sympathy—or anxiety.

He ran toward her and met her at the bottom of the steps.

"Nick!" The expression on her face was surprise, but her eyes were wet. She had definitely been crying. "What are you doing here?"

He slipped an arm around her shoulders and said, "Come on, I'll give you a ride home. What is it? Was it very bad news?"

"Oh, Nick, I *am* glad to see you." She swiped at her eyes again briefly with the handkerchief as he led her to his car. "I don't mean to be such a baby, but this day has just been awful. I can't tell you the trouble I had getting here, and it's so hot, and I spent almost two hours sitting in that reception room, and then he wouldn't even see me."

Nick stopped walking and stared at her. "He wouldn't *see* you?"

She shook her head glumly. "His secretary said he wasn't taking any auditions without an appointment, and I couldn't have an appointment unless I'd been recommended."

Nick's arm slowly left her shoulders. He said, "Audition?" And then he added carefully, "Just who were you here to see?"

"Why, Mr. Jarrod Wood. He's here auditioning actresses for a new film he's making in Hollywood and oh, Nick, I just know I would've been perfect! If he had just *seen* me, let me show him what I can do, but you can't get anywhere in this town if you're a no-body!"

It took a moment for the full impact of what she had said to register, and when it did, Nick laughed. He had no choice. He stood in the street and laughed until his shoulders shook, and when he looked at her again most of the desolation on her face had vanished, to be replaced by indignation.

"What are you laughing at?" she demanded. "It's not a bit funny! Oh, I should have known you were being too nice—you never take me seriously."

She started to stalk away but he caught her arm, gradually bringing his chuckling under control. "I'm sorry. I wasn't laughing at you. I was laughing at me . . . at how easily you can make a fool of me without even trying."

A line appeared between her brows and she looked confused, but Nick had no desire to explain. He turned her toward the car. "Now tell me about Mr. Jarrod Wood. I'll do my best to be sympathetic."

"I don't want to talk about it," she replied miserably, and climbed obligingly into the car when he opened the door for her. "I'm glad I don't have to walk home," she added irrelevantly, removing her hat and brushing her fingers through her curls. "I don't have any money left for the subway. How did you find me, anyway?"

"Your landlady."

She was silent until he started the engine and pulled into the street, and then she burst out, "The trouble is, I don't know *how* to do anything but act." She twisted in her seat to look at him, her expression despairing. "In the past two weeks I've had half a dozen jobs—selling pins at a five-and-dime, selling tickets at a movie house, chopping vegetables in a restaurant. But those jobs never last more than a couple of days, because every time I want to go on an audition they fire me and I don't know how to do anything well enough to have a *real* job. Even Molly knows how to sew, and she can always pick up extra money doing alterations at a dress shop. But all I know how to do is keep house and mind children and wash dishes, and you *know* all the good housekeeping jobs are taken by Irish girls! So what am I supposed to do?"

Nick was noticing the way the sun glinted on her wind-tossed hair and how her cheeks were flushed pink with emotion and how vulnerable her eyes looked, still moist with the residue of tears. He was thinking how good it was to see her, and wondering if the faint flowery aroma that always accompanied her was perfume or her own natural scent, and the significance of her speech was all but lost on him.

After a moment, he lifted an eyebrow and suggested, "Pretend to be an Irish girl?"

She slumped back in the seat and admitted dolefully, "I've thought about that. But I don't guess there are too many families who would give their maids the day off to audition for another job, so I suppose that wouldn't be much help." She sighed and leaned back against the seat. "I don't know. Maybe you're right. Maybe I should just give up."

He glanced at her quickly. "I don't recall ever saying you should give up."

"Maybe not. But you've thought it. Everybody's thought it."

It disturbed Nick to see her so despondent, and for more than selfish reasons. He wasn't used to solving problems, or even having them, and he didn't know what to do for her. But he didn't want to see her like this.

He said abruptly, "You can't give up. You just told me yourself you don't know how to do anything but act, and you don't want to end up pitching a tent on the streets, do you? Now stop depressing me and tell me what you want to do this afternoon. All you need is a little cheering up. Where shall we go?"

"I don't know. I don't care." Then suddenly she said, "Yes, I do. Let's go some place loud and noisy and a little dangerous. Some place," she decided grimly, "where they serve gin."

He glanced at her, amused. "Well, I'm not sure how many noisy dangerous places we'll find open this time of day. But Tony's serves gin. Shall we give it a try?"

"Yes," she said firmly. And then she added darkly, "I hope there's a knife fight."

Nick shook his head and chuckled as he made the turn.

ALICE HAD NEVER BEEN to Tony's, though she certainly had heard about it. It had always seemed to her the kind of exotic, disreputable place where anything could happen—and frequently did. Fights occasionally broke out there, and it was rumored to be a popular gathering place for men whose occupations were sometimes outside the law, but no one had ever been arrested inside. That might very well have been because the only policemen who were allowed inside owed too many favors to the patrons to risk arresting anyone.

Leaving his car on the street, Nick took Alice around a corner, into an alleyway and down a short set of stairs, where he knocked discreetly on a wooden door. Alice glanced at him, half suspecting that there was a more accessible entrance and that Nick had chosen this way for dramatic effect alone. She didn't care. A grand adventure in the form of something daring and forbidden was exactly what she needed to take her mind off the disappointment of the day, and a shiver of excitement went through her as Nick cast a surreptitious glance over his shoulder.

After a moment the cover scraped back over a peephole in the door, and in another moment the door opened. They stepped into a narrow, dimly lit hallway where a thin-faced man stood ready to take Nick's hat.

"Hi ya, Nick," he greeted him casually. "Long time, no see. You're starting kinda early tonight, aren't you?"

"I got thirsty." Nick handed over his hat and glanced around, though there was not so much as a picture on the wall to be seen. "Anybody here I should know about?"

The man chuckled. "Pretty slow this time of day, Nick. Anybody comes in you don't want to see, I'll steer 'em out of your way."

"Thanks, Sam."

Nick took Alice's elbow and guided her through the hallway, then down another, steeper set of stairs. "What did he mean," Alice whispered excitedly, "if 'anybody comes in you don't want to see'? Is somebody looking for you? Are you going to fight?"

He laughed. "You are in a bloodthirsty mood, aren't you? No, I'm not going to fight. That's just a routine with Sam and me, after I got into a couple of minor altercations here. At present I don't have an enemy in the world. Disappointed?"

"Of course not." She wrapped her hands around his arm and squeezed lightly. "I *am* glad to see you, Nick," she said, and suddenly shy, she withdrew her hands. "And I'm sorry I'm here in such a lousy mood. It was nice of you to bring me here."

"You may not think so after you get a look at the place." Though his tone was typically negligent, there was a softness to his smile that made Alice's stomach flutter. She looked away.

After the night on the rooftop Alice had not been entirely certain she would ever see him again, and she had spent too many hours remembering, wishing it had been different, wondering what she would do if he did not come back and telling herself there was no reason for him to come back. But he had. And now the taste of his kiss was as vivid as though it had happened only moments ago, and now even the polite touch of his hand on her back sent shivers down her spine, and now she was more confused than ever.

She could not allow herself to fall in love with Nick Crawford. Not when her life was crashing around her, when time was running out, when any day now she might be forced to admit defeat and return home and live out the life of plain ordinary Mary Alice Floyd. She could enjoy the time they had together and savor the sensation of carefree adventure he brought into her life, but she must never forget that was all it was. To hope for anything else, to *want* anything else, would be disastrous.

But still, when he smiled at her, her stomach weakened and there was a melting sensation in her chest, and she wished suddenly that she had not asked to be taken to someplace loud and noisy. She would have much preferred to be alone with him.

They emerged into a long, low room filled with tables covered in red-and-white checkered cloths, somewhat gloomy looking and smelling of Italian cooking. A piano roll rendered a jumpy version of Gershwin's "Rhapsody in Blue," and a man in shirt-sleeves and red arm bands was wiping off tables. There were no more than a dozen people inside, most of them men, and they looked up by turns as Alice and Nick walked in. Nick nodded to some and ignored others as he gestured her toward a table.

"Nick! Hey, Nick!"

Nick returned the greeting with a look of carefully disguised annoyance. The man who had hailed him wore a small black mustache and an expensive-looking blue suit. He was sitting with another, smaller man who looked slightly less prosperous, and both of them were smoking long cigars. Trailing blue smoke, the man with the mustache waved them over.

Nick hesitated, and Alice inquired, "Who is that?"

With a look of resignation on his face, Nick replied, "That's Tyler Bradford. Do you want to join him?"

Alice clutched Nick's arm with such force that he winced. "Yes!" she whispered. "Yes!"

Alice tried to compose herself as they crossed the room—she didn't want to look too eager—but inside her head a symphony was playing. Inside the dim, smoke- and garlic-flavored room the sun suddenly seemed to be shining, and confidence buoyed her every step. After all this time, and now, at her darkest moment, opportunity had not only knocked but had practically beaten down her door. She had no intention of letting it get away.

Bradford rose as they reached his table. His eyes swept over Alice lazily with a half grin that Alice didn't quite know how to interpret, then he turned to Nick. "Well, Nikki, old boy, who have we here?"

Alice stuck out her hand immediately and said, "Mr. Bradford, I'm Alice Fontaine. I'm an actress, and I want to work for you."

There was a moment of startled silence, then Bradford burst into laughter. "I like your little Sheba, Nikki. She's got brass." He took Alice's hand and kissed it gallantly, then, still holding her fingers, invited, "Come on, sit down. Let's have a drink."

Alice tried not to be too awkward about retrieving her fingers as they were seated, and she dared not look at Nick. She could feel her cheeks reddening and she knew she had made every mistake she could make: she had been too eager, too bold, too pushy. He had laughed at her. He would never hire her now. He *had* to hire her. He just had to.

She sat with her hands clutched stiffly in her lap while Bradford waved over the man with the red arm bands and ordered gin all around. When Bradford took out his cigarette case and flipped it open for her, it took her a moment to respond. She smiled nervously and snatched up a cigarette, but Bradford was too slow with the light. Nick's flame touched her cigarette before Tyler's did and the two men exchanged a look that resulted in Tyler's tucking his matches back into his pocket and settling back with a grin.

"So," he said to Alice, still grinning, "you want to work for me, do you?"

"Yes." Alice exhaled smoke, cleared her throat, and repeated, "Yes, I do." She didn't think she could do any more harm by being honest, so she added, "I know you've helped a lot of actresses on their way and I want to be one of them."

He nodded thoughtfully. There was a gleam in his black eyes that only increased Alice's nervousness. Nick lit a cigarette for himself and sat back, saying nothing.

"Well," Bradford said at last, and glanced at his companion. "What do you think, Leon? Could we use a girl like her?"

Leon replied only, "Whatever you say, boss."

Tyler looked back at Alice. "Pretty face," he observed. "Kind of innocent looking. Sweet."

Alice interjected quickly, "I usually look much better than this. With more makeup, I—"

Tyler waved a negligent hand. "You look just fine, doll. I like the way you look."

Hope swelled in Alice's chest like a balloon ready to burst.

And then Tyler turned to Nick and said conversationally, "So, Nick, old pal, haven't seen you around much lately. I figured by now you would've cut out to one of those fancy places where you rich kids like to spend the summer."

Alice couldn't believe it. A minute and a half into her big chance and he had forgotten her. The gin arrived and she sat there staring at it while he chatted with Nick about places and people she had never heard of, frustration clawing at her until she thought she would scream. Nick smoked another cigarette and kept up his side of the conversation a little reluctantly, it seemed to Alice, which couldn't help her chances any. Desperately she tried to think of some way to focus Tyler Bradford's attention back on her, but short of setting her dress on fire, she couldn't think of a single one.

If she was completely honest with herself, Alice would have had to admit that she was somewhat disappointed in Tyler Bradford. He wasn't at all what she had expected. His accent was coarse and uncultured, he wore too much hair tonic, and his manners seemed self-serving and convenient. The expensively tailored suit and immaculately manicured nails were like a heavy coat of veneer on a cheap piece of furniture, and the air of refinement he projected seemed a thin disguise for a man who was not too far from the streets. Not that any of that mattered, of course; he was still rich, he was still powerful, and Alice still needed him. The problem was how to convince him that he needed her.

And then, to Alice's utter dismay, Bradford pulled out his pocket watch and commented, "Well, I've got to be moseying on. I'm meeting some people in a few minutes. Nice running into you, Nikki. Don't be a stranger."

Nick said politely, "Don't call me that."

Tyler chuckled and turned to Alice. He said, "So, you think you can be a star."

Desperately Alice seized on her last opening. "I know I can. I know what it takes and I'm not afraid of hard work. All I need is a chance."

"It's going to take more than a chance," Bradford pointed out. "You're going to have to learn the ropes, make yourself known around town, be seen with the right people, all that kind of thing. You got to start out small and work up slow."

Alice clenched her hands in her lap, wanting to kick the table with sheer frustration. She did not need fatherly advice.

And then he said, "I've got a show I'm putting together at the King Club. We could start you out in the chorus, see how you do. Tell you what." He pulled out a card and handed it to her. "You be at this address tomorrow afternoon at three. Ask for Bennie. And here." While Alice was still staring at the card as though it were a magic wand, he took a folded bundle of bills from his pocket and counted out several. "You'll need some money for costumes and whatnot."

Alice took the money, too stunned to even thank him. He rose, Leon following his movements like a shadow. Tyler Bradford bowed to Alice, then grinned at Nick. "See you around, Nikki."

He was halfway up the stairs before Alice remembered to call, "Th-thank you!"

She sank back in her chair, her eyes darting from the bills to the card in her hand, ecstasy and astonishment bubbling inside her so that she could hardly speak. When she found her voice it came out almost as a squeal. "I did it! I've got a job! He actually gave me a job!"

Nick tossed down the remainder of his drink and pushed back his chair. "Let's go."

Alice was so engrossed in counting the money in her hand that she almost found herself left behind. She hurried after him, breathlessly examining and reexamining the bills Bradford had given her. "Fifty dollars!" she exclaimed. "He gave me fifty dollars! Oh, Nick, do you know what this means?"

"For God's sake, put that money away. Only one type of girl leaves a place like this counting money."

She was too excited even to take the insult. Nick retrieved his hat from Sam without speaking to him and strode through the door the man silently unlocked for them. Alice blinked in the late-afternoon light, which, contrasted to the dim interior they had just left, seemed exceptionally bright. In fact the whole world seemed sparkling bright, and she laughed out loud with sheer happiness.

"Oh, Nick, thank you, thank you!" She slipped her arm through his and squeezed. "I told you all I had to do was meet him, and if you hadn't introduced me—"

"Don't thank me." Nick drew his arm away and opened the car door for her. His tone was curt. "I never would have introduced you if I hadn't thought you'd have sense enough to see what a bad apple he was once you met him for yourself. I see I was wrong."

She stood on the sidewalk, staring at him. She had never seen his jaw muscles so tight before, and anger seemed to radiate from every inch of him. "What is the matter with you?" she exclaimed. "Don't you know this is a dream come true for me? What are you so mad about?"

"Get in," he said tersely.

Irritation and frustration began to seep into the edges of her delight, spoiling the moment of triumph, and she stood her ground stubbornly. "Not until you tell me what's wrong with you."

"Tyler Bradford, that's what's wrong with me. Now will you get in the car?"

After a moment, Alice stepped inside. But she didn't speak until Nick was settled behind the wheel with the engine running.

"So what have you got against Mr. Bradford?" She made every effort to keep her voice mild.

"I don't want you working for him, that's all."

She bit back a hasty, incredulous reply, taking several seconds to mentally declaim the eccentricities of men. Hadn't Nick known that working for Tyler Bradford was her life's main ambition? Hadn't she told him so practically the first moment they met? Hadn't she pleaded, cajoled and practically blackmailed him into introducing her? And hadn't he brought her over to Bradford's table on his own two feet and sat there in silence while the offer was made? Now he was in a pout because he didn't want her to work for Tyler Bradford. Was there any explaining the workings of a man's mind?

She inquired very calmly, "Why not?"

Nick made a reckless U-turn and slammed the car into forward motion. "Because he's a bootlegger, for one thing."

"Oh," replied Alice innocently. "Do you buy your bootleg whiskey from him?"

Nick scowled. "And he's got a reputation as a womanizer."

"Not as bad as yours, I hope."

"Blast it, Alice, it's not the same thing at all and you know it! The man's not a gentleman, and a girl like you has got no business getting involved with him."

Alice did not know whether to be flattered or enraged by his sudden display of protectiveness, and she was a little bit of both—as well as very confused. "Oh, for goodness' sake," she said irritably, "just because the man doesn't speak with a fancy Princeton accent and throw out two-dollar words every other sentence you've got him pegged as a bad character. Well, maybe he didn't come from a fine old family and maybe he wouldn't fit in with the European set, but let me tell you something, neither would I. Did you ever think of that? I thought that was what you liked about me. Have you changed your mind?"

Nick suddenly turned the wheel and slammed on the brakes, bringing the car to a jolting stop against the curb. Other automobiles squeezed their horns angrily and one man shouted an obscenity as he swerved past, but Nick ignored him. He turned in his seat to face Alice, his eyes churning.

"Will you listen to me?" he demanded. "Can you hear what I'm saying? The man is trouble and I don't want you getting mixed up with him!"

"I'd like to see you stop me!" Alice could not believe how quickly her ecstasy had deteriorated, how effortlessly he had turned the sweet taste of victory into something sour—any more than she could believe she was sitting here on the street corner yelling at Nick when they should have been celebrating. But the anger in his eyes shocked and disoriented her, and the only way she knew to respond was with anger of her own. "You're not my father, you know, or even my brother."

"Then what am I?" he demanded.

The question came at her with the force of a slap and seemed to echo between them for a long time after the words had been spoken. What was he? He was laughter and charm and good times and achingly sweet moments of unexpected tenderness. He was a smile that haunted her dreams and made her eager to start each new day. He was the man who gave purpose and excitement to her days and left a strange, empty spot when he wasn't there. He was the only man whose kisses had ever set her blood on fire and made her want to fall willingly into that deepest of all intimacies between a man and a woman. He was all that, and so much more. But it was the *so much more* that confused her, that made her heart beat faster and her stomach feel tight, and she knew she couldn't answer his question.

She looked away uncertainly, but not before she saw him drop his gaze. His arm, which had been half stretched along the back of the seat, contracted and relaxed. She could see the material of his jacket shift with the movement of his muscles.

"Never mind," he said. "Don't answer that." Then he looked at her again. His jaw was still knotted, but his eyes were calmer. "Tell me this instead. What if I told you that you had to choose between me and Bradford?"

Alice could not suppress a gasp. She thought he must surely be joking and she almost laughed, but there was no humor at all in his eyes. She started and stopped several sentences before they ever reached her lips and at last she managed, "But...but, Nick, that's crazy! There's no choice, no comparison! Whatever would make you say a thing like that?"

He didn't answer. He just continued to fix her with that pale, steely gaze and Alice felt trapped by it; she couldn't even think because everywhere her mind turned she saw the challenge in his eyes and she didn't know how to answer it.

"I don't even *like* Tyler Bradford," she insisted a little desperately. "Not in the way I—Nick, you know how important this is to me! You can't ask me to choose between you and my career."

"All right," he said sharply. He turned around, his hands on the steering wheel, and spoke to the air straight ahead. "I've changed my mind. I'll be your sponsor. I'll buy you a show. Hell, I'll buy you a whole theater! If you want money, I'll give you—"

He reached for his wallet and Alice shouted, "Nick, stop it!"

The shrill tone of her voice startled her as much as it did him, and she took a deep breath, trying to bring a quickly escalating situation back under control. "No," she said firmly, and a bit more calmly. "I don't want your money. I don't want you to be my sponsor."

"Why not?" he insisted. "You said before—"

She shook her head adamantly. "I don't want you to humor me, Nick. I don't want you to *buy* me anything. I want to earn it, I want a legitimate chance. Can't you understand that?"

"There's nothing legitimate about Bradford."

"I'm an actress and he has a show. That's all that matters."

He leaned back against the seat with a breath that could have been a stifled curse, or mere resignation. After a moment he turned to look at her. The anger had gone out of his eyes and been replaced with an emotion Alice had never seen in him before and could not quite define. It might have been apology, or exasperation, or just weariness.

He said, "This is all about independence, isn't it? That's all women care about these days, and will you tell me why? Men have been taking care of women since time began and they've done a pretty good job, haven't they? It all started with the vote, and don't you forget that it was *women* who voted in prohibition. If you ask me, the troubles of the modern world can all be traced back to giving women the vote."

Alice said weakly, "I thought all the troubles of the modern world could be traced back to underwear."

He looked at her for a moment, nonplussed, and then he grinned. The grin turned into a laugh. After a moment Alice joined him, and the tension between them dispersed like dust in the air. He took her hands and held them warmly in his. He shook his head, smiling. "Alice, Alice, you make me do the craziest things. Sometimes I don't even know myself when I'm with you. What kind of magic do you have?"

Her heart sped at his touch, and a flush of pleasure warmed her. She said softly, "No magic. You make

me crazy, too. Oh, Nick, what are we doing together?'

"I guess..." He lifted his hand and cupped her neck
gently, his fingers caressing her spine. His voice was
husky, his eyes deep with a tender light. "We don't
have sense enough to stay apart."

And then, there on the public street, he kissed her.
A rush of heat, a soaring dizziness, a sweet swift joining of bodies and tentative, unrealized emotions, and
then it was over. Nick moved away from her slowly,
and only a few inches. His fingers stroked her hair,
setting her hat askew. He smiled and righted her hat
and kissed her cheek.

"I just don't want anything to happen to you," he
said hoarsely. "Just promise me you'll take care of
yourself, okay?"

"I promise," she whispered. At that moment she
would have promised him anything, even if it meant
giving up her job and Tyler Bradford and all her
dreams.

But he did not ask her to do that again, and Alice
was secretly, selfishly glad.

Chapter Nine

Alice stood before the cheval mirror in the dressing room and could hardly believe that the reflection looking back was hers. The peacock-blue gown she wore bared the arms from a low, square neckline heavily embroidered with silver thread; a front panel of satin worked in seed pearls dropped to the hips where it gave way to a floating skirt of gossamer chiffon loosely drawn up in front to bare the knee, and trailing a three-inch train in back. A saucy silver bow was knotted high on the left hip and a single strand of waist-length pearls completed the ensemble. Her silver slippers sported stacked heels three inches high and crisscross straps fastened with a rhinestone-and-seed-pearl buckle. A scarf of shimmering blue chiffon embellished with silver threads was wrapped around Alice's forehead, knotted below the left ear, and dangling to her elbow. This was the way she had always dreamed of looking—elegant, glamorous, sophisticated. Yet she still couldn't believe the woman in the mirror was her.

And the best part was that the gown wasn't even part of her costume. For her part in the chorus at the King Club she wore a sequined white leotard with a "fru-fru" skirt and an enormous feathered head-dress. But after the show Tyler liked his girls to change and mingle with the customers; for that purpose he had ordered for each girl a number of elegant gowns like the one Alice was wearing—and he even encouraged the girls to wear the gowns outside the club. "I like my girls to look nice," he was known for saying. "Tyler Bradford takes cares of his girls. I want people to know that."

Alice had never felt so blissfully taken care of in her life. She felt like Cinderella, and she could hardly believe it was all real.

There was a knock on the door, and Alice hurried toward it, expecting Nick. Before she reached it, however, the door opened and one of the dour-faced men Tyler called his assistants stepped in, bearing a large bouquet of long-stemmed red roses. A man of his bulk looked stiff and uncomfortable in the tuxedo he wore, and with the addition of the flowers his appearance bordered on the ridiculous. But Alice felt no urge to giggle. Tyler's assistants always made her a little nervous.

He thrust the roses toward her. "From the gentleman at table six."

Alice felt a mixture of disappointment and excitement—disappointment that the roses were not from Nick, and excitement because she remembered that the gentleman at table six was rumored to be among the most influential men in America, on a par with the Roosevelts and the Astors. She recalled him as silver-haired and distinguished-looking, but she could not for the life of her remember his name.

"How sweet," she murmured, inhaling the fragrance of the roses. "Thank you."

Had Sarah Bernhardt or Lillie Langtry received tokens of admiration like this so early in their careers? Could Alice ever expect to live up to such distinguished company? After a moment's consideration, she decided she would have no trouble at all following in their footsteps if this kind of adulation was what she could look forward to.

Tyler's assistant stood by the door, scowling at her. "There's a card," he said tersely.

She looked inside the wrappings of the bouquet until she found the card. It read: "I would be honored by your company at a late supper this evening." Alice fought the urge to laugh out loud with childlike delight. Imagine Alice Fontaine receiving red roses and being asked to supper by wealthy strangers, performing nightly at the elegant King Club, wearing Worth gowns and silver slippers and dripping with pearls? This was better than a fairy tale. This was *real*.

And, with that in mind, she recovered herself and replied in what she thought was a suitably gracious tone, "Do give the gentleman my regards, and inform him that, as I have a previous engagement, I regret I will be unable to accept his invitation."

The scowl deepened. "Tyler ain't going to like this."

Alice lifted a haughty eyebrow. "I fail to see how my social life concerns Mr. Bradford at all."

The grim-faced assistant looked as though he would like to say more, but just then Nick appeared at the door. The two men locked stares for a moment, then the other man left the room without a word. Nick turned to Alice, noticing the roses with a lift of his eyebrow.

"Do I have competition already?"

Alice laughed and tossed the roses aside. "From one of my many admirers. Oh, Nick, isn't this exciting? Did you like the show tonight? Are we going someplace truly elegant? Oh, let's go to the fanciest place in town. I want to be shown off!"

Nick's face softened as he looked at her. "A man would be a fool not to want to show off a girl like you."

She picked up her cape, a matching blue satin embroidered with an intricate pattern of pearls across the back, and Nick settled it on her shoulders. His fingertips caressed her neck before leaving her, and he inquired gently, "You *are* enjoying this, aren't you?"

Alice looked up at him, her eyes glowing. "Oh, Nick. I've never been happier in my life."

And, alighting from Nick's white Rolls-Royce in front of the elegant Waldorf-Astoria, watching heads turn as she entered the restaurant on Nick's arm, she could not imagine wanting anything more. She was beautiful, she was glamorous, and she was Nick's. How could life get any better?

THE CINDERELLA DREAM that had begun when Alice crashed Nick Crawford's party reached its pinnacle over the next three weeks. Sometimes she actually woke up in the morning in a panic because she thought she *had* dreamed it. But then she would look around at the once dingy little room with its crisp new curtains and the matched ivory vanity set on the dressing table and the dozens of colorful beaded gowns and feather boas and patent slippers with rhinestone buckles and smart little hats with soaring multihued feathers scattered over everything, and she would sigh and settle back and know that the dream would never end.

The King Club was an elegant, by-invitation-only supper establishment where, it was widely advertised, no liquor was served, but that did not discourage the richly dressed patrons from flocking to its velvet-draped doors every night with secret bottles under their arms. Nightly except Sunday Alice danced and sang with six other girls on a stage that was painted gold against a backdrop of glittering black velvet that looked like a starry sky. The routine was exciting and well-received by the audience, and even though she was only in the chorus, Alice felt like a star. Afterward the girls were encouraged to mingle with the patrons, dressed in their glittering evening gowns and jazzy jewels, and more often than not someone would buy her supper. It was a party every night.

But even more exciting than having an actual job in show business was the fact that Tyler Bradford had plainly taken her under his wing. Often he took her to private parties at other clubs or in people's homes and introduced her to men he assured her would be very important to her career. He made certain her photograph was taken with him, and often with other equally influential types. Nick looked darkly upon these goings-on, but at no time had Tyler, or the men he introduced her to, been anything other than perfect gentlemen.

Nick was at the club every night—sometimes arriving late to see her home, sometimes staying only a few minutes—but he was always there. He said he found the show "mildly amusing" and occasionally they bickered about that. But just having him there, knowing that every night, rain or shine, he would make a point of reminding her of his presence, filled Alice with a fluttery elation that almost made her dizzy. Everything was so perfect that sometimes it frightened her, as though if she weren't careful some jealous god would look down on all her happiness and snatch it away out of spite.

That was exactly the way she felt when Tyler Bradford asked to see her after rehearsal late one afternoon. She knocked on his door timidly, her stomach clenched into a fist, certain that she had done something wrong, that she wasn't working out, that she was about to be fired just as she had been fired from every other job she had ever had.

When he called out she opened the door hesitantly, but there were three other men with him and she started to excuse herself and back out. But he rose from his desk, waving his big cigar and gesturing her inside.

"Alice, honey, come on in. Boys, this is one of my girls. You've probably seen her out front, prettiest one in the line. This one's gonna be a star, all right."

Encouraged by his jovial tone, Alice came inside and smiled tentatively at the three men who half rose, unsmiling, and then sank back down into their chairs. Tyler flung an arm around her shoulders and gestured at the men with his cigar. "Some of my associates."

"I don't want to interrupt," Alice began quickly. "I can come back."

"They can wait. I've always got time for you." With his arm still companionably around her shoulders, he turned her toward the window and away from the three. "I'll tell you what I've been thinking, Alice. You got talent. I'm real proud of the way you're coming along and I wouldn't be surprised if inside a month you was out front, leading the show."

Color rushed back into Alice's cheeks as her pessimistic expectations shattered into so many points of light. It was true. Just when she thought things could not get any better they always did, and how could a dream be any more exciting?

She looked up at Tyler, drawing a breath for effusive thanks, but he went on, "I was thinking it's about time we started you on some voice lessons—singing, diction, all that. A star's got to have a trained voice, you know, so's people can hear you even in the cheap seats."

"Oh, yes, I know! I—I'd be very happy to take lessons." Voice lessons! A man didn't waste money on voice lessons unless he planned for that voice to be heard, did he? She was on her way. It was finally happening.

"Now, I'll tell you what I want you to do." Dropping his arm he went over to his desk, picked up a thick envelope and brought it over to her. "You take this to the address that's on the front there and give it to a man named Lou. Now, you've never met him, but he'll be expecting you." At her questioning look, he added, "Lou does some accounting work for me sometimes. It's the receipts from last night's show, so you be real careful with them now."

"Oh." Alice looked at the envelope with new respect. "Oh, I will."

"And after that—" Tyler draped his arm around her shoulders again, leading her toward the door "—I want you to take the night off. Spend some time with your boyfriend Nikki. He'd appreciate that, wouldn't he?" And he laughed, looking over his shoulder toward his three associates. "How about that, boys? The lady's a good friend of Nick Crawford's. Pals around with the Princeton set. She's got looks *and* class."

He opened the door and ushered her through. "Have a good time. Give Nick my regards."

"Oh, I will and . . . thank you!"

STUART LOOKED AROUND the dim little room uneasily. "Come on, Nick, let's go someplace else. This ain't our kind of club."

Nick smiled thinly and leaned back in the hard wooden chair. "Which only goes to show it's not who you are, but who you know."

"I'm not sure I want to know anybody who'd come in here."

The Village cellar was musty smelling and none too clean, and catered to the type of customer who, more likely than not, carried a machine gun in his rumble seat if not on his actual person. The men were hard-eyed and tight-lipped, the women were tired-looking whores in limp feathers and paper jewels. Nick said the food was good, but Stuart was not particularly anxious to try it. Even the gin tasted a little off.

Since they had been here a fight had broken out over a game of cards, and a separate incident had involved a knife and the drawing of blood; no one seemed to know what had started that one. Nick not only had taken it all in stride, but actually seemed to thrive on the element of danger, drinking up the seedy little dive with its unpleasant smells and disreputable-looking occupants and the promise of mayhem lurking just beneath the surface, the way another man would savor a vintage wine. Stuart preferred to spend his leisure hours in slightly more civilized company.

"Seems like every time I'm with you I end up being someplace I shouldn't," Stuart muttered. "I'd like to know what it is that fascinates you so about this kind of joint. A man like you has got everything—plenty of money and lots of women to spend it on, a high-class name, folks that stay out of your hair, blue-haired mamas chasing after you to marry their daughters ... And what do you want to do but sit in a filthy place like this with men who look like they'd cut your throat for the change in your pocket. Why, Nick? Can you just tell me why?"

"For the sensation, of course," Nick replied lazily, narrowing his eyes against the haze of blue smoke that permeated the room. "That's the trouble with having everything, you see. It gets harder and harder to find something new." His lips tightened slightly as he lifted his glass and added, "To *feel* something new."

Stuart was silent for a moment. Nick had been moody for several weeks now, and it seemed to him the mood was getting darker as time went by. Though he knew it was probably wiser not to push his friend just now, he had to know. He asked earnestly, "Are you mad at me, Nick?"

Nick looked startled, and then oddly tired. He said quietly, "No, Stu, I'm not mad at you." His gaze shifted away, and he lifted the glass again. "I don't know who I'm mad at. Myself, maybe."

The truth was, Nick could not even say that the turmoil clawing at him these past weeks was even anger. Confusion, yes. Unhappiness, certainly. But beyond that he didn't know.

He kept waiting to get over Alice. The longer he waited the stronger his feelings grew, and the truth was that he had not come to this despicable place today to try to feel something, but to *stop* feeling, if only for a few hours, the frustration and dissatisfaction that had been churning in him since Alice had gone to work for Tyler Bradford.

He was acting like a fool, and he knew it. What he didn't know was *why* he was acting this way. Stuart was right; there were dozens of girls who would be more than glad of his company for a night or two, and doubtless they would not be inclined to limit their favors to a kiss. It wasn't as though he ever expected anything serious to develop with Alice Fontaine, did he?

And how could he? She had given no indication that she cared for him as anything other than a dear friend and a sometimes passionate, sometimes chaste, companion, and that unbalanced Nick. He was used to women becoming much more involved much more quickly than he did, and that Alice Fontaine would put her job—her career, as she called it—ahead of him was something he simply could not fathom.

She had defied him outright on the matter of Bradford and he had never expected to tolerate that from any woman. Not that he gave orders often, but when he did he always imagined that the woman concerned would easily concede to them. A rather foolish notion in this day and age, as he had found out. Of course a part of him admired her independence, but he just wished she had chosen another matter on which to make her stand.

And he wished he had never asked her to make a choice between him and Bradford. Because when she'd hesitated, there had been a gut-wrenching moment when he had felt that nothing had ever mattered so much to him as what she might say, and he had been afraid to hear her answer.

Every day he told himself this had gone on long enough. The best thing for him to do was to get on a ship for Europe, or travel south to Florida, or at the very least look up one of his old girlfriends and spend a warm night reveling in the pleasure of what it was supposed to be like when a man and a woman were together. But every night he went to the club, just to make certain that Alice wasn't having any trouble, that she got home safely. And that was what disturbed him the most. That he should care so much.

"Do you know what my sister said?" he said thoughtfully. "She said Alice was just another one of my hard-luck cases. That if she were rich and successful I wouldn't look at her twice, but because she's down and out I can't stay away from her." He looked at Stuart. "Do you think she's right?"

Stuart looked uncertain, perhaps because he wasn't used to such confidences from Nick; perhaps because he couldn't quite figure out how the conversation had gotten around to Alice.

"Well," he ventured after a moment, "sounds like a queer thing for her to say. I didn't know she was back."

Nick shrugged. "Every once in a while she likes to pretend to be a deep thinker. She got back last week."

Stuart nodded, then offered, "At any rate, I wouldn't say Alice is down and out anymore, would you? I mean, every time I see her she looks fine. Dressed to the nines, chipper as a jaybird."

"Yeah," Nick said slowly. He examined the liquid in the bottom of his glass as though debating whether to drink it. "She's got what she wanted."

Stuart looked at him closely. "Say, you don't think something's going on between her and Bradford, do you? I mean, she wouldn't two-time you, would she?"

Nick looked up, an irritable scowl appearing between his brows. "Don't be an ape-brain. Alice isn't that kind of girl. You should know that."

Stuart looked uncomfortable. "Well, *I* know that. What I don't know is what's bothering you if it ain't Bradford."

"He's like a bad smell that rubs off if you get too close. I know he's popular with some of our set and I don't mind dealing with him now and then, but I just don't want Alice getting too close."

And it was just that very protective feeling that confused and annoyed Nick. He was not Alice Fontaine's keeper; she had made that very clear. He had no claim on her nor she on him, and he was too old for fighting dragons.

"Of course," he added negligently, draining his glass. "It's her life."

Stuart looked at him silently for a moment. Then he said, "You know what I think, Nick? I think you better figure out what you want."

Nick frowned at him sharply. "What do you mean?"

"What I mean is..." Stuart looked down at his hands and even in the dim light Nick could see a pinkish color stain his cheeks. "Well, the thing is, I brought Molly home to meet the folks the other night, you know. She didn't want to—she was afraid they wouldn't like her or something, like she wasn't good enough for them. Isn't that the craziest thing? A girl as sweet and mannerly as she is—what difference does it make if she lives in a hotel and sometimes sings in public? I mean, it's a ladies' hotel, isn't it? And it's not like she sings in saloons or anything.''

Nick nodded impatiently, wondering if there was a point to this story.

''But my folks really liked her, and afterward Pop said to me it was about time I started making some sensible choices about my companions and he was glad to see I was using good judgment for a change. My mother even invited her back for tea next week— no men allowed, you know how that goes—and I think Molly really liked them, too.'' He must have seen Nick's attention straying, because he went on more purposefully, ''But the thing is, I was sitting there at the dinner table across from her and all of a sudden I knew that was what I wanted. To see her face across from me at the dinner table every night.''

He took a breath and said courageously, ''I'm going to ask her to marry me, Nick.''

Nick didn't know what to say. Surprise was the least of his emotions. He and Stuart had been together since prep school and he could no more picture Stuart getting married than he could himself. The thought simply had never occurred to him.

At last he managed, ''Well. That's fine, Stuart. Really fine.'' And it was, he knew immediately. Molly was the kind of girl men married, and Stuart would make a good husband.

''I'm glad for you,'' he added with more enthusiasm. ''I know you'll be very happy.''

Stuart looked pleased, then anxious. ''Well, I haven't asked her yet. Didn't seem proper, so soon. She might think I'm, you know, fast. I thought I'd give it a few more weeks. Of course she might say no. She might not want me.''

That thought seemed to disturb him so much that he couldn't bear dwelling on it, so he turned his attention rather forcefully back to the original point of the conversation. "Anyway, what I'm saying is that, since it came to me what I want, since I kind of got things straight in my mind, I sleep a whole lot better at night. Maybe that's what you need, Nick," he suggested guilelessly. "To get things straight in your mind."

Nick looked soberly at Stuart. Sometimes his friend amazed him. Most of the time Stuart went bumbling along, doing the best he could to keep up with a life that was generally too fast for him, holding few opinions and voicing even fewer. But occasionally, as now, he would surprise Nick with some unexpected wisdom or insight, and Nick never knew exactly what to make of it.

Except that he knew Stuart was right. Everyone needed to know what he wanted. It was a question Nick had never asked himself before...and maybe now he was afraid to.

He took a breath to answer Stuart, and a movement over Stuart's head caught his eye. He stiffened, hardly believing what he saw, then he said softly, "God."

Alice Fontaine had just come into the room.

DURING THE SUBWAY RIDE Alice had been too excited to think much about the nature of her errand. But the closer she got to her destination, the more uneasy she became. She started thinking about just how much money she was carrying, then she looked around at the neighborhood, then she grew really nervous. She wondered why Tyler had wanted her to deliver the money in person. She wondered why Lou—whoever he was—couldn't come and pick it up. And the more she thought about it, it seemed to her that an accountant's job would be to keep the books. Why was Tyler delivering cash to this man?

Of course it was none of her business; she was just an errand girl. But the entire interchange bothered her.

She spent almost twenty minutes looking for the address, then found it painted in faded letters on a curb in front of a nondescript, almost ramshackle little building. She knocked on the front door for almost five minutes, and no one answered. She was ready to give up when she remembered the amount of cash she had been entrusted with, and the confidence Tyler must have placed in her to allow her to deliver it. Besides, it was getting dark, and she did not want to walk all the way back to the subway carrying so much money.

She bravely squared her shoulders and went around to the back. She knocked four times before the door opened a crack, and one eye, belonging to a face she could not see, peered out.

She said, "I . . . I'm looking for a man named Lou. Tyler Bradford sent me."

The door opened just wide enough to admit her, then closed quickly. She heard the sound of the bolt turning, metal snapping into metal. It was then that she realized Tyler had sent her to one of those secret speakeasies, much like the one Nick had taken her to, Tony's. But this place was darker and dirtier, and without Nick, she did not feel very adventurous. She could not, in fact, remember why she had ever thought there was anything glamorous or appealing at all about the inside of a gin mill, and she wished she were safe at home.

The man who'd admitted her led her down a dark corridor and into the saloon proper, where he silently pointed out a large man in a tight brown suit sitting alone at the far end of the room. The smoke was so thick and the lighting so poor that she had to keep her eyes on her steps lest she trip over something; nonetheless she could feel the eyes of every man in the room following her as she passed. They were not the kind of looks a woman wanted to receive when she entered a room, and Alice's skin crawled as, head held high and eyes straight ahead, she made her way over to Lou's table.

The first thing Nick noticed about Alice was how striking she looked in her white summer dress with its draped back and the matching hat, worn slightly to the side and pinned with a discreet pearl broach. She was a woman who was made to wear beautiful clothes, and he wanted to be the one to supply them for her. The second thing he noticed was how out of place she looked in this filthy little room where the air was so thick with corruption that a sensitive palate could choke on it, and how all eyes followed her as she passed. The speculative looks in those eyes made his fists clench.

She walked past him without seeing him, and when Stuart started to hail her, Nick stopped him with a hard grip on his arm. Stuart gave him a confused look, but Nick's eyes were on Alice.

She stopped at the table of a man Nick did not know, but whose type he knew very well. There was a sick feeling in Nick's stomach as Alice spoke to him, and the man looked at her with cold eyes.

"Who's that fellow, Nick?" Stuart asked, puzzled. "Do you know him?"

"No. But I can make a pretty good guess what he does for a living."

"What?"

Nick watched as Alice took an envelope from her purse and handed it to the man. "Let's just say he's probably not a banker."

The man opened the envelope and glanced inside, running a thumb over a collection of what could only be cash in bills. He gestured for Alice to sit down, and she shook her head. He said something to her, and Alice took a step backward.

Nick said absently, "Pay the tab, will you, Stu? I'm going to take Alice home."

The man grabbed Alice's wrist, and when she tried to pull away he jerked her forward, eliciting a little cry of pain from her. He took her face in one hand and pulled it toward his. Alice tried to twist away but his grip was firm.

The muscles in Nick's eyes were so tight they ached; his hands contracted into fists. He made himself maintain a leisurely pace as he moved toward the table, concentrating on keeping his senses alert and his temper under control. He took Alice's arm and said smoothly to the man at the table, "Excuse me. The lady is with me."

It was probably nothing more than surprise that caused the other man to release her. Alice snapped her head around to look at Nick, and the fear in her eyes almost made him forget his firm resolution for self-control. But the fear was replaced almost immediately by a relief so total, so desperately complete, that Nick felt a renewed surge of helpless rage when he thought about what might have happened had he not been here. How could she have put herself in a position where she would have to depend on a miracle for rescue? Didn't she know how vulnerable she was? Didn't she know how *valuable* she was?

The man at the table was looking at Nick with slow calculation. He was heavyset and powerful, but in his present frame of mind Nick could have torn him limb from limb or died trying, and perhaps the other man sensed as much.

He muttered, "What the hell. I got what I came for." He shoved the envelope into his pocket and pushed his chair back with a loud clatter. He gave Alice a dark look and deliberately brushed Nick's shoulder as he strode past.

Alice could not take her eyes off Nick. Now that it was all over she could feel fine tremors deep within her muscles, and her voice was breathless as she said, "Nick! What are you doing here?"

But Nick's face was grim and his grip on her elbow hard. "Walk," he said, turning her urgently toward the door. "Just walk."

Chapter Ten

By the time they reached the street Alice's heart had stopped pounding, but Nick did not stop walking, nor did he speak. His fingers remained clamped on her elbow and he did not take her to his car, but abruptly turned left and kept on walking.

His stride was so long that Alice had to double her steps to keep up, her ankles wobbling in the high-heeled shoes. His face was dark and closed and she dared not speak to him. She knew he was angry with her and she didn't blame him; she had been foolish to make that trip alone, even if Tyler had sent her. Those men in the speakeasy had frightened her, and Lou was certainly no accountant. She did not like to think how she would have handled herself if Nick hadn't been there. The only thing that mattered now was that Nick *had* been there, just as though she'd wished him out of thin air, and she was so glad to see him that she wanted to stop in the middle of the street and fling her arms around him and cling to his neck and hold him tight. But he wouldn't even look at her.

Her side began to ache with exertion but he kept on walking. She dared not complain or ask him to wait; she had a feeling that if she slowed her steps he would drag her along heedlessly, and she didn't have the breath to protest, anyway. She had no idea how many blocks they had covered, but suddenly he turned onto a quiet side street lined with neatly kept shops and painted storefronts. She was relieved when he headed toward a small coffee shop, but rather than going inside, he pulled her around the building and toward a flight of stairs.

Gasping, she managed to question, "Where are we going? What is this place?"

He didn't answer, but started up the stairs at a rapid pace. Alice struggled to keep up with him, her shoes clattering on the wooden steps.

At the top of the stairs there was a door, which he opened with a key from the ring in his pocket. He pushed Alice unceremoniously inside and slammed the door behind them.

She stood just inside the threshold, regaining her breath. The curtains were drawn so she could tell very little about the room, but she could make out the shadows of furnishings. There was a faint stale odor of old cigarette smoke and dust, underlined with a warmer, welcoming smell—coffee, she realized, coming from the shop below.

Then Nick switched on an electric light and she realized he had taken her to someone's apartment. It was simply, though tastefully, furnished in dark chintz and polished wood, with embroidered rugs on the floor and an open fireplace. A small kitchen area, dominated by a white porcelain stove and sink, had been carved out of the space at the far end of the room. The walls were a rough, unpolished brick, which added a sense of coziness, and they were hung with landscapes that, to Alice's untutored eye, looked expensive. There was an archway in the center of the far wall covered by a forest-green print drapery, beyond which, Alice supposed, was the bedroom.

Nick flung back the curtains and opened a window, admitting a plethora of street noises and a faint breeze scented with cooking smells and automobile fumes. He stood there with his hands braced on the sill, shoulders squared against her, looking out.

Alice asked hesitantly, "Whose place is this?"

He turned. There was a light film of perspiration on his face, and his hair was disheveled. Alice could not recall ever having seen him look so rumpled before.

He answered without expression, "Mine."

She opened her mouth to ask why he would need an apartment when he had that huge mansion on Fifth Avenue, and then she understood. Of course. He brought women here. Every young bachelor needed a place of his own.

She dropped her eyes, embarrassed, not knowing what to say. "Oh."

"My friends think it's very bohemian." His voice sounded odd, strained and flat.

"I imagine they would."

"What do you think?"

She looked at him. "Why did you bring me here?"

He smiled without humor. "To have my wicked way with you? Don't worry. You're safer with me than you were with that shark back at the saloon."

She winced, and he walked over to the door, turning the bolt. The lightness in his voice rang false. "Maybe I brought you here to lock you up until you come to your senses. Maybe I'll feed you supper and send you home. Maybe..." There he hesitated, and his voice tightened. "I just want to keep you safe."

He turned on her. "For God's sake, Alice, what were you doing in a place like that?"

She wanted to be flippant, or brave, or nonchalant. She wanted to turn the question back on him in a display of bravado and self-defense, but the accusation and confusion in his eyes wouldn't let her, and the memory of her own fear was too fresh. She shook her head helplessly, hugging her arms with a latent urge for self-protection, and though it did not quite answer his question she had to say what was foremost on her mind. .

"I don't understand it," she burst out. "Why would he send me to a place like that? He must have known—"

Nick's eyes sharpened. "Who sent you? Tyler?"

She nodded miserably, wishing she'd remained silent.

"What were you delivering?" he demanded flatly. "Money?"

Again Alice nodded, and tried once more for self-defense, though the words rang hollow even to her. "Just the receipts from last night's show for...for accounting."

She fell silent under Nick's steady, expressionless gaze, and finally she had to drop her own gaze.

Nick walked over to the window again, took out a cigarette and lit it. "Well," he said after a moment, "I guess that answers your question." His voice sounded casual, almost disinterested. "He sent you there to test your loyalty, and to see how stupid you were. And if you really believe last night's receipts were in that envelope, you passed his test."

Alice didn't want to hear any more; certainly she didn't want an answer to the question she was about to ask. But some instinct caused her to jerk her chin up stubbornly and insist, "I don't know what you're talking about. What else could it have been?"

Nick walked over to an end table and carefully tapped a sliver of ashes into the ashtray there. The twist of his lips was dry, the set of his shoulders hard. "Ill-gotten gains, I believe, is the common phrase. I wonder just how many illegal games old Tyler is into, anyway. Extortion? Prostitution? Execution for profit? I've got to hand it to him. I knew he was rotten, but I never guessed he was high enough on the ladder of success to be paying people to do his dirty work for him."

A shudder went through Alice as she realized what Nick was saying. With every fiber of her being she knew his speculations were grounded in truth, and with every fiber of her being she rejected that truth.

"You don't know that," she said sharply. "The money in that envelope could have been from last night's show and you have no proof that it wasn't. Neither do I. If Tyler Bradford were a criminal he'd be in jail, wouldn't he?" She took a deep breath, desperately trying to reassure herself. "I mean, criminals have their names in the paper and their pictures on post-office walls. They don't get invited to society parties and operate high-class supper clubs where all the rich people go. You're wrong about Tyler, Nick," she said vehemently. "You just don't like him so you think the worst about him, but you're wrong."

The expression in Nick's eyes could only be described as pity. Alice wanted to shrink from it.

He asked quietly, "Is being a star so important to you that you'd work for a gangster to do it?"

Alice wanted to reply, she *should* have replied, with an immediate and resounding *no*. But as his words echoed in her head, all she could think of was the applause after every show, the finely dressed, elegantly decadent men and women who crowded in to see her every night, the sparkling gowns against her skin and the little pile of money that grew week by week in its safe resting place under her mattress.

A vision of her mother's face came to mind and she pushed it away. The picture of the pride in her father's eyes as he watched her train pull out of the Chattanooga station was just as urgently squelched. How could she go back to them in defeat? How could she turn their pride into disappointment, their hope into resignation? How could she go back, after all she had done and seen, to being a nobody in a town no one had ever heard of?

But how could she work for a gangster?

She couldn't, that was all. If Tyler Bradford was a criminal she would have to leave him; her dream would be over, her last chance spent. She was on her way; she knew it, she could feel it. Voice lessons, the lead at the club, more and more people coming to see her every night... A few more weeks, a month, and all of New York would be talking about her. She didn't have to stay with Tyler forever. In just a matter of time she would have her own show, she'd be the sensation she'd always known she could be, she could write her own ticket. In the meantime, she could not give up. Not when she was so close.

She turned away, hugging her elbows. "Tyler Bradford is not a gangster," she said firmly to the door. "And it's going to take a lot more than an envelope full of money that you can't explain to convince me otherwise. He runs a legitimate club and there's no law against dancing in a show, and he pays my salary on time and that's all that matters. That's all that *can* matter, Nick.''

To her absolute chagrin, her voice broke with the last and she felt her throat burning with tears. In a moment Nick was beside her, his hands on her shoulders, turning her gently to his chest. Alice wrapped her arms around him and held him tightly, as though he was her shield against all the ugliness, all the uncertainty and all the fear that threatened her world.

Nick stroked her hair, aching for her, burning with helplessness and anger—at Tyler, at Alice, at himself. Most of all at himself. Because when he thought back over the dubious moral choices he had made in his lifetime he knew he couldn't stand in judgment of Alice; he couldn't even blame her. How many times had he closed his eyes to certain incriminating facts because it wasn't convenient to recognize them? How many times had he reached out and taken what he wanted regardless of the consequences?

One of the perils of the time in which they lived was the blurring of the line between right and wrong, between fantasy and reality. When everything was possible it was sometimes hard to make the right choices, and Nick had never realized how dangerous a state that was until now.

He wanted to grip her shoulders and shake her; he wanted to lock her in this apartment until the world was clean enough and safe enough for her to walk the streets again; he wanted to kiss her until all thoughts of Tyler Bradford and stardom left her head and the only sensation she cared about was the one she felt in his arms. And since when had he started living other people's lives for them? What had happened to him that he could care so passionately and so intensely about something that was, essentially, none of his business? Was he still fighting dragons ... or was he falling in love?

Abruptly he stepped away from her, and tried to smile. "Say, how did life get so serious all of a sudden, anyway? Come on, cheer up. Sit down. I think what we need is something to drink."

He went into the kitchen and started opening cupboards. Alice sat down, but she couldn't cheer up. Even more devastating than the speculations gnawing at her about Tyler Bradford was the possibility that Nick would think less of her for what she had done. She had never realized before how important his opinion of her was.

"Guess what I've got," Nick called from the kitchen area. "Coca-Cola. Can you drink it warm?"

She took off her hat and her gloves and forced a smile, trying to match his light tone and failing. "Sure. Sounds good."

He returned in a moment carrying two glasses of the dark bubbly liquid and sat beside her. Alice glanced at him as she accepted her glass. "I've never seen you drink Coca-Cola before."

"Another one of your bad influences on me." He tasted his drink and made a face. "God, this stuff is foul warm, isn't it?"

He put the glass aside and leaned back, stretching his arm along the top of the sofa so that it cupped, but did not touch, Alice's shoulders. It was a relaxed gesture that was doubtless meant to reassure, but for Alice his nearness was only a reminder of how uncomplicated things had once been between them, and how much she wanted them to be so again.

Alice looked down at her glass and took a breath. "Nick, I want to explain something to you."

He said quickly, "You don't owe me any explanations."

"Yes, I do. I mean, I want to." Her hands tightened on the glass, and she looked up at him anxiously. "I know that you think my ambitions are silly—" he looked as though he wanted to interrupt, but she fluttered her hand to silence him and went on determinedly "—but I want you to know I'm not driven by greed or selfishness, or because I think more of myself than I should."

She gave a painful little smile and admitted, "I know I can't sing. And maybe I'm not the greatest actress in the world—but I *can* act," she was quick to add, "and I can dance, and I can learn to be even better. You see, I was raised to believe that hard work is all it takes to get what you want, that you can be anything or do anything as long as you keep trying. I know that sounds naive," she said at the look of reluctant disagreement in Nick's eyes, "but you've got to understand that where I come from, I was the best. I was the prettiest and the brightest and, yes, even the most talented, and everyone expected great things from me. I knew it would be different in New York, but I always figured that even if there were girls prettier than me, and smarter and more talented, at least there wouldn't be anyone who would work harder, and that had to count for something.

"I was used to being somebody special," she said earnestly, and her eyes were half-insistent, half-pleading. "And I've got to be somebody special again. I don't know how to be anybody else."

Nick didn't know what to say. Didn't she realize that she *was* special, simply by virtue of being Mary Alice Floyd of Haven's Hollow, Tennessee? How could she not realize that everything about her set her above and apart from everyone else he had ever known? Her determination, her resilience, her quick honesty and quirky wit, and the bold, grim-eyed way she had of taking on the world single-handedly and ignoring the odds. She didn't need newspaper headlines to proclaim her uniqueness, nor her name on a billboard to make her a star. She was Alice, and she did not need to be anything else. But Nick did not know how to make her see that.

Alice put her glass aside and touched Nick's hand. "You're always asking me why my career is so important to me," she said, "and now I'm telling you. Because it's not just for me, but for everyone who ever believed in me and—" Her breath caught, as though better judgment was, at the last moment, trying to prevent the next words from being spoken. But the words were out almost before she had thought about what she was saying. "For you, too."

Nick looked startled. "For me?"

She nodded, and dropped her gaze. But it was too late to back down now. "I know you know women who are more exciting, and well traveled and well educated, and more, well, everything than I am. They're part of your set, and I know I'll never be a part of that. But if I can be successful and, well, sophisticated . . . if at least *I* know I'm good at something no one else is—" hesitantly she raised her eyes to his

"—then maybe you'll look at me differently, and won't grow bored with me so fast."

Nick stared at her for the longest time. She felt her cheeks grow warm under his silent, unreadable gaze, and Alice felt like a gangly eighth-grader confronting the object of her first crush. The hesitant, bumbling speech kept replaying in her head and she squirmed with the memory. Why couldn't she have kept quiet? Hadn't she learned by now that it was not always necessary to say what she was thinking?

And then Nick released a long breath through slightly parted lips, and leaned his head back against the sofa so that he was looking at the ceiling. He said with soft incredulity, "Bored with you? Lady, I've been trying to get bored with you ever since I met you. It just isn't working."

Alice's heart beat several quick, stuttering steps, then settled into a more cautious rhythm.

Nick turned his head on the sofa to look at her. His eyes were as soft as pale satin, stripped of artifice yet hesitant. He said quietly, "You don't have to try to impress me, Alice. Of all people, not me."

He wrapped his fingers around hers, lowered his eyes for a moment to their entwined hands, then looked back to her. "All this noise I've been making about your working for Bradford, it was just to cover up the real problem, and that's me. I'm the one who's trouble for you, Alice, and if I had any decency I would have let you go a long time ago. But I don't have any decency, and I can't let you go."

A wild, incredulous emotion started to form inside Alice: joyful, unsure, a desperate hope that what she thought she saw in his eyes was true, yet knowing it couldn't be. She opened her mouth to speak, but Nick stopped her with a finger laid lightly across her lips.

"No. Listen. Just let me finish."

He sat up straighter, still holding her hand securely in his, covering it with his other hand and lightly stroking the back of her wrist. The warm, whispery caress traveled on prickly waves of pleasure from her skin to the center of her chest.

"All my life," he said slowly, "I've known there was something wrong with me. Something missing. Call it a sense of purpose, of commitment . . . I don't know. Maybe it's just that ability to care. To get involved. I know you think that what I do for the poor is noble and that it makes me a good person, but there's nothing noble about it at all. Helping out those people is just a way to make the emptiness inside me go away for a little while. I feel connected to something important for a time, I feel involved . . . but it's only temporary."

His hands tightened on hers and his eyes held hers firmly, as though in a warning, or a plea. "*Everything* is only temporary with me, Alice," he repeated. "That's all I'm capable of feeling, the only way I know how to live. Moment to moment."

There was a choking sensation in Alice's throat, an aching that began in the pit of her stomach and spread upward through her chest and her arms and her fingertips, reaching for him. Needing him. She said hoarsely, "I never asked any more from you, Nick."

"You deserve better. You deserve promises and plans and permanence. You deserve a man who knows right from wrong and cares enough to do something about it. At the very least, you deserve a man who knows what he wants."

Alice's throat was so tight she could hardly swallow, and her breath seemed a shallow, slippery thing in her lungs. She looked at him and felt engulfed by the gentleness in his eyes. ''Don't you know what you want, Nick?''

His eyes went over her face, carefully, slowly, examining it in minute detail. He said softly, ''Right now...I want to make love to you. That's what I want every time I'm with you. I want to make you mine and keep you safe.''

Alice heart was pounding. At that moment it seemed so simple. She wanted to be safe in his arms. She wanted to be held by him, close to him, a part of him. There were no more secrets between them, no invisible barriers, and she needed no promises. A moment, an hour, a single thrilling interlude that would last forever in memory—she had no right to ask for more. She didn't need any more.

She was almost certain of it.

She slowly extracted her hand from his and lifted it to touch his face. His skin was smooth and warm, slightly coarse where the shadow of his beard began, and her fingers trembled as they explored the changing textures. She whispered, ''Maybe that's all I want, too, Nick.''

She heard his intake of breath and saw the slight lowering of his eyelids as her fingers moved down, tracing the shape of his jaw, the line of his throat, cupping to caress his neck and the silky brush of hair that fell there. Her fingertips felt mesmerized by him, controlled by a power not her own, tingling with each new exploration and hungry for more. She traced the shape of his cheekbone, the gentle puffy flesh beneath his eyes; she felt the brush of his eyelashes on the backs of her fingers. She touched the soft fullness of his lips, the indentation of his chin, the dimple that edged the corner of his mouth. Dimly she was aware of the beating of her heart and the whisper of her own breath, slow and shallow, and time seemed to stop, frozen in expectation.

He lifted his eyes to her, and they were lit with a deep rich glow that made her breath stop in her throat. He took her fingers and brought them to his lips; a kiss, the warm moist flood of his breath, the brush of his tongue across her fingertips. He said huskily, "No promises, Alice."

She whispered, "No promises."

His hand slid around her neck and his lips pressed against her throat with a slow rush of heat that seemed to melt her spine. She threaded her fingers through his hair as his lips moved to cover hers, and dizzy, pulsing light surged through her.

His hand caressed her waist and the curve of her hip, the length of her outer thigh. Each lingering stroke sent a new wave of weakness through her, tightening desire, and she could feel the urgency rising in him as it did in her. Her fingers tightened on the back of his head, she opened her mouth beneath his and greedily sought the taste of him, losing her breath in the hot mating play of their tongues.

He slipped his arms beneath her and shifted her onto his lap, but she hardly felt the movement. She clung to him, whirling in a vortex of pleasure and need. Each separate sense was filled with him yet ached for him: the salty taste of his skin as her tongue swept across his lower lip and his chin, the abrasive texture of his jaw; the uneven flutter of his scented breath across her cheek and the misty-jewel blur of his shaded eyes. She wanted to drink him in, to lose herself in him, to wrap herself around him, body and soul, and hold him forever.

She arched her neck against the pressure of his lips on her throat, light butterfly touches of his tongue tracing a downward path, drawing a helpless, muffled moan of pleasure from her. His mouth covered the material over her breast and her nipples tautened and ached, while his hand lightly caressed the shape of her leg, pushing aside her skirt, moving above the rolled top of her stocking, molding the naked flesh of her thigh. The muscles of her legs seemed to liquefy; her breathing grew shallow and then stopped altogether as every sense she possessed was concentrated on the upward movement of his hand. A burning ache gathered between her legs, which she knew instinctively only he could satisfy, and when his fingertips slipped inside the flared leg opening of her underpants she went very still, rapt with anticipation and desire. His fingers explored the dark heated secrets of her inner thigh, tantalizing and promising with whisper-touches against her aching flesh, and when she thought she would cry out loud from pleasure and need he withdrew his hand and shifted her in his arms, making her look at him.

His face was flushed, his eyes hazy with intensity and desire. His lips were slightly parted for breath, and several curls of hair were caught in the dampness of his forehead. She reached to push them back with trembling fingers. He whispered, "Alice—"

But she could not let him finish. She lifted her mouth to his with a hunger he matched, clinging to him, drinking of him, pulling him closer, completely abandoned to the sensations and the need. Between their bodies his hand worked to free the buttons of his collar, which she pushed aside impatiently, and then he opened the buttons of his shirt, pulling his shirt tails free from his trousers with a careless urgency, until Alice felt the heat of his bare chest against her, the firm muscles of his abdomen beneath her hand, tasted the texture of his shoulder with her tongue.

She hardly knew when he lifted her in his arms and got to his feet, holding her against his chest as he pushed aside the curtain and carried her to the bedroom. Her skin was on fire and her muscles were watery, and all she knew was the strength of his arms around her, his scent engulfing her and his taste infusing her. All that existed for her was Nick and the need never to be separated from him.

He lowered her onto the bed, and kneeling beside her, he stroked her hair away from her face with both hands, kissing her lips, her cheeks, the corners of her eyes. His face filled her vision, his eyes alight with the hazy glow of passion—and something else, something deeper, something that filled her and drew her to him even though she dared not name it, nor even recognize it.

He said softly, "You *are* special to me, Alice. You're the only special thing I've ever known."

She lifted her arms and drew him to her, knowing no other way to give expression to the choking sense of wonder that flooded her in that moment.

Making love with Nick was everything she had ever imagined and more than she could have expected. Not once was there a moment of hesitance or regret or uncertainty, for with him her whole being was involved, her body and her mind and her senses given over completely to his keeping and to the pleasure they shared.

He undressed her slowly, rolling down her stockings and caressing her naked legs each in turn; unbuttoning her dress and kissing every inch of flesh exposed as he slipped her garments down over her arms and cast them aside. His tongue swept slowly down her inner arm, causing her to writhe with pleasure, then circled her nipples in slow, maddening caresses. His lips traveled down the centerline of her chest and pressed deeply into her abdomen, causing the ache of need in her womb to flare and spread downward in a rush of moisture and heat. Urgently, she pushed aside his shirt and caressed the defined muscles of his chest, tangling her fingers in the damp mat of dark hair there. His eyes closed and his breath caught with the pleasure of her touch, and the surge of joyous wonder she felt was heady.

She had always expected some awkwardness when a man and woman lay naked together, the embarrassment of uncertainty, the shock of newness. But with Nick it was all so easy, so natural, as though it had been ordained before the beginning of time that on this night they should be together like this.

He held her and touched her as though he could never have enough of merely being near her, and by his own tender leisure encouraged her to explore his body—the lean thighs and smooth shoulders and flat abdomen; the straight line of his spine and the hollow of his knee and the firmly sheathed muscles of his arms. She had never known there could be such pleasure in simply touching a man's body, never imagined the sense of intimacy and discovery and belonging that would fill her in claiming this man, this special man, as her own.

When he entered her it was like a blending, a joining, an expansion of sensation so intense that Alice could barely comprehend it. Time stopped and nothing existed in the world except Alice and Nick and the ecstasy of the moment they had created together. His heart beat slow and heavy against her breast. His hands pressed against her back, his lips caressed her face. His hair brushed against her forehead, his breath flowed into her parted lips. She opened her eyes and saw only his face, and the wonder that filled her was so sweet, so powerful and all-encompassing that she wanted to cry out with the joy of it. Slowly at first and then more powerfully, he began to move inside her, and the pleasure had only begun.

Afterward Alice lay in his arms, dazed with the power of emotions she had only dreamed of before, filled with things so new and so wondrous she could not begin to know their meaning yet. She lay on her side with her head on Nick's shoulder, her arm across his chest, holding him, unwilling to break the contact with him even for a moment. She felt different, new, as though some alchemy had occurred between them, mixing their blood and making her more than she had been before, as though he were still a part of her, and always would be.

She could feel the beat of his heart and the warmth of his body and the slippery texture of his skin as she caressed his arm, and all of it was special to her, magical, filling her with a joy that was as clear and simple as a high, resonating musical note. She pressed her face into the hollow of his shoulder, inhaling the rich masculine scent of him.

He bent his head to her hair, his hand stroking her back. He said softly, "Are you sorry?"

She lifted her face to him, smiling. "Oh, Nick, how could I be sorry? I'm so happy I'm almost afraid to feel this good. I wish—" And there she broke off, for the words that were rushing to be said were *I wish it could be like this forever.*

But there were no promises between them, and no forever. She had wanted it that way, and so had he. From the beginning she had known she could not serve two masters—love and her career. An hour ago there had been no choice to make, for Nick had asked nothing of her and she had asked only for the moment. Now it did not seem so simple.

Nick was looking at her intently. There seemed to be a slight quickening in his muscles, an urgency and a tension that had not been there before. "What?" he inquired. "What do you wish?"

She turned her head to rest again on his shoulder, hiding her expression from him, determining to be content with the moment. "Nothing," she answered, and ventured a quick smile at him. "Besides, I already used up my wish that night on the rooftop, remember?"

Nick remembered. He settled back against the pillow, again stroking her back, surprised at the disappointment he felt. He murmured, "Maybe I shouldn't have given that wish away. I think I could have put it to better use."

She looked up at him. "I thought you didn't believe in wishes."

He hesitated, then smiled, bringing his hand up and running his fingers through her hair, ruffling it lightly. "I don't." But suddenly, surprisingly he wanted to.

For the first time in his life he knew what he would wish for.

They were silent for a time. Distantly the sounds from the streets below drifted up to them, wheels moving and bells clanging and doors slamming and voices calling, but they were a world apart, separate and indistinct and having nothing to do with the secure cocoon in which they rested.

After a time Nick turned his head toward her and inquired, "Do you want a cigarette?"

But he made no move to reach for one, and Alice shook her head. She was content.

"Are you thirsty? Or shall I try to find something to eat?"

She smiled. "No. I have everything I want—" she kissed his shoulder "—right here."

Nick slipped his forefinger under her chin, lifted her face to his and kissed her. They made love again in slow, beautiful languor, each sensation a memory unto itself, each touch of the lips or hands charged with magic, as though they touched for the first time.

When again they lay in each other's arms, their heartbeats steady and their hands entwined, Alice looked up at Nick. Distant streetlight shadowed his face, gleaming softly in his hair. It was a face that meant all that was beautiful in the world to her, all that was perfect and desirable. She was happy. She was content. Physically, she wanted for nothing. Yet there was a pinpoint ache just beneath her breastbone, a need for something she couldn't even define, and when she thought ahead to the time she must leave this bed and the warmth of his arms, the ache became a sadness, an emptiness she could not put out of her mind no matter how hard she tried.

"Nick...if you could have your wish back, what would you wish for?"

He looked at her, and again he hesitated. Then he smiled and gathered her in his arms. "Nothing," he said, holding her close. "I have everything I want, right here."

But there seemed to be a hollowness to his words, and a shadow hovered over them, darkening the edges of their happiness. He held her tighter, and she clung to him, each of them knowing, in their own secret ways, that it was not enough.

Chapter Eleven

Alice timed her arrival at the hotel the next morning carefully: late enough that the door would be unlocked but early enough that Mrs. Handley wouldn't have noticed she hadn't slept in her bed. Molly would know that Alice hadn't been home, of course, but despite Molly's tendency to get flustered, Alice knew she could be counted upon to cover for her in a pinch. Nick let her off at the corner and there were too many people on the streets to even share a kiss. Alice felt bereft when he was gone.

She let herself silently into the front hall and heard the sounds of the other girls' voices gathered at the breakfast table. They seemed distant and unreal to her, inconsequential; even the elaborate steps she had taken to sneak back into the house unnoticed seemed unnecessary. She was a different person from the one who had left here yesterday, her life had new meaning and focus, and it was difficult to concentrate on mundanities. Whether or not she got caught almost did not matter.

She started up the stairs to her room, then heard the door to Mrs. Handley's room close as the heavyset woman approached the top of the stairs. Alice turned around quickly so it would look as though she was coming down, instead of going up.

"Good morning, Mrs. Handley," she said.

But the other woman passed her on the stairs without looking at her, without even appearing to notice her. Two bright spots of rouge stood out on her pale cheeks, and her eyes were unfocused, almost stricken, as she strode toward the dining room.

At first Alice thought with a lurch of alarm that her landlady had discovered she'd spent the night out, and she hurried after her to try to make some sort of excuse or apology. But when Mrs. Handley entered the dining room with Alice at her heels, she simply stood there until the chatter died down and all eyes turned toward her. Alice knew then that something much more serious was on her mind.

She could see the trepidation on the other girls' faces as the silence lengthened. And then Mrs. Handley spoke.

"Ladies," she said in a high, unsteady voice, "I've just heard it on the radio. Valentino is dead."

LOOKING BACK, it seemed to Alice that everything began to change from that day. It almost seemed as though the untimely death of the film legend heralded the twilight of an age; the gaiety began to dim, and nothing was quite as carefree as it once had been.

The world went into mourning. There were reports of suicides and attempted suicides from around the globe as desolate women saw in the death of their hero the death of hope. In New York a crowd gathered outside Campbell's funeral home, where the Sheik, attired in full evening regalia, lay in state; before the doors even opened to the public the line stretched for nine blocks, completely blocking traffic on Columbus Circle and making movement impossible for seven blocks to the south and all the way up Broadway to Seventy-second street. Before noon impatience and hysteria reached their peak; the mob surged forward and broke through the plate-glass window, pushing the line-guard of policemen with them. A riot broke out that kept ambulance and police sirens screaming until almost midnight, at which time the toll of injuries exceeded a hundred.

The next day more than ten thousand lined up again in front of the funeral home and stood sobbing in the rain, only to be informed that, due to a lack of proper reverence, the actor's body would not be available for viewing. More rioting was expected, but by the third day the mood of the crowd had become more subdued, and order was restored.

Though none of the residents of the Handley Hotel took the loss of the legend with quite such unmitigated displays of grief, each of them shed their own tears and recognized in their own way the passing of something from their lives that would not come again. When Jane heard that Jim had been assigned to crowd control she rushed to the police station and waited there for twenty-six hours until he returned safely. The King Club was closed for three days, not due to any particular show of respect, but because the dancers refused to work and traffic in the city was all but immobilized. And even when the furor had settled down and the tabloids turned their attention to other sensational events, there remained a sense of something lost, something changed, as though in a matter of a few days the world had somehow gotten immeasurably older. Perhaps Molly summed it up best when she said pensively, "It makes you wonder, doesn't it, what he ever lived for?"

Alice thought about that a lot the next few days. A man had been born, had achieved greatness and, at the age of thirty-one, had died. He had left behind the adoration of hundreds of thousands and his image captured on celluloid, but at the moment of death had that been enough? Was it ever enough to live for one's own glory, to know no lover except the faceless crowd? Wasn't there more to life than to be able to say at the end, "He will be remembered"?

When the club reopened, Tyler announced that he was putting together another show and selected several of the girls—Alice among them—to headline it. In another lifetime Alice would have been thrilled beyond endurance, and there was a part of her that was, but mostly what the new arrangement meant to her was that until the new show opened she did not have to work at night. She had voice lessons in the morning, rehearsals in the afternoon, and her nights were free to spend with Nick. Tyler did not ask her to run any more errands, and in fact she rarely saw him at all, so it was easy to pretend the disturbing episode with the man called Lou had never happened. When she was with Nick it was easy to pretend nothing in the world existed except the two of them.

Each time they met it was as though Alice lost a little more of herself to him and gained, in return, more of him to fill in the spaces. There was no part of her life that did not touch his; whether she was awake or dreaming, her secret thoughts and private plans were all somehow entwined with him, and there were times when she wondered if she would ever again be able to really tell where she left off and he began. Already she could not remember when he had not been an integral part of her life.

It was a little unsettling to be so totally involved with another person, so dependent on his presence. She wondered if this was a common phenomenon; if, every time a man and woman made love there occurred some exchange of vitality that bonded them together and made them more and more a single entity. If so, it seemed to Alice that the intimacies she and Nick shared in the bed of his apartment over the coffee shop were more than magical; they were also a little dangerous.

And at last, lying in his arms in the fading sunlight late one afternoon, she had to ask, in a very subdued tone, "Is it always this way, Nick?"

His hand caressed her shoulder. "What?"

"Sleeping with someone. Making love. I mean, people talk about it all the time like it's the chic thing to do, but they never talk about how it feels afterward."

"How does it feel afterward?"

"Like...I don't know. Every time I'm with you something changes inside me. I feel different, and the difference doesn't go away when we're apart."

She wanted to say more. She wanted to tell him how she had never expected it to be like this; how she felt as though the essence of him was implanted in her heart and could never, ever be uprooted; how she couldn't envision herself without him; and how sometimes in the dead of night she would awake in a panic because he wasn't beside her, and she was afraid, just for that moment, that he would never be again. But they did not talk about things like that.

After that first time in Nick's apartment, they had an unspoken agreement that there was a list of things they would never talk about: Tyler Bradford, Alice's job, the future…love. In that way they maintained the fragile net of fantasy that shielded them from the real world and allowed them to pretend that the moments they shared were all they needed, all they wanted, and that, while they were together, nothing from the outside would ever intrude.

Nick's hand stopped moving against her shoulder and he was silent for a moment in which Alice thought he would say something: something important, something life-altering. But, because of their unspoken agreement, because of the fantasy they held so tenuously between them, the only reply he could make was a quiet, "No. It's not always like this. Sometimes nothing changes at all."

Alice closed her eyes and threaded her fingers through his and pretended that answer was sufficient. But it was growing harder and harder to pretend, and she knew that one day soon she would not be able to pretend at all.

BARBARA WAS THE FIRST to leave. Because it was Barbara—the only one among them who wasn't afraid to wear eye makeup in public, the first one to experiment with a home permanent, the girl who talked such a good fight and knew all the tricks and always had a job—the news was all the more shocking.

"I'm going home," she simply announced one day, and started packing her bags.

Alice had never even thought of Barbara as having a home outside the bustle and glamour of New York

City. "But where is home?" she asked, almost too stunned to react.

"Kansas City," she answered, folding lingerie into her weathered brown suitcase.

"What will you do there?" Jane demanded, more than a little shaken over the prospect of losing her roommate.

Barbara shrugged. "I've got an aunt. She's old, and not in very good health, and she needs somebody to take care of her. It's room and board, and it looks like she's named me her only heir in her will. I wouldn't want her to change her mind at the last minute, so I figured I'd better get out there and protect my interests."

Molly, Alice and Jane were silent as they watched her pack. Alice could tell the other two girls were having as much trouble as she was picturing Barbara as a nursemaid to a frail old woman.

And then Barbara burst out, "Well, what do you expect me to do? Spend the rest of my life going from one sleazy joint to the other, singing for my supper? Painting over my wrinkles and hoping nobody notices until I'm too old to do anything but sell myself on the waterfront to nearsighted sailors? I'm twenty-eight years old and I don't have a lot of time left to waste."

She took a breath, looking from one shocked face to the other, and then said simply, "It's just not as much fun as it used to be."

They saw her off at the station in a light September rain. There was a great deal of hugging and crying and promises to write, which they all knew they would never keep. And as Alice watched the train pull away, she wasn't sure whether it was pity or envy she felt for Barbara. She did know she was very, very sad.

Jane was next. She got a job as a nanny in a family with three young children.

"I really can't afford to keep the room without Barbara," she explained. "And I like children and—" She gave a wry little smile. "Let's face it, I was just marking time here until the right man came along. Whoever would have guessed that the right man would be a cop with fifty dollars in the bank and a smile to break your heart? Life sure can surprise you sometimes."

For a moment, as she considered this, even she looked startled, then she blushed a little and added, "Anyway, Jim won't be on the force forever, and since I'll be saving every penny, we should be able to afford a place of our own in a year or two and..."

Her eyes filled unexpectedly with tears as she hugged Molly and then Alice. Sniffing, she smiled and added, "It's not as though I'll never see you again, you know! I'll only be over on Park Avenue, enjoying the good life in a big mansion while it lasts!"

Her smile became laced with a hint of nostalgia as she said, "It's funny, isn't it? I was just thinking how we all were sitting here that night reading about Nick Crawford's party in the newspapers and how it was the most exciting thing in the world to think Alice could actually meet him and then if she hadn't I never would've met Jim and... It's just funny how things turn out. And," she declared suddenly, "you know what I want to do tonight? Let's get all the scandal sheets together and stay up all night drinking Coca-Cola and painting our nails and doing each other's hair and reading the papers like we used to, okay? One last time, for old time's sake."

And that's what they did, but it wasn't as much fun as it used to be. Nothing was.

Then, only two evenings after Jane had left the hotel to start her new position, Molly came home with shining eyes, a stunned look on her face, and a diamond on her finger.

All the girls came down to the parlor to "ooh" and "aah" over the ring; Mrs. Handley shed a few tears and even broke out a secret cache of elderberry wine, which she kept for "medical emergencies." Molly had always been her favorite, and hers was the best kind of success story—the modest young lady who caught the eye of the handsome prince and was swept away to live happily ever after.

Alice joined in the celebration, repeatedly telling herself how happy she was for her friend, and wondering why there was a burning spot in the pit of her stomach that felt so much like jealousy.

The wedding was scheduled for June, allowing for a respectable period of engagement, which met the approval both of the demanding Mrs. Handley and Stuart's parents, who liked to do things right. When the lights were out and Alice and Molly were in their nightgowns, sitting up in bed and whispering secrets as they had done so many nights before, Molly said, a little hesitantly, "I wanted to tell you first, Alice, even before Mrs. Handley...."

Alice looked at her curiously. Surely the most important news had already been told, and she could not imagine what was causing that uncertain tone in Molly's voice.

Molly said, "It's just that, well, it really isn't proper for an engaged girl to be living by herself, in a hotel, that is, even though it is a very respectable hotel...."

Alice felt her heart sink. She knew what Molly was going to say.

Molly went on quickly, "You know how long it's been since I've seen my family. I mean, there's just never enough money for a train ticket even though they're so close, and getting married is such a big step I'd really like to spend some time with them and—" she took a breath "—well, I'm going back to Connecticut for a while.

"The exciting part," she went on in a rush, "is that Stuart's parents have a country place in Westchester, which is close enough for Stuart and me to see each other every day, and they're opening it for the holidays. And I think it's really important for our families to get to know each other, and all my friends are back there, and besides, I won't be leaving until the end of the month and I'll be back in the spring to shop for the wedding. Of course I'll probably be staying with Stuart's parents then. But," she insisted, "you'll be my maid of honor and we'll have loads of fun picking out the gowns and the flowers, and then Stuart and I will be living in the city—he's taking a job at his father's bank—so we'll see lots of each other then! Oh, Alice."

She caught Alice's hands and held them, her expression earnest and pleading. "I know it feels as though we're all deserting you, but you always wanted such different things from the rest of us. And look," she said, injecting cheerfulness into her voice, "you've got them! I mean, here you are on your way to being a real star and making tons of money and wearing gorgeous gowns and going to the fanciest restaurants in town with a man other girls only dream about! Of all of us you're the only one who actually went out and *got* what you wanted, just like we always knew you would. So please don't be lonely, Alice.'' Molly slipped her arms around her and hugged her hard. ''We've all got so much to be happy about.''

Alice kept trying to remind herself how much she had to be happy about, but despite Molly's admonitions, what she really felt was lonely.

Until the day she arrived at the club for rehearsal and there was a message saying that Mr. Bradford wanted to see her. Then everything changed again.

Alice recalled the last time she had been summoned to Tyler Bradford's office, and her heart was in her throat as she knocked on the door. At his muffled ''Come in,'' she pushed open the door and stopped in her tracks, staring.

On an easel in the center of the room was a full-color, poster-size painting of a girl in a red, spangled dress and gold feathers—exactly like the costume Alice had been fitted for only the day before. The dress was slit up the side and the girl's leg was propped on a stool, revealing a long, provocative length of shapely flesh. Her head was thrown back gaily, her lips drawn into a provocative pout . . . and, Alice realized slowly, the girl in the poster looked a great deal like her. In fact, it must have been her, because the script across the top of the poster read: ''Tyler Bradford Productions Proudly Presents the New Entertainment Sensation . . .'' And there at the bottom in huge black letters: ''Alice Fontaine.''

Grinning broadly, Tyler Bradford came around the desk, the perpetual cigar in his hand. ''Do you like it?''

She couldn't take her eyes off the portrait. ''Is . . . is that me?''

He chuckled. "Close enough for jazz, anyway. What do you think?"

Alice took a step closer, feeling eerily as if she was caught in a hall of mirrors—not because the portrait was so much like her, but because it was so much like the way she had dreamed of looking ever since she had come to New York. Her image, all dressed up in sequins and feathers, larger than life and portrayed for all the world to see. The New Entertainment Sensation.

Her voice was thin and breathless as she said, "I don't understand. What does this mean?"

"It means, my dear—" Tyler put his arm around her shoulders and stood back with her, surveying the poster "—a hundred of these spread all over New York between now and opening night. It means red velvet ropes to hold back the crowd, and in front of those ropes, this poster blown up to life-size, with your name in letters as big as mine right there where everybody can see it."

He looked down at her and squeezed her shoulders. "It means you're going to be the star of my new show, honey. What do you think of that?"

Alice's hand went slowly to her throat, as though in search of the voice she had suddenly lost. She stared at the poster. She stared at Tyler. She didn't know what to think. She was going to be a star.

Tyler walked back over to the desk, grinning at her reaction. "That's what I like about you, doll. You're sweet. Real sweet. You didn't think old Tyler would come through for you, did you?" He sat on the edge of the desk and interrupted her stammering protests with a wave of his hand. "Well, let me tell you something. I saw from the first you had potential and you haven't disappointed me yet. I always do right by them that do right by me."

She did not know exactly what he meant by that and was glad she didn't have to think about it for long, because he went on, "You've worked real hard and you've come a long way. I think you're ready. All the crowds'll be coming back to the city next week from wherever it is they go for the summer, and they always expect something special from Bradford Productions when they get home. You're going to be that something special."

Something special. Alice Fontaine, in a glittering red dress and her name spelled out in letters a foot tall. It was happening. It was really happening.

"We open Friday night," Tyler said, and it was with difficulty that she made herself focus on what he was saying. "You'll start rehearsing for your big number today. Picture this. A long, white staircase, you in that hot little red number there with feathers dripping all over you, four guys in white tuxedos carrying you down the stairs while the band plays a big, booming number..."

Alice did not have to picture it. She had been dreaming that very dream since she was ten years old.

NICK ARRIVED HOME from the prize fights with just enough time to change and meet Alice at the apartment. It had been her idea that he not pick her up at the club anymore, almost as though she was afraid of what might happen if he and Tyler met. That was a ridiculous fear, of course, and Nick wasn't too happy about Alice going all the way out to the Village alone, but she insisted she always took a cab and it was perfectly safe. Nick had learned long ago the pointlessness of arguing with Alice about anything that threatened her independence, so he'd conceded. Besides, there was a not-very-admirable part of him that preferred not to meet her at the club. It was easier for him to forget that she worked for Bradford if he didn't have to see her there every day.

He tossed his hat on the hall tree and started to stride past the parlor when a glimpse of something from the corner of his eye caused him to stop. Cynthia was in the parlor, flipping through a magazine. That she should be at home and idle at this time of day was unusual enough in itself, but a second glance gave him the reason. His father was standing near the fireplace, putting a match to his pipe; his mother was just replacing the receiver of the telephone.

Cynthia glanced up as Nick came in. "Well," she drawled, "if it isn't the prodigal himself."

Nick's mother extended one graceful arm toward him. "Nikki, darling, I was just telephoning a few people to see if I could get together a little dinner tonight. So glad you could join us. It simply wouldn't be the same without you."

Nick's mother was perpetually "getting together a little dinner." Nick did not know why he should be surprised to come home and find her, after a three-month absence, just hanging up the telephone—precisely as she had been doing the last time he saw her.

He bent and kissed her cool, powdered cheek. "Welcome home, Mother. How was ... ?"

He paused questioningly, and his father supplied with a scowl, "Crete."

Nick nodded acknowledgment to his father but no further greeting was necessary.

"Dreary, darling, simply dreary," his mother replied, patting the place on the sofa beside her. "If it wasn't pouring rain it was blistering hot. Can you imagine the nerve of that Marilee Stephens telling me the weather on Crete was never less than divine?"

Nick sat down tentatively beside her, hoping his mother would soon be distracted by the preparations for her "little dinner" and he could go on with his plans. "You should have told us to expect you—we'd have had a party," he said. "When did you arrive?"

"We docked last night—or was it the night before?—but I was really too exhausted to face a homecoming, so we put up at a truly charming hotel, quite as nice as we've seen outside of Europe, I do believe. But enough of us. Tell me what you've been doing with yourself all summer."

Nick glanced at Cynthia, who looked very much like the cat who'd swallowed the canary. No doubt she'd been filling their parents' ears full of tales, but that did not irritate Nick as much as it might once have done. He said, "Nothing much. I stayed in town most of the time. Went to see the horses run once or twice." Anything more elaborate than that would have bored his mother; he had learned early to condense his life into short sentences for his parents' benefit.

But his mother surprised him by commenting, "I heard your friend Stuart has gotten himself engaged to a little nobody. Little more than he deserves, no doubt. I never did understand, Nikki, why you insisted upon cultivating that boy's friendship. You have nothing at all in common, and breeding will always tell."

Nick felt himself stiffen, and he smiled thinly. "Yes, won't it? I've always known Stuart was too honorable for my taste, but I never suspected why until now. Thank you for enlightening me, Mother."

His mother's eyes reflected shock and his father said sharply, "Is that any way to talk to your mother?"

His mother fanned herself vigorously with a sheet of engraved notepaper. "Which is exactly what happens when you associate with the wrong kind of people."

Nick rose. "Excuse me, but I see no reason to stay here and have my friends maligned before my ears. I don't wish to be impolite, but we've had this conversation before—"

Nick's father interrupted, "We have never had this conversation before, you may thank your lucky stars. And we're not talking about your so-called friends."

"Then what, pray tell, are we talking about?"

"Do you see, James?" Nick's mother turned dramatically despairing eyes to her husband. "This is what comes from letting all those wild ways go unchecked when you insisted he would grow out of them. I *told* you we should have sent him to a European university! Now I defy you to do anything with him. I turn him over completely to your hands."

She rose with a graceful swirl of silk skirts. "Come along, Cynthia."

Cynthia looked as though she would balk, but her mother extended her hand and repeated firmly, "Come along."

The door closed quietly behind them, and Nick turned to his father, not knowing whether to be exasperated or amused. He often felt that way in the presence of his parents, but today he was also in a hurry. He said, "I take it you've been instructed to give me a lecture." He lifted his shoulders lightly. "Seems as good a way as any to celebrate your homecoming."

Customarily his father's response would have been an uncomfortable look, a few gruff words and a brusque dismissal. It was a ritual they had been going through periodically since Nick was eighteen: every six months or so his mother would take it into her head that he needed reforming, his father would make a token attempt to do so, and it would all be over in a matter of minutes.

But this time his father's gaze was steady and he said, "Yes. Sit down, will you, son?"

Nick said cautiously, "I'll stand, if you don't mind."

His father nodded absently. "To tell you the truth, I wasn't happy with the idea of having this little talk with you. Frankly I don't think this latest pecadillo of yours is any worse than the others you've done, and probably quite a few we've never even heard about, but you know your mother—she flies off the handle at the least thing, and it's easier to appease her than argue with her." He smiled faintly. "These man-to-man talks of ours have never been particularly successful, have they?"

Nick hesitated. Those sentences constituted the longest string of serious words his father had put together for him in almost ten years, and Nick did not know quite how to react. He said, "No, sir." Then, "What have I done to upset Mother this time?"

His father waved a dismissing hand, frowning at the thin stream of smoke issuing from his pipe. "Oh, this chorus girl of yours. I know it's not the first and won't be the last, but your sister wanted to make a melodrama out of it, and sometimes I think your mother just looks for excuses to play out her maternal instincts. Makes her feel useful."

He smiled a little and Nick found himself reciprocating. It was the first time Nick could remember that he and his father had ever shared anything even vaguely resembling a joke.

"Like I said, I wouldn't even think it's worth mentioning except I've been thinking about you a lot this past year, Nick." His father raised his gaze from his pipe and met Nick's eyes. "And what I've been thinking hasn't made me very proud. To tell you the truth, I've been worried."

Nick reached in his pocket for a cigarette, then changed his mind. Until now, meetings with his father had never lent themselves to the kind of informality in which he felt comfortable smoking. He couldn't imagine where the impulse to do so now had come from.

He said, "I'm sorry if I worried you."

His father nodded slowly. "I don't think you are, but that doesn't matter. How old are you Nick? Twenty-five?"

"Twenty-six."

The older man gave an impatient shake of his head. "A father should know a thing like that," he muttered. "Maybe that's part of the problem. Go ahead, smoke if you want to," he added, and walked over to the fireplace. He emptied his pipe, then added fresh tobacco, tamping it firmly. "Maybe I should take up cigarettes. Seem to be a lot less bother than this damn pipe."

Part of Nick was impatient to get on with it, but another part was curious and didn't want to rush. He found himself actually wanting to hear what his father had to say. After a moment he lit a cigarette and sat down.

When his pipe was relit, his father turned to Nick again and said, "What bothers me is this restlessness of yours. Oh, I know it's all part of the crazy world we live in—young people running uncurbed, girls with no modesty or shame, rumble seats. But let me tell you something, son. If you think the twenties are wild, you should have been a young man in the nineties, because I'm here to tell you there's nothing new under the sun. You think the world is yours for the taking and there's so much you can't make up your mind what you want first, so you think you'll try it all because it'd be a damn shame to miss out on anything. Am I right?"

Nick stared at his father, speechless.

His father merely nodded. "And after a while none of it means anything, nothing seems to satisfy, and you start to feel like a man who goes to bed hungry at a feast."

Nick studied the tip of his cigarette. He said slowly, "Yes."

"Everybody sows wild oats. It's only natural. The trouble comes when you don't know when to stop. Then you go the rest of your life looking for something you haven't tried, wanting something you've never had. There are men like that out there, Nick, and they're sad, empty men. I would have been one of them, if I hadn't found your mother when I did."

Nick looked at his father as though seeing him for the first time. And in fact, he did feel as though he were meeting a stranger. How could his father have changed so much in only three months? Or was it perhaps that he, Nick, had changed? Was he hearing things from his parent that had been said before, perhaps for years, but he had never chosen to listen until now?

Nick asked suddenly, "Did you love her, Pop?"

His father smiled. "Oh, yes. From the day I met her and every day of my life since."

Nick found that dimly amazing. Somehow one never thought of one's parents as sharing passion.

"How did you know?"

"That it was love?"

"And not . . . infatuation."

"Simple. She made me want to change. I married her when I was twenty-three and haven't regretted a moment of it since." He examined his pipe thoughtfully, puffed on it, and added after a moment, "Oh, I could have lived without her, I suppose. But I wouldn't have been *alive*. Because from the day she became my wife I knew what it was I'd been looking for and could never find—and it wasn't just love. It was responsibility. A sense of being a part of something bigger than myself, of caring for something beyond the moment, of building something that would outlast the two of us. That's what your generation lacks, Nick. A sense of responsibility. And that's why I worry about you."

Nick felt as though he were on the verge of a discovery, as though he were standing before a thin veil of curtain that, once lifted, would reveal clearly something very important. The cigarette burned between his fingers and he made no move to lift it to his lips. He thought he would remember this moment— hazy afternoon light slanting through the windows, a clock chiming in the hall, the rich cherry smell of his father's pipe—for a very long time.

He said, without looking up, "How do you get this sense of responsibility?"

"Simple," his father replied. "You just make up your mind to be responsible. And then you do it."

Nick looked up at him slowly. "Why are you telling me all this?"

His father met his gaze evenly. "Because of something your sister said. Your mother didn't hear it—sometimes I think she's like those sob sisters in the papers and only hears what makes good copy. It was about this girl of yours. Something that made me think she might be more than just a chorus girl. Cynthia said, 'I think she's been good for him.'"

Nick could not hide his surprise. "Cynthia said that?"

His father nodded. "And on that subject I'll say just one thing. If she's good for you, it doesn't matter what she does for a living. The only question you should be asking yourself right now is, is it time for a change?"

Nick slowly extinguished his cigarette and got to his feet. "You know, Pop," he said, "sometimes I think you're pretty smart."

His father nodded gravely. "I'm only sorry you couldn't have taken advantage of that sooner."

Nick smiled and extended his hand. His father clasped it warmly. "So am I."

Chapter Twelve

All the way to the Village, snatches of insight kept floating and flashing through Nick's head. It was so simple; he was only amazed that he had not understood it before. *What have I done with myself over the summer, Mother? I've discovered a future, that's all.*

That was why Alice was different from any other woman he'd ever known. When he was with her he thought in terms of tomorrow, of consequences and choices. He had never done that before. He had never needed that before. But with Alice, no matter how hard he tried to make each moment sufficient unto itself, that was never enough. He loved her. And when the physical act of loving was over he loved her even more, he needed her even more desperately. He wanted to build his life around her.

All these weeks he had fought the urge to make promises. He had thought he was incapable of caring for Alice in the way she deserved. He had been afraid that when the moment came he would not be able to give her the commitment she needed, that he would make the wrong choice just as he had been making the wrong choices his entire life. And all the time he had been unable to see that there was no choice at all; the commitment had already been made.

A light autumn rain had begun to fall by the time he reached the apartment, and when he parked around the back of the building he could see Alice waving to him from the top of the stairs. He bounded out of the car and took the steps two at a time, catching her to him in a brief swift kiss. She tasted of raindrops and flowers and the sweetness that was simply Alice.

"You should have waited downstairs inside," he scolded her, brushing the light film of rain that sparkled on her skin with his fingertips. "You're all wet."

"Not yet," she assured him. Her eyes were shining and her cheeks were flushed with excitement, "But I will be if you don't open the door. Oh, Nick, I have the most exciting thing to tell you."

Nick looked at her glowing eyes, her rapt little-girl expression, and though he had never been prescient before he suddenly knew he did not want to hear what she had to tell him. He smiled, though, and turned the key in the lock. "Sounds important."

"It is." She stepped into the darkened apartment, whipping off her hat and shaking the dampness out of her curls. "It's only the most important thing that's ever happened to me in my whole life, ever." And she gave a little laugh of bubbling excitement, bending to turn on a lamp. Then she did a little pirouette that ended in a pose, and she declared, "You are looking at the star of Tyler Bradford's new show, opening next Friday night to record crowds! Oh, Nick, aren't you excited for me?"

Nick closed the door and leaned against it, trying to maintain his smile. He said, "Congratulations. It's what you wanted."

Something in the subdued tone of his voice made Alice pause, and she realized suddenly how hard she was working to keep the smile on her face, the excitement in her tone. It *was* what she wanted. Wasn't it?

The uncertainty confused her, and she glanced away. "I thought you'd be happy for me."

Nick took out his cigarettes and offered one to her. She shook her head. He walked over to the easy chair by the fireplace and sat down, looking at the cigarette case for a moment before putting it away. He seemed different, Alice noticed then. Calmer, older somehow. The rain was beginning to fog the windowpanes, sealing the two of them inside in an atmosphere that was not so much cozy as ominous. Trepidation formed inside Alice, the source of which she could not quite define, and she had to force herself to go over to Nick.

She sat on the arm of his chair and cupped the back of his neck with her hand. He slipped his arm around her waist. "Nick, don't you want me to do Tyler's show?"

He looked at her, and with a shock that went right through her soul, Alice knew that she wanted him to say no. And that if he did she would agree; she would turn her back on Tyler Bradford and the dreams of stardom that once had been so important to her, because she could not bear to see the sadness in Nick's eyes, because nothing was worth having if it threatened the precious moments they had together. Because she knew now, and had known for a long time, that there was something more important to her than being a star.

Nick's lips curved in a faint smile of absent introspection and he said, "You know, it's funny. I've spent all my life thinking about what I wanted, what it would take to make me happy. It never occurred to me that the day might come when the only thing I would ever want was someone's else's happiness.''

Alice caught her breath and everything inside her seemed to stop—the flow of her blood, the beat of her heart. Everything was suspended and waiting for what she knew instinctively would be the most important moment of her life.

With a gentle caress of her waist, Nick got up and crossed the room. He stood before the window, looking out, and he said simply, ''I love you, Alice. I never thought I'd hear myself say those words and mean them, but I do. And the funny thing is I thought all I had to do was race over here and tell you that, and everything would be perfect.'' He turned. ''But it's not that easy, is it?''

Yes, Alice wanted to cry. *Yes, it is that easy, just that easy, because I've waited so long and wanted so badly to hear you say those words, to say them to you, and now they're said and nothing else matters. Nothing at all.* She wanted to rush from the chair and fling herself into his arms; she wanted to hold him and kiss him and know that this time the moment could last forever. But there was a pounding in her chest and a tightening in her throat, and the sadness in his eyes held her back.

She stood slowly and took a single step toward him. Her voice was choked, though whether with happiness or anxiety she could not be sure. ''Oh, Nick, I love you, too, I always have, and I want...'' And there, inexplicably and to her utter horror, her voice broke. What did she want?

She wanted a big church wedding like Molly's, or she wanted a few minutes before a judge with only

Nick at her side. She wanted to lie down at his side at night and awake to his face every morning. She wanted her name in lights and her picture in the papers and the sound of applause. She wanted to walk on the beach with Nick and she wanted to ride in a parade given in her honor. She wanted the view from the rooftop, and she wanted the world at her feet.

She *knew* what she wanted, and he was standing right before her, within the reach of her arms. But the dream she had held so tightly and so long kept creeping in the way, blurring her vision and shadowing her perspective. It should have been easy. Why couldn't she speak?

Nick watched her, and it was as though he read every thought that went through her head and accepted what he saw. He said quietly, "I want you to do the show, Alice. Because if you don't you'll spend the rest of your life wondering what would have happened if you had. Because there are some choices you have to make for yourself, and that's the only way you'll ever know what you really want."

She shook her head mutely, wanting to argue with him, wanting to insist that there was no choice, that all she needed she already had and she could not—she dared not—risk losing it. But she could not make him a promise that was given with only half her heart.

She walked slowly into his arms, closing her eyes against the pain that tore at her. He enfolded her gently; he kissed her lips.

He said softly, "I'll be waiting, when you make up your mind."

He walked out of the apartment, leaving her alone.

ALICE WENT THROUGH the motions of the following week numbly: voice lessons, grueling sessions with the choreographer, rehearsals. She came home at night with her body aching and a hollowness deep inside that nothing could fill. This was her moment of triumph, the fulfillment of an ambition for which she had worked all her life. How could anyone in her right mind turn her back on an opportunity like this?

It was only one show, she kept telling herself. One taste of stardom, one moment in the sun, and then she would have done it. She would have lived her dream and she could walk away with no regrets.

"It's not like I was doing something wrong," she told Molly as she soaked her feet late one night. She was aware that she was trying to convince herself more than Molly. "Nick knows I love him and…and I want to marry him. But I've worked so hard for this, Molly. Don't I at least deserve to do the opening show?"

Molly carefully poured more steaming water from the kettle into the Epsom salts mixture that covered Alice's feet. "I don't know," she said worriedly. "A man has a right to ask the woman he's going to marry not to dance in a nightclub."

Alice shook her head impatiently. "But he wanted me to do it. He told me to."

Molly said, "Sometimes what men say and what they mean are different things."

Alice shook her head firmly. "Not Nick."

"Is he coming to your opening?"

And that was when the sinking, hollow feeling started in Alice's stomach again. "I don't know." Then, hopefully, "Are you and Stuart coming?"

Molly looked embarrassed and uncomfortable. "I don't think so, Alice. It's not as though we wouldn't like to see you, but you know I've never been very comfortable in places like that and, well, I don't think so.''

Alice tried to smile and assure her friend that it was all right, but it wasn't all right. What good was it to be on top of the world if there was no one to share the view?

All during that week she kept expecting to hear from Nick, to find him waiting outside the club, to see his familiar yellow roadster parked at the curb when she got home. Once, on impulse, she even went by the apartment, but it was dark and silent and locked up tight. She was fighting back tears as she turned away.

There were moments when she was angry. Why had he done this to her? He had said he loved her; why couldn't he just be happy for her? Why had he insisted on turning her moment of triumph into an ordeal? And then she was confused. He had known how much this meant to her. And even so, if he had asked her not to do it she would have agreed without hesitation, because she loved him and couldn't bear to lose him. Wasn't that enough? What more did he want from her?

But most of the time she was desolate, because deep down inside she knew Nick was disappointed in her, and she was afraid that there was nothing she could do that would ever take that look of sadness out of his eyes.

Opening night came, and for those few hours of intense bustle and frantic excitement before the doors opened, the agony and uncertainty Alice had endured to reach this point almost seemed worth it. She was fitted into her skintight red costume, painted her eyes and rouged her cheeks and went over the dance steps in her mind, and it was all exactly as she'd expected it to be. She watched as the finishing touches were put on the scenery—the curving white staircase, the shimmering gold backdrop, the raised center platform from which she would do her solo dance. She looked out over the empty tables draped in red velvet and imagined them full of happy, exuberant people, rising to their feet in enthusiastic applause when the show was over, and she told herself it was all worth it. This was her night. Nick would be here, she knew he would. Nothing had ended for them. Tonight was only the beginning. Tonight they would celebrate. Tonight, for once in her life, she would have it all.

And there was Tyler Bradford, sleek and handsome in his tuxedo, grinning and coming toward her with his hands outstretched. "So, the big night, eh? Let me look at you." He caught her hand and twirled her around gracefully. "A living doll. You're gonna knock 'em dead, sweetie. So, how do you feel? A few butterflies?"

"A few," she admitted. "Mostly from excitement."

"Sure, you got star quality, I told you that. We've got a crowd lined up outside already. It's going to be a full house. Showtime in less than an hour."

Alice wondered if Nick was in that crowd outside.

"And listen, afterward we're having a little party over at Jack Brady's place. You remember Jack, don't you? He sure was taken by you."

Alice wasn't sure she did remember Jack, and she was sure she didn't want to go to a party. The only person she wanted to celebrate with tonight was Nick. She said, "I don't know about a party. I was kind of planning to—"

"Well, whatever you were planning, bring it along," he said jovially. "The party's in your honor!" He started to turn away, then added casually, "By the way, I won't be able to break away till later, so I was wondering if you wouldn't mind taking a package over there for me when you go."

Everything within Alice went very still. She said in what she hoped was a perfectly normal tone of voice, "More receipts?"

There might have been a slight narrowing of his eyes, or she might have imagined it. His smile remained intact. "No," he answered easily. "Just some papers. Names and addresses, that sort of thing. Jack's been kind of anxious for them. You don't mind, do you?"

Alice smiled. "No. Of course I don't mind."

Tyler looked at her for a moment longer, then gave her a friendly pinch on the cheek and walked away, calling out something to a waiter about the candles on the tables.

Alice brought her hand to her cheek, feeling as though she wanted to rub away a stain. She looked at the stage, which only a moment ago had been the epitome of enchantment and glamour. Now it was only plywood and painted cardboard, tawdry and cheap. Moments ago she had been standing on top of the world, and now she was standing in the middle of an overpriced, overdecorated speakeasy where dreams were bought and sold for the price of a drink. And now she understood everything very clearly.

It wasn't just one show. Just a taste of stardom, one night of glory from which she could easily walk away. It was Tyler Bradford, who always did right by those who did right by him. It was the lure of bright lights

and the thrumming of applause, so thrilling, so se-
ductive. It was a matter of choices in a world in which
the lines between right and wrong were too often
blurred, and in which nothing worthwhile ever came
easy. And that was what Nick had meant when he
wanted her to decide for herself.

OFFICER JIM WILLIAMS made his way through the
crowd of disreputable-looking, poorly dressed people
who partially blocked the street corner until he caught
sight of the familiar yellow roadster at its center. Un-
shaven men smelling of grain alcohol and filth, women
dressed in rags and half-starved-looking children with
thin, straggling hair all pressed closed, some of them
shouting, some of them laughing, all of them scrambling for the boxes that were piled high in the back of
the automobile and scattered on the street beside it.
The contents of some of those boxes had already
spilled out, and the less-ambitious ones crawled between other people's legs and under the car to retrieve
the cans of food and articles of clothing scattered
there.

Jim called out, "I might have known it was you."

Nick Crawford sat on the hood of his car, a bottle
in his hand, watching the proceedings with a mixture
of amusement and dismay. At the sound of Jim's
voice he turned, then extended a hand to help the policeman up onto the hood beside him.

"I tried to distribute it all in an orderly fashion," he
explained, gesturing at the mob scene before him and
raising his voice a little to be heard. "It was hope-
less."

Jim scowled and reached for his nightstick as
someone grabbed at his leg. "You'll be lucky if they

don't tear this little machine of yours apart right underneath you.''

Nick shook his head. "No. They like me."

Jim regarded Nick the way a disapproving but indulgent parent might look at a precocious child. "You're a wonder in this world," he muttered, and as a second bump from below scuffed his boot, he followed Nick's example and drew his legs up on the hood of the automobile. "What's that you're drinking?" he demanded suddenly, staring at the bottle. "Coca-Cola?"

Nick lifted the bottle. "I think I'm addicted. Want some?"

"No, thanks. Gives me gas."

The two men watched in silence as the last of the boxes were dragged out of the car and dumped on the street, the mob converging to tear through their contents. Then Nick said quietly, "It's a stupid thing to do, isn't it? I mean, it doesn't really change anything. Tomorrow they'll just sell the clothes for a drink or a doorway to sleep in and still be wondering where their next meal is coming from. There's never enough to go around."

Jim was thoughtful for a while. Then he said, "I don't know. You give them a moment of happiness. That's something. For them, that's a lot."

Nick drank again from the bottle and said nothing.

After a moment Jim said, "I see Alice is still working at the King Club. Posters all over town."

Nick replied, looking straight ahead, "That's right."

"I take it you won't be going down there tonight."

Nick didn't answer. All week he had been arguing that very question with himself and had finally answered it by coming here with a carload of canned foods and useless pieces of clothing and children's toys, which would be broken or sold before morning. The gesture had proved to be no answer at all; just another way to avoid the question.

And that was not the only question he had been unable to answer. His eyes were bloodshot and dark-rimmed from tossing in bed, and he had grown so irritable that his mother had begun to make pointed references to the reputed benefits of the waters at Saratoga Springs; his mother believed that any ill could be cured with enough pampering and mineral water. Even Cynthia had begun to give him sympathetic looks, and his father went out of his way not to pry. Nick had briefly considered moving in to his apartment to avoid inflicting himself on his family any further, but the apartment was so filled with memories of Alice that he had not even been able to stay an hour.

Why had he left her there that day with so much unsaid, so much unanswered? Who did he think he was, setting himself up as her moral judge? What difference did it make whether she came to him in a moment of passion, or after cold-sober reflection, as long as she came to him? He should have swept her off her feet. He should have demanded that she choose at that moment between a lifetime with him and an ephemeral career on the stage. He should have driven her to Maryland and married her on the spot. He should never have walked away from her.

Every day since she had gone to work for Tyler Bradford he had expected her somehow to suddenly see the light; to realize that the kind of fame she wanted did not come without sacrifice, and that the life Bradford offered was not for her. He could not make that decision for her. He had wanted her to come to him willingly, to turn her back on the bright lights and walk into his arms because that was what she wanted, not because he insisted.

Now he wondered if he had been wrong. Maybe he should have insisted. He loved her; he should take care of her. And maybe his refusal to make demands, disguised as it was under the noble emblem of allowing her freedom of choice, was just another way of avoiding responsibility. It was easy to love an independent woman, he had learned, but not so easy to hold on to one. And by insisting that Alice make her own choice he had risked the one thing in the world he could not afford to lose.

Jim muttered beside him, "Ah, hell."

Nick turned his head. For a moment he had almost forgotten the other man's presence.

Jim focused his attention on the crowd, which was now beginning to disperse into the dying light with their trophies. He said, deliberately not looking at Nick, "Listen, I want you to know it could mean my job if it ever gets out I told you this. I've been hoping all day I wouldn't run in to you. I don't know why you always have to do your little tricks on my beat."

Nick was in no mood for playing games. "What are you talking about, Jim?"

Jim glanced at him uneasily. "It's just that if Jane ever found out I didn't try to do something... Well, I don't want to think about what she'd do. So, this is for Jane."

Nick finished off the cola and discarded the bottle in the back of the car, regarding Jim impatiently.

Jim rubbed his lower jaw. He looked very uncomfortable. He said, "Look, this Tyler Bradford—you may not know it, but he's involved in some pretty big-league stuff. Not just bootlegging, but racketeering with the heavyweights. He's got a whole organization spread out under him that covers everything from race-fixing to land fraud, with muscle to enforce his rules, if you know what I mean.''

Nick could feel his heart beating more swiftly and heavily in his chest. The voices of his beneficiaries were dying away with the scuffling of footsteps. The last of the autumn twilight was whisked away with a chill breeze, and night came abruptly.

''The problem is we've never been able to pin anything on him,'' Jim went on. ''Can't even get him for serving liquor in his own club that's got a sign posted out front plain as day saying he doesn't. But the reports are that he keeps records of all his transactions—names and dates that would put half the gangsters in this city away for a good long time—right there in his office. And I guess that's worth the embarrassment to a few wealthy patrons because, well, there's a raid scheduled for tonight. And anybody caught in there is going down.''

It was a long time before Nick managed hoarsely, ''What time?''

Jim shook his head. ''I can't tell you that.''

Nick made a quick move toward him and Jim flung up a hand to ward him off, alarm mixed with the anger on his face. ''Dammit, Nick, I don't *know*! Nobody does but the men on the team, and I'm not one of them.''

Nick did not have to look at his watch to know how late it was. The club had been open for an hour, maybe more. Maybe they would wait until the show started, when the place was packed and everyone's attention was diverted. Maybe they wouldn't. Nick swung over the windscreen and into his seat.

Jim leapt off the hood. "Just get her out of there!" he called against the roar of the engine. "Just get her outside and she'll probably be okay!"

Nick drove off blindly, praying without much hope he wouldn't be too late.

ALICE WAITED until she saw Tyler deep in conversation with a group of customers at a table before she slipped silently into his office. There were only a few minutes left before the show started, and her heart seemed to pound in her throat. She would have to hurry.

She could have waited, of course, until after the show. Until Tyler gave her the papers he wanted her to deliver and sent her on her way. On the other hand, Tyler could have delivered those papers himself. He had his little tests; she had hers.

A green shaded lamp burned on the desk, casting shadows on the dim, yellow walls. There were shelves with ledger books on them, wooden file cabinets in a corner. She went over to the desk. She did not even know what she was looking for. She wasn't entirely sure what she would do with it when she found it. She only knew that she had to have proof in her hands before she went on stage tonight. The time for pretending was over.

She tried the top drawer and found it locked. She looked anxiously at the door. Her palms were sweating. The right-hand drawer was locked, too, but the left one slid open easily. There was nothing inside but a sheaf of paper and some pens.

Quickly she looked around the room. *Stupid,* she berated herself. *What did you expect to find? What difference does it make, anyway? You know the truth. You've known it from the first. Nick tried to tell you, but you wouldn't listen, didn't want to listen.*

Her eyes fell again on the desk. There, covered by a stack of order forms and payroll sheets, was a small bound book. Of course. Names and addresses. He had intended to give it to her tonight. He had left it out, and why wouldn't he? Tyler Bradford had nothing to fear in his own office. She reached for the book.

She heard a noise, a small click, and her eyes flew frantically to the door. She watched in stupefied horror as the doorknob began to turn.

No more than a couple a seconds passed, but it seemed forever that she stood rooted to the spot like a trapped animal. Why hadn't she locked the door? She should have locked the door. How would she explain what she was doing here? Where could she hide?

The door started to swing open and she ducked behind the desk, scrunching herself up as small as possible on the floor. A trickle of cold perspiration slid down her spine and she dared not breathe; she tried to smother the thunder of her heartbeat as, in the space between the desk and the floor, she saw a pair of black patent men's shoes advance into the room.

She squeezed her eyes shut and hugged her knees, trying to make herself smaller, invisible. She never should have hidden here. Tyler would come straight to his desk and be sure to see her. She could never explain why she was hiding. Her heart was pounding so hard she couldn't hear. She wouldn't even know he was near until he grabbed her and then it would be too late. *Oh, God,* she thought. *Oh, God...*

A man's voice called, ''Bradford?''

Alice opened her eyes cautiously. The black patent shoes were still in the center of the room, several feet from the desk. They hesitated there a moment, then turned back toward the door. A moment later the door snapped shut.

For a moment she couldn't even move. She remained huddled on the floor, weak with relief, breathing shakily. And then slowly she got to her feet.

She should get out of here right now. She couldn't be that lucky twice. And there was no guarantee that man had not seen her and hadn't gone to report to Tyler. She was crazy to have come here. She should get out *now*.

She actually started for the door, and then her eyes fell on the desk again. The book. Could she leave it behind now after having come so close?

A cowardly little voice inside her shouted *yes!*

She glanced quickly toward the door, biting her lip. Then she snatched up the book.

But then she hesitated. It still could be nothing. She had to be *sure*—for her own sake much more than Tyler's.

She opened the book slowly and began to read.

The door opened abruptly to the clamor of voices and the clink of glasses and Alice looked up with a gasp. The book almost slipped from her fingers. Tyler Bradford stood there watching her for a moment, then he closed the door lazily behind him.

''Why, Alice,'' he said smoothly, ''you're due on-stage in a couple of minutes. What are you doing in here?''

After a few seconds of painful slamming against her ribs, her heart settled down into an amazingly calm rhythm. She met Tyler Bradford's cold, unreadable gaze evenly, and with an innocence in her tone that matched his own she inquired, "Are these the . . . papers you wanted me to take to your friend?"

The corner of his lips moved, imitating a smile. "That's right. But you didn't have to come in here for them. I told you I'd see you after the show."

He came toward her, reaching for the book, but Alice took a step backward, holding it against her chest. His hand fell and his face went hard for a moment, then settled into its usual smooth, inscrutable lines.

Alice said, "I want to ask you something, Tyler."

After a moment Tyler smiled and leaned against the desk with a conciliatory gesture, "Of course. Anything you like."

"Why did you hire me? Why did you decide to make me a star?"

The smile deepened and appeared almost genuinely amused. "That's easy. You were bright, willing…ambitious. Really ambitious. That's the kind of raw material I like to work with. And you were well-connected, too."

For the first time, Alice felt her courage falter. "Nick?"

"Of course, Nick. A man like him, old money, friends from the mayor's office on down—I would have liked to've had him on my side. You could go far in this organization, Alice. You've got what it takes."

"Ambition," she repeated dully.

"Knowing what's important," he clarified. "It takes a smart girl to know how to hitch her wagon to the right star."

Alice felt the cold leather of the book against her breast, the whisper of feathers against her neck. She looked up at Tyler. She said, "There were some real interesting names in this book. And figures right after them. You know what I think? I don't think this is a regular address book at all. I think this is a list of people you've collected money from, and people who haven't paid you yet. And I think when I give this book to your friend Jack he's going to pick out some names and give the list to some other men, and the people on that list are probably going to end up with broken arms and legs, or maybe even dead."

She shrugged. "Of course, I could be wrong. It could be a list of people you've paid off for doing things you don't want anybody else to know about. Or it could be a list of people who've made bets on things they shouldn't have. But whatever it is, I'm pretty certain that it's illegal."

As she spoke she watched the tolerance fade from Tyler's eyes, the placidity from his face. Now there was little left of the man she had known except his pose—still carefully cultivated, but only a veneer. He said, "There, you see? I always knew you were a smart girl." His voice was as smooth as silk, as cold as a blade. He extended his hand. "Now, give me the book."

Alice replied quietly, "No. I don't think so. I have a friend who's a policeman. I think I'll give it to him instead."

Tyler rose. "You disappoint me, Alice. You don't really think I'm going to let you just march out of here with my important papers in your hands, do you?"

She managed a smile that was almost normal. "Why not? An hour ago that's exactly what you were *asking* me to do."

His smile was utterly without warmth. "Don't be a fool, Alice. You cooperate with me and the good life is yours. Look what I've done for you already. I made you a star, didn't I? And that's just the beginning. You can be the hottest thing in show business just as soon as you learn to play by the rules."

Alice swallowed hard and lifted her chin. But the words were surprisingly easy to say. "I don't want to be the hottest thing in show business. I don't think I can afford the price."

He took an impatient step toward her. "I'm tired of playing with you. Do you want to give me the book nicely and get out on stage where you belong, or do I have to take it from you and slap you around once or twice for good measure?"

Alice's throat convulsed, but she lifted her head. "I know you can take it from me," she said. "You're bigger than I am and you're not afraid to beat me up. But you're forgetting something. I'm an actress, remember? I'm used to memorizing lines in a hurry. I've seen this book, Mr. Bradford, and I'm not going to forget what I've seen."

He stopped, his eyes narrowing as they went over her. Outside, the band began the intro of the opening number. "Well, now," he murmured. "That does put an entirely different complexion on things, doesn't it?"

The desk still separated them, and Tyler leaned back on his heels, his fist against his chin, a small, cold smile toying with his lips. "You know, I've got to admire a girl with spunk. Maybe I've been thinking too small in my plans for you. We could really go places together, you and me. Big places."

Alice stiffened. "Thank you, but I don't want to go anywhere with you."

The band began its second intro. Tyler cocked his head toward the door. "Your cue, I believe, my dear. Sure you won't change your mind?"

"No."

"Then you leave me no choice."

NICK SCANNED the interior of the club and knew immediately something was wrong. The band was playing something the leader seemed to be making up as he went along, and the customers were starting to glance around impatiently. He skirted the tables quickly, pushing toward the front, making his way toward the stage entrance. He pushed through the curtain and into the backstage area, where a group of irritable, anxious-looking costumed dancers were gathered.

"Alice," he said, looking from one face to another. "Alice Fontaine. Where is she?"

"You tell me," one of the male dancers snapped, peering through the parted curtains. "They're gonna start throwing things out there in a minute."

"She's supposed to be on," said a girl. "Somebody find Mr. Bradford."

"He's probably looking for her."

Nick pushed through the crowd of young people, running the length of the narrow hall, flinging open a dressing-room door, and running back.

"Where's Bradford?" he demanded.

"Wait a minute—I think I saw him go into his office a minute ago. Hey, ask him what we're supposed to do, will you?'' one of the young men called out, but Nick was already gone.

His heart was beating in asynchronous rhythm with the music as he moved back into the club area and began to make his way quickly, but far too slowly, through the crowd of tables again. Maybe she had left. Maybe Jane had warned her. Maybe she had just quit.

But Alice wouldn't quit on opening night, and if Jane had known about the raid Jim wouldn't have felt it necessary to warn Nick. Something was wrong. Something had happened to Alice, he knew it as surely as he had ever known anything in his life, and Nick had let it happen. He had practically forced it to happen. He had set her on the road to disaster, and when he might have pulled her to safety he'd merely stepped aside. Being in love meant being responsible, not only for yourself and your own feelings, but for the person you loved; that was what his father had tried to tell him. Why hadn't he been able to understand that before it was too late?

He bumped into a woman who was getting up to leave and pushed her aside without even apologizing. Her companion grabbed his shoulder but Nick shrugged him off. He didn't even hear the angry challenge that followed him as he reached the door to Tyler's office and burst inside without knocking.

Tyler had his hands on Alice; she was struggling. The door bounced on its hinges and slammed shut as Nick lunged toward them. Nick seized Tyler's shoulders and dimly heard Alice's cry as he flung the other man away. A red haze of fury blurred his vision and stripped his judgment and he couldn't even focus long enough to make a fist. He simply grabbed Tyler and threw him.

Tyler staggered against the desk, and Nick lurched backward with the release of the other man's weight. Breathing hard, he started forward again, and suddenly Tyler straightened and turned, a gun in his hand.

"Well," Tyler said. His breath was choppy but he held the gun steady on Nick. "Isn't this romantic?"

Alice's hand flew to her lips but she made no sound. The scream was lodged in her throat. She looked at Nick, his tie askew, his hair rumpled, his hands clenched into fists. She looked at Tyler, holding the short, ugly black weapon. She thought irrationally, almost incoherently, *Is this it, then? Is this what it all was for, all those girlhood dreams, all the hope, all the plans to end in the back room of a speakeasy at the point of a gun?* How far away the rest seemed now, how unimportant. Outside the band played on, richly dressed people lifted their glasses and waited for the show, but none of it was real. There was only one thing that mattered, and that was that the man she loved was facing the barrel of a gun and there was nothing she could do to help him.

She whispered, "Nick," and took a step toward him.

"Stay there!" Tyler barked, and turned the gun in her direction. He shifted around the desk, so that he could cover them both, and with an absent motion he pushed back a strand of hair, which had fallen from its neat center part.

Nick looked at Alice. "It's all right," he said softly. "Do what he says."

She believed him. Looking at him, drinking in the strength and reassurance in his eyes, she believed everything was going to be all right. She nodded.

Tyler smiled. "Good advice." He turned his gaze to Nick. "Now this is an interesting situation. I was just trying to figure out what to do with your girlfriend, here, and now it looks like I've got the two of you on my hands. They say trouble comes in twos."

Alice said, fighting the tremor in her voice, "That book, Nick." She nodded to where the book had fallen on the floor. "It's got names in it, and numbers. You were right about him. He's nothing but a common criminal, and he was using me."

Tyler lifted an eyebrow. "A common criminal, Nick? Did you say that about me? And after I've valued our friendship so." Still holding the gun on Nick, he began to edge slowly toward the door. "Well, I'd like to have a talk with you about that someday, but right now I've got a business to run, and a show to put on, and as it happens—" he glanced at Alice with mock regret "—our star performer will be unable to appear tonight. I'm afraid I'm going to have to ask one of my boys to put you in a safe place for a while, Nick, just until I decide what to do with you. I've got more permanent plans for your little Sheba, here."

He tilted his head toward Alice, still smiling that cold, humorless smile. "That's show business, doll. They come and they go, and nobody ever misses yesterday's stars."

He had reached the door and put his hand on the knob. Alice's eyes drifted desperately to Nick, but she dared not move. There was no chance to move, for Tyler did not take his eyes or his gun off them. And suddenly Tyler froze.

The disturbance from outside was loud enough to be clear through the muffling walls—people shouting, heavy movements, scuffling, tables being over-turned. "What's that?" Tyler demanded sharply.

"Threes, Tyler," Nick said. "Trouble always comes in threes."

They heard a woman scream, more muffled shouts. And Alice saw the panic cross Tyler's face as they heard the voice, clearly amplified by a bullhorn, commanding, "Stay where you are! This is a raid! Stay where you are and raise your hands over your heads!"

Tyler cursed viciously and pushed away from the door. The next sequence of events took only a matter of seconds, but Alice would remember it in vivid detail for the rest of her life.

She saw the book lying on the floor and Tyler rush-ing toward it. Afterward she was never quite sure what she was thinking except that that book was her proof, her reason, the truth she had waited too long to dis-cover, and he was getting away with it. She flung her-self toward the book, and Nick shouted, "Alice, no!" Her hands were on the book, but Tyler tore it from her fingers and pushed her down. Nick rushed toward him, and as Tyler swung in a half crouch, the gun ex-ploded.

Alice screamed but she never heard it. She only saw Nick fall backward and the blood on his jacket, on the floor. Mere inches separated them, but it seemed like miles; she stretched out her hand toward him, but she couldn't move, she couldn't make a sound.

Tyler ran toward the window, the book clutched under his arm. The door burst open. Someone shouted, "Stop! Stop in the name of the law!"

Tyler turned and fired the gun again and then the room was filled with the sound of thunder. Blood splattered, wood chips flew. And Tyler Bradford was flung back against the wall, his eyes open, his expression stunned. The book slid from his limp fingers and fell open onto the floor.

In the silence Alice was sobbing. Her face was pressed against Nick's chest and the policemen kept trying to make her move away, but she wouldn't budge. "I thought you were dead," she whispered brokenly over and over. "I thought you were dead."

Someone had cut away Nick's jacket sleeve and tied a crude bandage around his arm, but it was stained with blood already, and every time Alice looked at it a dry, choking shudder went through her. He held her securely with his uninjured arm, caressing her shoulder, kissing her hair. She couldn't get close enough, couldn't hold him tightly enough.

"It's all right," he murmured. "It was only a scratch. I'm all right. Everything's going to be all right."

"N-no," she whispered, and held him tighter. "Not all right. Never...all right again."

Outside the closed door the muffled sounds of disorder gradually being brought under control occasionally seeped through. Against the far wall a blanket covered the body of Tyler Bradford. No one could do anything about the bloodstains on the walls and ceiling, nor the acrid smell of gunsmoke that still haunted the room.

Alice swallowed a final sob and looked up at Nick. She tried on a brave smile, but it wavered and disappeared in horror before it even reached her lips. "Well," she said shakily, "I'm going to have my name in the papers. It's what I always wanted. People will be talking about me and remembering me and—"

Nick's arm tightened about her shoulders as her voice broke on the edge of hysteria. "Don't," he said swiftly, pressing her close. "Hush."

She caught a ragged breath, stiffening her muscles against the shudders that went through her. But she couldn't stay silent. She couldn't turn away from the truth; she couldn't pretend it didn't exist. She would never be able to do that again. "It's my fault," she said clearly, as steadily as she could. "My fault that you're hurt and Tyler is...is..." She swallowed hard. "If I hadn't been here you never would have come and he..." She looked up at Nick in agony and helplessness. "He was a bad man, Nick, but he didn't deserve to die! Not like this, not..." She couldn't say any more.

Nick's face was hard, lost in his own struggle with a pain that went beyond the physical. "Men like Tyler take their chances, I guess. He must have thought it was worth it. Or maybe—" his tone dropped, becoming so low it was almost inaudible "—he just never thought he'd get caught."

Alice whispered, "Just like me. It was all like a...a game to me, a grand and glorious game, and I was so sure I could win it. I never thought I'd get caught by...real life." She squeezed her eyes tightly closed and tried hard not to let the tears begin again. "Oh, Nick," she said brokenly, "it's never going to go away, is it?"

Nick's face was very sober. "No," he said. "I wish I could say something that would make it better, but we're both going to have to live with this for the rest of our lives. And maybe that's not such a bad thing. I think we've all been playing a game too long, like children who refuse to come in after it's dark. But it's time to come in now, Alice. Time to grow up."

He stroked her hair with a light, unsteady touch. The feather headband was dislodged and tumbled to the floor. She let it lie.

He tried to smile, but it was a vague, distant effort that held only sadness. "I never thought I'd hear myself say that. But I'm tired of playing. I want to be a grown-up now. To have a family, and a place to come home to. Someone to come home to. To stop living like there was no tomorrow and start building a future." The expression in his eyes was hesitant, questioning. "I'd like it if you wanted that, too. And if you wanted it with me."

Slowly, Alice bowed her head against his shoulder. Until he spoke the words, until she felt the warmth and the life of his muscled arm against her face, she could not believe that she would ever know peace again. But there it was, a small kernel of something solid and secure growing within her, a bud of hope, a promise of joy. It was enough to build on.

"Yes," she whispered. "That's what I want. I think that might be the only thing I've ever really wanted."

A policeman came over and said quietly, "I'm sorry, Nick, but I'm really going to have to ask you two to leave now. We've got to get our people in here."

Nick nodded and looked down at Alice. His face was pale and tight with pain, but he smiled. "Can you make it now?"

Alice drew one last gulping breath and brought her hand up, wiping the tears. She nodded and summoned her strength. "Yes."

She slipped an arm around Nick's waist to support him. In the end, she leaned on him as much as he leaned on her, each of them taking from the other's strength.

But at the door, she had to look back. The shudder that went through her shook her very soul, and she had to close her eyes before she could breathe again. "It wasn't worth it," she said in a small, stunned voice.

"No," Nick agreed slowly. "None of it was worth it."

She looked up at him, and they shared in that moment all that words could never say, all that either of them needed. Sorrow, guilt, bitter regret... hope, courage, resolution. And love. Quiet and simple, it flowed through them and around them, sealing them together and making them strong.

"It's over now," she said softly.

"No." He kissed her hair. "Only the bad things are over."

"I love you, Nick."

He smiled. "Let's go home."

The policeman opened the door for them. "Have somebody take a look at that arm," he advised. "And we'll need to talk to you both." He looked from one to the other, hesitated, then added, "But I guess that can wait until morning."

Nick said, "I hope it won't take long. We're planning to go away."

Alice looked up at him as they moved through the disgruntled crowd that littered the interior of the club. "Where are we going?"

Nick waited until they were outside in the cool, open night to reply. He breathed deeply of the damp autumn air and turned his face to the stars. "Someplace quiet," he answered, "and faraway." He tightened his arm around her, holding her close. "Just the two of us, for a long, long time."

HARLEQUIN
American Romance®

ABOUT THE AUTHOR

Short skirts, free love, women's liberation, the "Twiggy" look... Does this sound like a description of the 1960s? Rebecca Flanders thought so, too, until while researching the 1920s, she discovered that the Woodstock Generation had nothing on its wild and reckless forebears from the Jazz Age.

Rebecca first became interested in the Roaring Twenties when her daughter did a high school paper on the music of the period. She was fascinated by the way the emergence of jazz reflected the social turmoil of the time, much the way rock and roll defined the spirit of the '60s. In studying the social history of the decade she describes as "one of the most glamorous and decadent in modern history," she found other similarities between that generation and her own, all of which eventually became *The Sensation*. Even the love story Nick and Alice share, Rebecca says, "is timeless and the lessons they learn are familiar to us all, proving once again that the more things change the more they stay the same and that we are all united by the threads of history."

One of the original authors for the Harlequin American Romance and Harlequin Intrigue series, Rebecca Flanders is the author of over twenty-five novels. She also now writes mainstream historical and contemporary fiction. Extraordinarily versatile, she is a master at breathing life into her characters and evoking the spectrum of readers' emotions. Rebecca lives in the mountains of Georgia with her daughter, Ginny.

CARS-1A

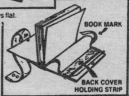

PASSPORT TO ROMANCE VACATION SWEEPSTAKES

OFFICIAL RULES

SWEEPSTAKES RULES AND REGULATIONS. NO PURCHASE NECESSARY.

HOW TO ENTER:

1. To enter, complete this official entry form and return with your invoice in the envelope provided, or print your name, address, telephone number and age on a plain piece of paper and mail to: Passport to Romance, P.O. Box #1397, Buffalo, N.Y. 14269-1397. No mechanically reproduced entries accepted.

2. All entries must be received by the Contest Closing Date, midnight, December 31, 1990 to be eligible.

3. Prizes: There will be ten (10) Grand Prizes awarded, each consisting of a choice of a trip for two people to: i) London, England (approximate retail value $5,050 U.S.); ii) England, Wales and Scotland (approximate retail value $6,400 U.S.); iii) Caribbean Cruise (approximate retail value $7,300 U.S.); iv) Hawaii (approximate retail value $ 9,550 U.S.); v) Greek Island Cruise in the Mediterranean (approximate retail value $12,250 U.S.); vi) France (approximate retail value $7,300 U.S.).

4. Any winner may choose to receive any trip or a cash alternative prize of $5,000.00 U.S. in lieu of the trip.

5. Odds of winning depend on number of entries received.

6. A random draw will be made by Nielsen Promotion Services, an independent judging organization on January 29, 1991, in Buffalo, N.Y., at 11:30 a.m. from all eligible entries received on or before the Contest Closing Date. Any Canadian entrants who are selected must correctly answer a time-limited, mathematical skill-testing question in order to win. Quebec residents may submit any litigation respecting the conduct and awarding of a prize in this contest to the Régie des loteries et courses du Quebec.

7. Full contest rules may be obtained by sending a stamped, self-addressed envelope to: "Passport to Romance Rules Request", P.O. Box 9998, Saint John, New Brunswick, E2L 4N4.

8. Payment of taxes other than air and hotel taxes is the sole responsibility of the winner.

9. Void where prohibited by law.

PASSPORT TO ROMANCE VACATION SWEEPSTAKES

OFFICIAL RULES

SWEEPSTAKES RULES AND REGULATIONS. NO PURCHASE NECESSARY.

HOW TO ENTER:

1. To enter, complete this official entry form and return with your invoice in the envelope provided, or print your name, address, telephone number and age on a plain piece of paper and mail to: Passport to Romance, P.O. Box #1397, Buffalo, N.Y. 14269-1397. No mechanically reproduced entries accepted.

2. All entries must be received by the Contest Closing Date, midnight, December 31, 1990 to be eligible.

3. Prizes: There will be ten (10) Grand Prizes awarded, each consisting of a choice of a trip for two people to: i) London, England (approximate retail value $5,050 U.S.); ii) England, Wales and Scotland (approximate retail value $6,400 U.S.); iii) Caribbean Cruise (approximate retail value $7,300 U.S.); iv) Hawaii (approximate retail value $ 9,550 U.S.); v) Greek Island Cruise in the Mediterranean (approximate retail value $12,250 U.S.); vi) France (approximate retail value $7,300 U.S.).

4. Any winner may choose to receive any trip or a cash alternative prize of $5,000.00 U.S. in lieu of the trip.

5. Odds of winning depend on number of entries received.

6. A random draw will be made by Nielsen Promotion Services, an independent judging organization on January 29, 1991, in Buffalo, N.Y., at 11:30 a.m. from all eligible entries received on or before the Contest Closing Date. Any Canadian entrants who are selected must correctly answer a time-limited, mathematical skill-testing question in order to win. Quebec residents may submit any litigation respecting the conduct and awarding of a prize in this contest to the Régie des loteries et courses du Quebec.

7. Full contest rules may be obtained by sending a stamped, self-addressed envelope to: "Passport to Romance Rules Request", P.O. Box 9998, Saint John, New Brunswick, E2L 4N4.

8. Payment of taxes other than air and hotel taxes is the sole responsibility of the winner.

9. Void where prohibited by law.

PASSPORT TO ROMANCE
WIN 1 of 10 Vacations SEE INSIDE

VACATION SWEEPSTAKES

Official Entry Form

MONTH 1 ENTRY

Yes, enter me in the drawing for one of ten Vacations-for-Two! If I'm a winner, I'll get my choice of any of the six different destinations being offered — and I won't have to decide until after I'm notified!

Return entries with invoice in envelope provided along with Daily Travel Allowance Voucher. Each book in your shipment has two entry forms — and the more you enter, the better your chance of winning!

Name _____

Address _____ Apt. _____

City _____ State/Prov. _____ Zip/Postal Code _____

Daytime phone number _____
Area Code

☐ I am enclosing a Daily Travel Allowance Voucher in the amount of **$** _____ Write in amount revealed beneath scratch-off

© 1990 HARLEQUIN ENTERPRISES LTD.

PASSPORT TO ROMANCE
WIN 1 of 10 Vacations SEE INSIDE

VACATION SWEEPSTAKES

Official Entry Form

MONTH 1 ENTRY

Yes, enter me in the drawing for one of ten Vacations-for-Two! If I'm a winner, I'll get my choice of any of the six different destinations being offered — and I won't have to decide until after I'm notified!

Return entries with invoice in envelope provided along with Daily Travel Allowance Voucher. Each book in your shipment has two entry forms — and the more you enter, the better your chance of winning!

Name _____

Address _____ Apt. _____

City _____ State/Prov. _____ Zip/Postal Code _____

Daytime phone number _____
Area Code

☐ I am enclosing a Daily Travel Allowance Voucher in the amount of **$** _____ Write in amount revealed beneath scratch-off

CPS-ONE